"I'm under a curse."

Bruce's eyes opened wide at Sandor's pronouncement.

"You didn't believe me." His mouth curved in an ironic grin. "In this day and age, who would believe such a thing?" Sandor said. He looked away as the horrors came rushing back at him. "At first I dismissed the very idea of a family curse, but soon accidents began to happen. I knew it was my fault somehow."

"But how? And why?" Bruce asked.

"I began to consider that it might be the curse. I chartered a plane for myself alone." His hand tightened until his knuckles were white.

The silent suffering Bruce understood. Softly she said, "That was the plane that crashed, and your back was broken."

"That plane crash made a believer of me. The curse is real. You must leave, Bruce. Go back to New York where you will be safe."

ABOUT THE AUTHOR

Madelyn Sanders lives in North Carolina. The things she finds most fascinating in life are, in order of importance, her writing, large bodies of water and old houses. All three are combined in her second novel for Harlequin Intrigue, *Sarabande*.

Books by Madelyn Sanders

HARLEQUIN INTRIGUE
158—UNDER VENICE

Sarabande
Madelyn Sanders

Harlequin Books

TORONTO • NEW YORK • LONDON
AMSTERDAM • PARIS • SYDNEY • HAMBURG
STOCKHOLM • ATHENS • TOKYO • MILAN
MADRID • WARSAW • BUDAPEST • AUCKLAND

Acknowledgments

I wish to thank the following people for their help in the
writing of *Sarabande:* Frank Efird, friend of the family
and excellent guide; Margaret Pfaff, for her advice and
companionship on my research trips; Kathy Beckwith of
the New Bern Historical Society; Barbara Howlett of the
Historic Preservation Foundation of New Bern; and Lou
Proctor of the ARTS Gallery on Pollock Street, whose
exuberant entry into my life at the time I was thinking
about writing a novel of intrigue made me decide to choose
New Bern for the setting.

Harlequin Intrigue edition published June 1992

ISBN 0-373-22187-8

SARABANDE

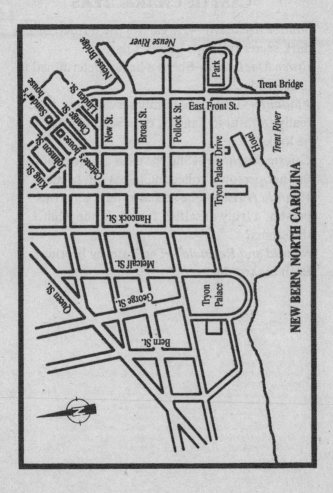

NEW BERN, NORTH CAROLINA

CAST OF CHARACTERS

Sandor Szelazeny—He carries the burden of a dark secret from his family's past.

Bruce MacLaren—She is a healer determined to heal Sandor.

Vladimir—Longtime family servant, but is he really faithful to Sandor, or is he as sinister as he looks?

Celeste Stanhope—She owns an antique shop, but her personal collecting tastes run to men.

Virginia Hassel—She seems to be a generous person, a truly unselfish friend. Is she what she seems?

Ronald and Reginald—The Ramsay brothers. Both are trouble.

Chapter One

The door seemed implacably closed. She had already knocked three times with no response. Well, she'd been warned; she knew this would not be easy. The spark in her blue-gray eyes matched the fiery color of her hair. She had never been one to back off from a challenge, which was how she came to be here in the first place. She lifted the old bronze knocker and brought it down hard, again.

The door jerked inward. A man stood there, leaning on a cane and glaring at her. His voice was deep and harsh. "Whatever it is you want, I'm not interested, and I resent you disturbing my peace with your infernal knocking!"

"You must be Sandor Szelazeny," she said quickly. "I'm Bruce MacLaren, from New York. You're expecting me."

He was tall, a good couple of inches taller than her own rather unusual height of five-ten, though the recent injury to his spine made it impossible for him to stand fully erect. His famous face was familiar, though it, like his body, had been changed by his accident: high cheekbones, more prominent now than in his many newspaper and magazine photos; an arresting, hawklike nose; dark hair which he habitually wore longer than was the fashion, now shaggy and with new touches of silver at the temples; a mobile, expressive mouth that at the moment curled back from very white teeth in mixed disbelief and derision.

"Bruce MacLaren? *Bruce?* You can't be Bruce, you're a—" he looked her up and down "—a girl!"

Bruce grinned. She usually went through a similar routine whenever she met someone new. It was not her masculine name that had gotten her this job, but the name had helped in the subterfuge, which Sandor's manager had assured her was necessary. "Blame it on my father," she said. "He's a nut about our Scots ancestry. Besides, I'm not a girl, I'm a woman. Fully qualified and sent by your manager to be your personal assistant." *Overqualified,* she added silently to herself.

"Well, you can't stay," said Sandor more harshly than before. Without thinking, he tried to straighten, to arrogantly assume his full height, and pain sliced through him like a hot knife through butter. He swallowed a curse. He willed his facial muscles to stillness, allowed himself only a quick intake of air through his nostrils when what he wanted was to gulp great heaving breaths to cool the burning agony in his back. He grasped the edge of the door with his left hand, while he leaned his weight more heavily on the cane in his right. A moment more and this would pass, and he would slam the door in her face. If only his legs weren't threatening to give out on him! Through clenched teeth Sandor growled, "I won't have a female in my house! I don't want an assistant anyway, my man Vladimir can do whatever I need. I wish to hell my bloody manager had never found me!"

Bruce was qualified to be much more than a personal assistant, she was a licensed physical therapist who specialized in difficult cases—but Sandor Szelazeny was not to know that. Not until he trusted her, his manager had said. It was up to Bruce to win her way into his house and into his confidence. She disregarded the hostility in Sandor's words and voice, and attended instead to subtle cues a person without her training might have missed. The fine sheen of moisture that broke out upon his face, the almost imperceptible shaking of his right hand upon the cane, the whitened knuckles of the left hand, that gripped the edge of the door, and most telling of all, the desperation buried in the depths of his golden brown eyes. He hid it well, but this man was in great pain. His legs wouldn't support him much longer, she was certain.

Bruce moved swiftly, with an ease borne of skill. In one fluid motion she was through the door and at Sandor's side, her strong arm circling his back, her legs slightly bent to take his weight against her thigh. "Let's not stand in the door arguing," she said as she pivoted and took him with her. The wheelchair was, as she had hoped, only a couple of feet away, and she had neatly deposited him in it and placed his cane across his knees before he had time to react. "That's better," she said, going behind the chair, bending to release its brakes.

She pushed decisively down the hallway toward a patch of sunlight, after a glance over her shoulder assured her that the front door was closing of its own accord. From experience she knew it was best to continue in charge for a few minutes. Most people, especially men, instinctively resented being handled the way she had just handled Sandor, even if they knew they needed the help. Each person had to recover from such an "insult" in his own way, in his own time.

So, although she hadn't the slightest idea where she was going, Bruce pushed the wheelchair down the hall toward the patch of sun, and ended up in a room that was part kitchen and part cozy living space, with a round oak table and chairs, a fireplace, and a plump sofa under a row of tall, small-paned windows.

At first Sandor felt too relieved at being off his feet to be astonished or offended by the way this female stranger had taken him over and put him in his wheelchair. He shifted against its soft, embracing leather and released a little sigh as the pain subsided. He was never without pain now, but most of the time it was dull if ever-present, and he had learned to live with it. However, he could walk only a few steps and stand only a minute or two before the agony gripped him and forced him down like a defeated animal.

Sandor reflected, as he saw that she had managed somehow to find his favorite room of this rented house, that in a curious way he'd been glad of this woman's strength. It would have been worse, far more humiliating, to shake and grope his way to the chair, very possibly to fall before reaching it. At least she had spared him that embarrassment.

She parked him at the oak table and took a chair herself. Sandor looked at the woman. Bruce. A Scot, indeed! One side of his mouth curved upward in unconscious appreciation. She looked the Scotswoman, with thick, shoulder-length hair the color of bright copper and eyes gray as a cloudy sky, pale fine-textured skin, full lips above a determined chin, and a tall, long-boned body. Every inch of her spoke strength. With little effort he could imagine this Bruce taking her highland castle in hand while the laird was away, managing her household with no less skill and ferocity than that with which her husband the laird fought his clan wars. Sandor admitted grudgingly that she had also managed *him* well. Perhaps too well.

"How did you do that?" he asked.

"Do what?"

"You know what!" He scowled.

Of course she knew what he meant, but she said, lightly, "It's not important," and tossed her head so that her hair swung, brushing her shoulders.

Bruce had had a lot of experience in getting started with difficult patients, even though she'd never accepted a live-in job before. Just these few minutes with Sandor Szelazeny had taught her a good deal about him: he was innately strong, because he was able to withstand the pain that, to her practiced eye, appeared fairly constant; he was also stubborn, locked in denial of that very same pain. Denial could be hard to handle. The best thing to do in such cases was to establish a momentum and keep on rolling. Coming quickly to this assessment, Bruce jumped up and crossed the room. "I'm going to get my things out of the car. I'll be back in a flash."

"Now just a bloody minute," Sandor warned, but she paid him no mind. He thought of yelling after her but he didn't. Instead he watched her go. She wore jeans tucked into calf-high leather boots, and a long yellow sweater that rode on the motion of her hips as she walked. He liked the way she moved, with a clean, crisp, certain sort of grace. He felt a sudden flood of warmth in his groin that astonished him. He was attracted to her! Impossible, he'd just been celibate for too long. This Bruce was not at all his type of woman—he preferred elegant, small-boned creatures, expertly coiffed and made-up, cosmopolitan yet compliant. Bruce MacLaren was clearly none of the above.

Recognizing the futility of the way his thoughts were going, Sandor scowled. It did not matter whether this Bruce was his type of woman or not. There would be no more women in his life, just as there would be no more music, no more orchestras to conduct, no more feeling the exhilaration, the power surge in an audience's applause—things that had once, not too long ago, been as important to him as breathing. The plane crash, and the terrible thing he had learned about himself not long before the crash, had robbed him of all that.

I should have died, Sandor thought. *I was meant to die in that crash and it would have been better if I had.* He struck the table hard with his fist, and the sudden flare of anger subsided. Fear came in its place, fear that he quickly drowned in the dark gray dullness that had become his usual preferred state of mind. Depression. He knew that was what people—the doctors, the nurses, his manager, even his man Vladimir—thought, that he was depressed. They expected him to be, and in part they were right. But only in part. He assumed the cloak of depression as a place where he could hide from pain that was more than physical. This was not easy for him—it went against his very nature to hide and suppress feeling.

Sandor was a man of unusually strong will and extreme emotional sensitivity, both qualities important to his choice of career as a symphony orchestra conductor. Both qualities had come to him as naturally as the color of his eyes or the hawklike bone structure of his face. The ability and, more than that, the need to be both fierce and tender was a genetic inheritance from his parents who had fled Hungary before the Second World War. They had been aristocrats who, as far as Sandor ever knew, had gladly left their titles behind though they took with them considerable wealth, which he had inherited on their deaths years before.

Not until that final, near-fatal trip to Europe had he known what else, besides the genes and the wealth, he had inherited. Sandor's true inheritance was a horror so ugly— or an ugliness so horrible—that simple knowledge of it threatened not only his existence but also his very soul. The plane crash had come too close on the heels of learning about the inheritance to have been an accident, or so it seemed to Sandor. Before then, he had never known fear; he had based his whole life on love of beauty and pleasure, pursuing both with the passionate strength that had been his hallmark. Now he pursued only safety, hidir.g from feelings and emotions as well as people. He was hounded by a fear he didn't quite understand, because such ugliness, such horror, was as incomprehensible as it was unspeakable.

Sandor shuddered and withdrew further into the protective cloak of his depression. He would ignore the woman, Bruce; there was no possible place for someone like her in the kind of life he must have now.

Bruce deposited her soft-sided luggage and a carton of books at the foot of the stairs. Then she stretched, pulling the kinks of six straight hours of driving out of her muscles. She had purposely broken the trip from New York to North Carolina into two days because she did not want to arrive at night.

New Bern, which she had never heard of before taking this job, was a pleasant surprise. The town was practically surrounded by water, being at a point where two rivers came together, and it was full of beautiful little old houses. Sandor Szelazeny lived in one of these, on East Front Street. She was itching to explore both the town and the house, but first things first. She wasn't even sure yet that she'd be allowed to stay—she had to get back to her recalcitrant new patient. She strode down the hall to the room where she'd left him, peering into rooms on either side, noting with approval that there were no rugs on the hardwood floors to trip up the wheelchair.

He didn't hear her enter. He had turned his chair away so that she saw him in profile, a famous profile with that arch of nose and full hair falling over the high brow, the shadows under the cheekbones. But his posture was all wrong. The set of his head, the slump of his shoulders, not to mention the brooding expression, spoke volumes to Bruce. In spite of the defiant attitude toward his pain that he had displayed earlier, Sandor Szelazeny was depressed. She was not surprised, most of her patients started out that way. Especially the most difficult ones, the ones who did not really want to get better. His hopelessness thickened the air of the room and squeezed her heart.

"I left my stuff at the bottom of the stairs," she announced, planting herself in front of him where he would have to look at her. But he didn't. He continued to gaze at a point that was nowhere, at nothing. He didn't move a muscle.

How to get a handle, how could she reach him? Bruce searched through the things his manager had told her. Not much. Sandor Szelazeny, an American orchestra conductor of Hungarian descent, was thirty-eight years old—young for one of his profession. He had been on the first wave of fame in what promised to be a brilliant career when the accident occurred nine months ago. Bruce didn't know much about symphony orchestra conductors, country music was more her style, but with a little prodding from Sandor's manager, Mr. Gross, she had remembered his making a splash as guest conductor of the New York Philharmonic a couple of years ago.

Sandor's striking dark good looks and arrogant manner had captured the attention of the press at the same time that his musical interpretations and command of the orchestra had impressed the critics. For a few weeks his face had been everywhere. Bruce had seen him on one of her favorite television shows. Charles Kuralt's *Sunday Morning*. Sandor had fire in his eyes then, she remembered, passion in the way he gestured with expressive hands as he talked about his music.

The rest of the story, leading up to Sandor's injury, had been told to her by Mr. Gross: how Sandor had gone on a European tour, the tour starting out so triumphantly that the world seemed to be at Sandor's feet. But then something had gone wrong. Exactly what, nobody seemed to know.

During a hiatus in the tour Sandor had gone off without telling anyone his destination, gone alone except for his servant Vladimir; they'd rejoined the group in time to resume the tour as scheduled. But, according to others in the party, Sandor had seemed unlike himself after the hiatus. And on the way to a concert in Brussels, Sandor had separated himself from the others, who traveled by train, and without giving an explanation had chartered a small private plane. The plane had crashed along the Swiss/Belgian border, and the pilot had been killed. Sandor had sustained multiple injuries, some of which could have been fatal, but he had survived . . . with a broken back.

Bruce shuddered. She wrapped her arms around herself and quietly moved around the table to take a chair and place it where she could sit near Sandor. She could imagine very little that would be worse for her, or for anyone, than the kind of confinement forced upon a patient to heal a broken back. Absolute immobility. A full body cast. The best one could hope for was a torturous-looking rotating device called a Stryker frame. In spite of such daunting obstacles, Sandor Szelazeny had done well. Bruce knew that his back had healed remarkably, she'd read his medical records and talked to his doctors before she had accepted this unusual job. Sandor had left the hospital AMA—against medical advice—as soon as he could move about enough to do so. Presumably the servant Vladimir had helped him. Why had Sandor done that? And why had he turned up in New Bern,

North Carolina, a place so out of the way that most of the world had never heard of it?

Bruce looked at Sandor, locked in his brooding silence. He seemed so alone. True, the manager, Bernard Gross, cared enough to hire Bruce on the doctors' recommendation. Bruce's services did not come cheaply, especially in this live-in arrangement. At twenty-nine, she already had a reputation for being able to succeed with the most difficult patients and she set her fees accordingly.

But Bruce privately thought the manager was motivated more by greed than by really caring about his client—if Sandor didn't conduct again, then Gross was out a hefty percentage. Bruce had asked about friends, family, because both could be important to recovery, and she'd been told that there were no friends and Sandor's parents had died some time ago. There were no brothers or sisters, only the family retainer, Vladimir, who had come to Sandor after the parents' death.

Sandor not only seemed alone, he really *was* alone. By his own choice? Why had he, in effect, run away? This job was not only a challenge, it was a mystery. There were more questions than answers, and after reviewing everything she knew about the man, she still hadn't a clue how to reach him. No matter, it was time to get to work.

"Well, I guess a good place to start," she said, disliking the false brisk tone she heard in her own voice, "would be for you to tell me where my room is."

Nothing. Silence. No response.

"Or," she went on doggedly, "do I have to wait for, uh—what's-his-name—Vladimir, to come back and tell me? Where is he, by the way? He obviously isn't in the house." Suddenly Bruce was alarmed, not for herself, but for Sandor. What if Vladimir had gone off and abandoned him? Had he been trying to cope without help? He couldn't, it would be too much for him! With an edge of panic in her voice, she grasped Sandor's arm. "Vladimir hasn't gone off and left you, has he?"

With an effort, Sandor pulled himself out of the dark gray place where lately he spent so much time. This woman's energy was a bother, it pulsed around her like a flame, it was disturbing. He grimaced distastefully and pulled his arm back from her touch, then abstractedly rubbed at the spot where her fingers had been. It felt warm, tingly. His answer came out automatically. "Vladimir would never leave me. He'd be lost without a Szelazeny to look after."

"Oh." Well, that was just as well, thought Bruce, though she wondered if she hadn't heard a hint of bitterness in Sandor's voice. At least he had finally said something. Now, to keep him talking. "So he's just out somewhere, is that it?"

"If you must know, if it's any of your business, Vladimir has gone shopping. Grocery shopping." Irritated now, Sandor in a vigorous motion spun one wheel of his chair and turned it away from her, barking over his shoulder, "Why are you still here? I told you I'd have no females in this house, and I meant it! I'm sure that when I told Gross—an appropriate name for that bloody interfering manager!— that I'd have this personal assistant he was so insistent I needed, he knew I never meant a woman! If this is his idea of a joke, hiring you just because you have a man's name so that he can play a trick on me—"

"Now wait just a minute, Mr. Szelazeny!" Bruce interrupted, stalking around so that once more she stood in front of him. A part of her knew that this was good, a verbal battle was a great way to break him out of his depression. But a larger part of her was darned if she'd let anybody, no matter how much in need of help, devalue her that way! "Your Mr. Gross didn't hire me just because I have a man's name, he hired me because I was the best applicant for the job! Though he did warn me that you were a male chauvinist and that my name would help me get a foot in the door!''

"Maestro!" Sandor barked, managing to ignore virtually everything she'd said. "When you speak to me, do not call me Mr. Szelazeny, call me Maestro!"

"I'll be darned if I will," Bruce shouted. "I'm not one of your fawning little musicians!"

"You don't have to be a musician, little or fawning, or otherwise. Everybody calls me Maestro!" Now they were both yelling.

"Uh-uh. No way." Bruce shook her head, enjoying the fight now. Sandor's golden eyes were snapping, his old arrogance returning. This was it, the handle: to fight with him, to challenge him, this was her way into his isolation...and his way out. She nailed him with a steely blue-gray gaze. "That word, 'maestro' means master. And I'm not calling anybody Master, not for any amount of money, not for anything in this whole wide world!"

"Is that so?" Sandor's eyes locked on hers. A wave of energy coursed through his body and he relished it, he didn't remember that only minutes ago he had found Bruce's energy a bother. He straightened in his chair, his shoulders went back, his chest swelled and his chin came up in a gesture his orchestra members would have recognized. "Not for *anything?*"

"That's right. No man is my master!"

"How about," said Sandor cunningly, his expressive lips curving, "if I tell you that you can stay here, you can have this job as my assistant that you seem to want so much, if you agree to call me Maestro...and not otherwise?"

Bruce blinked. She hadn't seen it coming, but she should have. She could almost hear him say "Gotcha!" Well, she'd just have to call his bluff, have to hope that he enjoyed the verbal sparring as much as she thought he did, that he wouldn't let her go. She pulled a chair over and deliberately sat, leaned back, crossed a long leg so that one booted ankle rested on the other knee, and steepled her fingers under her chin. "Let me get this straight. I came all the way down here from New York, was chosen as the best person out of all applicants to, ah, assist you, and you don't care how intelligent I may or may not be, you don't care how well I type or write or any of those things. I guess you already figured out that I'm strong and if you'll let me I can make you look as if you get around better than you do." He bristled. She was skating on thin ice, and she knew it, but she went on. "You don't care about any of those things. The job is mine on one condition—one, if I may say so, *asinine* condition—I have to call you Maestro."

Sandor nodded, smiled a sardonic smile and leaned back, steepling his fingers in intentional mockery of her pose. "Precisely."

Bright, rosy spots of color bloomed high on Bruce's cheeks. She unfolded her long body out of the chair slowly. Her eyes, full of challenge, never left his face. "Well, *Mr.* Szelazeny, it's been nice meeting you. Hardly worth driving the better part of two days for, but what the heck. Easy come, easy go." She walked a few steps and felt him watching her. She turned, her voice now cold as ice. "I'll expect a month's pay for my trouble in coming down here."

Sandor felt his heart pound. His mouth was dry. He knew this feeling, it was how he often felt before a performance—anxiety, or excitement, caused by an excess of adrenaline in the blood. Obviously he cared very much about the outcome here. He gripped the arms of his wheelchair and made his voice match hers for coldness. "Bernie Gross hired you, he can pay you off."

Bruce nodded, apparently satisfied. She turned again and continued on her way out of the room. She reached the doorway. He hoped she would pause, turn back, but she didn't.

Sandor's thoughts whirled. His whole body felt alive, more alive than he'd felt in weeks, months, he couldn't remember how long. He was confused. This tall, strong, handsome woman with the unlikely name would disrupt everything, he knew she would, and yet…and yet he didn't want her to go! It made no sense, but he didn't care. He threw off the brake levers and wheeled his chair as hard as he could after her. He yelled, "Wait! Hell and damnation, wait!"

In the hallway Bruce let out her breath. She hadn't realized she was holding it. She heard the thrum of his chair's rubber tires as he wheeled himself into the hall, but she didn't turn around. She forced herself to bend toward her bags, to close her hand on a handle. Then, through the copper curtain of her hair, which swung forward to hide her face, she looked back.

Sandor winced with the effort it took to bring his speeding chair to a halt. He suddenly felt the ignominy of his position. He was a man, or he had been one once, but he was crippled, and the woman towered over him. This was not right, not how it should be. He almost gave it up. But as he struggled with his feelings, wanting her to stay but unwilling to humble himself further to say so, Bruce dropped to one knee beside her bags. She no longer towered over him. She looked at him with a tiny, knowing smile, as if this were a farce they'd been playing and they'd both done their parts extremely well. She made it easy.

"I don't really want to go," she said.

"I suppose you could call me Sandor," he offered, "I really hate *Mr.* Szelazeny. It sounds so *common.*"

She laughed, a rich, throaty sound that made him want to touch her. She said, "I'd be delighted, Sandor. And you can call me Bruce."

"Bruce." The name suited her, and he liked saying it. He was a connoisseur of sounds, of language as well as music; to find a word that described anything or anyone absolutely perfectly gave him an almost sensual pleasure. The name was different, in precisely the same way that the woman was different: refreshing and strong. He said the name again, "Bruce." And then he smiled. He held out his hand.

Sandor's smile transformed his face, like sun coming out of shadow, and Bruce was warmed by it all the way to her toes. She clasped the hand he offered firmly. Hands held, eyes met, a bargain sealed. Yes. She would stay.

... INTENSE in him, the passion and tenderness that welled up inside by the wild ... The delight I saw ... And you fill me like a ...

... The letter urged her ... to be less trusting, to use a common-sense standard of judgment, or it will be harder to find a way that described ... anything to anyone else. Every particle gave him an aspect untouched ...

Chapter Two

Bruce awoke and listened to the quiet of the house. Her room was upstairs at the back, with windows that looked out over the wide expanse of the Neuse River. Clear, pale, early sunlight streamed through the sheer curtains. She sighed, for the moment content. She had slept well, unlike her first night under Sandor's roof, when she had tossed and turned and fretted and thought she would never get to sleep. It had seemed too quiet here, and too dark; she missed the city sounds of traffic and people and various clankings in the street, and although she knew that New Bern had to be a million times safer than her apartment on the fringes of Greenwich Village, the inky blackness beyond her windows had felt threatening. Not to mention the sinister-seeming presence of Vladimir a couple of doors down the hall!

Bruce began the stretching routine that she always did before getting out of bed in the morning. This was the beginning of her third day at her new job, and she felt optimistic. Unlike yesterday when she hadn't seemed to be able to do anything right. Vladimir had followed her around all day, glaring at her with his beady black eyes, and Sandor had been sullen and withdrawn. She wasn't going to let Vladimir throw her, even if the man seemed to have decided she was the enemy without so much as trying to get to know her.

Part of Vladimir's problem, thought Bruce, is just that he's old and he's been with the Szelazenys a long time. Sandor wouldn't talk to her about Vladimir—not that there'd been much of a chance, with the man constantly hovering about. But she didn't need Sandor to tell her that Vladimir had known him since childhood—Vladimir's attitude made it loud and clear. He was both possessive of Sandor and jealous of the new person in this previously two-person household. Unfortunately for Bruce, Vladimir's kind of overprotective solicitousness was exactly the wrong approach, would hinder rather than help his precious Maestro's recovery.

Yes, Vladimir was a problem. Not just how he acted, but how he looked. And sounded. With his thick foreign accent and his too tall, too thin, stooped body and beaky features crowned by sparse white hair, he was like some ancient Transylvanian bird of prey. A flesh-eating vulture of the Old world, thought Bruce, rolling out of bed with a wide smile on her face. *At least I haven't lost my sense of humor!*

She went to the window, held back the filmy curtain, and looked out. A faint mist hung low upon the rippled waters of the river; the sky above, just yielding to sunlight, looked clean and fresh as a newly washed pale blue handkerchief. The lawn, sloping down to the river, was scattered with tender green shoots of new grass. It was early March, and Bruce had left the city still locked in winter's death grip, but here already there were signs of spring. Good. A good time for all sorts of new beginnings.

A good time for her to begin her own routine in this new place, even if she didn't yet have any idea how she was going to get a therapeutic regimen started for her patient. Quietly, quickly, Bruce zipped in and out of the bathroom and into her running clothes: silver-gray spandex tights, an old navy blue turtleneck leotard that had seen better days. A navy sweatshirt, which covered her from collarbone to thigh, and gray leather running shoes. She tugged a white terry sweatband around her forehead to keep her hair out of her eyes and pinned her new house key inside the sweatshirt's kangaroo pocket, then crept down the stairs and out the front door into the fresh morning air.

Turning to her left, Bruce started out along East Front Street in an easy warm-up jog, keeping to the sidewalk. Soon she was running steadily, following the curve of the street along the water, past bridges over both rivers and a waterside park, past a large, new-looking hotel, past an old railroad station that housed a farmer's market, past brick walls and imposing iron gates where a sign said Tryon Palace. Palace? What in the world was that?

It was hard to keep running, she continually wanted to stop and gawk. Everything was fascinating. With the exception of the hotel, all the buildings and houses looked very old. Bruce was no authority on architecture, or history, either, but as she ran past she was reminded of a time she had visited Boston and gone on a walking tour of the historic part of that old seaport. New Bern, too, must have been a kind of colonial seaport, but it certainly didn't look a thing like Bruce's idea of the Old South!

Beyond the palace she swung up a street to her right, past more lovely old houses, some of which now housed businesses and an art gallery or two, and then she skirted a small business district and zigzagged through more residential streets until she reached East Front Street again. There she slowed to a walk, warming down. She had run herself into an invigorated, glowing sweat and felt wonderful.

"Hey, there!"

The voice, a woman's, came as something of a shock in the quiet street. Bruce had just peeled off her sweatshirt and was tying it around her waist as she walked.

"Hey, over here!" the woman called again.

Bruce turned her head in the direction of the voice, curious but not really glad of the interruption. She still didn't see anyone.

"Up here! Wait, I'm coming down."

Bruce looked up just in time to see a dark head disappear from a second-story window in a house directly across the street from Sandor's. This house, unlike his and most on the street, looked more like her idea of a Southern mansion—large, square, and white, it had a porch all the way around its two stories and fat columns in the front.

What now? Bruce wondered as she obediently waited, stretching one leg and then the other. Her muscles still quivered from the run.

The front door of the house across the street opened and a woman came out onto the porch. From where Bruce stood she could see only that the woman was small and dark-haired. The woman called, as if they had known each other for years, or at the least weeks, "Can you come in for a while? I've got coffee perking."

"I, uh, thanks but I don't think so," Bruce called back. Was this the famous Southern hospitality everyone has heard so much about? She added the obvious, "I've just been out for a run. I have to get back."

That brought the woman off the porch, down the steps and across the street, talking as she came. She had a Southern accent but it wasn't exaggerated as on TV or in the movies, it was soft and pleasant. "I saw you leave a while ago, so I watched for you to return. Since we're neighbors, I thought I'd introduce myself. I'm Celeste Stanhope."

"How do you do," said Bruce. Since Celeste held out her hand, Bruce wiped her own sweaty palm on a slippery, spandexed thigh and shook hands, saying, "I'm Bruce MacLaren." Though Bruce was confident in her professional life, in social situations she was by nature cautious and reserved. Celeste had caught her off guard; she wasn't prepared to meet the neighbors at barely eight o'clock in the morning when she was all sweaty and wearing her oldest leotard.

Besides, Celeste Stanhope was exactly the type of woman who made Bruce feel like a female Incredible Hulk. To Bruce's five-ten she was maybe five-three at the most, with a perfectly proportioned petite figure clad in a turquoise sweater and a full, paisley print skirt, with a matching paisley shawl artfully draped around her little shoulders. Her hair, so black that it had a blue sheen in the sun, curved around a very pretty face, with a rosebud mouth and black-fringed violet eyes. She had flawless ivory skin, perfectly made up, and she was wearing high heels...before breakfast!

Bruce unconsciously backed up a step before this paragon of femininity, but Celeste reached out and looped her arm companionably about Bruce's elbow. In a low, confiding voice Celeste said, "I just know we're going to be friends. I was so glad to see you arrive the day before yesterday. Why, those two men in that house need a woman's hand, I'm sure!" She pulled back a bit and looked Bruce up and down. "Are you a relative?" Her expression said, clear as words, You can't be, you don't look a bit like either one of them.

"No, I'm not a relative." Bruce wiped at her forehead below the sweatband. This wasn't Southern hospitality, this was pure intrusiveness. But still, it wouldn't do to get off on the wrong foot with a neighbor. Sandor needed friends, and

Bruce was sure he wasn't going to make an effort on his own to make any. But perhaps she was wrong. She asked, "Do you know Mr., uh, Maestro Szelazeny and his man Vladimir?"

"Oh, everyone knows who he is, of course, but he keeps very much to himself. Hardly goes out at all. I called with an invitation and I took a cake over, I mean I couldn't have a new neighbor and not be welcoming, could I? But I never got to talk to the Maestro and that strange-looking manservant refused both the invitation and the cake. I gather there's been some sort of difficulty and they haven't felt like being sociable. Maybe now you're here, you'll change all that, Bruce."

She gave Bruce's arm a little squeeze. "Such a nice name. It sounds rather Southern. You know, Southern girls often have their mama's last name for a given name. I think it sounds so distinguished! I can call you Bruce, can't I? And you must call me Celeste. We women have to stick together!"

Bruce reflected that she'd have to introduce Sandor to Celeste—he'd like her right away, she called him Maestro before she'd even met him! "Sure, Celeste," she said. "Look, I think I'd best get back inside. I'm Sandor's personal assistant, that's why I'm here, and I have to shower and change and get to work."

"Oh, of course. I'll just walk with you to your door. That way we can talk a little longer. You're from up north, aren't you? In spite of your interesting name."

Bruce nodded, her long legs impatient with Celeste's small steps.

"I thought so. Now I don't want to seem pushy, but I do want us to be friends. I know absolutely everyone in New Bern, I've lived here practically all my life, and if there's anything going on here I don't know about, then it isn't worth knowing!''

They reached the steps and Bruce smiled down at her. "That sounds interesting."

"I can introduce you and the Maestro to anybody you want to meet. I know for a fact that he hasn't met anybody yet but the realtor who rented him the house. And of course I'm just dying to meet him myself! He can't stay in there all to himself forever."

"I intend to see that he doesn't," said Bruce.

"Good. You come over and see me any time. You saw where I live, right across the street. And I have a little antique shop over on Pollock Street—that's a couple of blocks up that way."

Bruce nodded, she'd crossed Pollock Street twice on her run. "I know where it is."

Celeste smiled. She really was very pretty. "My shop is called Celestial Antiquities, a little play on words. You come around sometime, you hear?"

"I will," Bruce promised, smiling. She felt warmer toward the woman, who was obviously genuinely friendly and understandably curious about Sandor. After all, Celeste couldn't help being small and beautiful and dark-haired, everything that Bruce in her fantasies would like to be when she was dissatisfied with herself.

With a final squeeze to Bruce's arm, Celeste said brightly, "I'm going to hold you to that. Bye, now!"

WITH HER HAND on the banister, thinking how good it would feel to get out of the sticky leotard and tights and into a warm shower, Bruce stopped. She thought she'd heard something. A groan. There! It was a groan, she heard it again. It was Sandor, and he was in pain.

The shower forgotten, Bruce ran up the hall. The former dining room had been converted into a bedroom for Sandor, since he couldn't manage stairs. The only thought in her mind was that Sandor was in pain, so she paid no attention to the closed door. She burst through without knocking and reacted instantly to what she saw.

"Let me do that!" she commanded, pushing the inept Vladimir out of the way. "Can't you see you're hurting him?"

"I beg your pardon, miss," said Vladimir stiffly, closing fingers like claws on Bruce's shoulder. "You should not be in here. The Maestro is not dressed."

Bruce shrugged her shoulders, and when Vladimir did not release his clawlike grip, she turned angry gray eyes on him. "No, and he won't be dressed without being hurt, the way you're going about it!" Vladimir, startled, dropped his hand and backed off.

"You think you can do better?" Sandor growled through clenched teeth.

"I know I can. Here." Bruce went into a crouch beside the bed where Sandor was sprawled in a half sitting position. He had been supporting his weight on one arm while Vladimir attempted to put on his trousers. Bruce reached behind Sandor and placed one hand firmly at the base of his spine to provide support, while with her other hand she disentangled the trousers from around his ankles. "Put your arms on my shoulders," she said, "lean on me and sit up straight, with your feet on the floor. Any lateral pull on your back muscles is too much for you right now!"

Sandor did as she said. The pain in his back immediately lessened, and the pressure of her hand on the base of his spine felt good. Reassuring, not to mention intimate, he thought as the pain subsided to its usual dull ache.

Bruce raised her head and found herself looking straight
into Sandor's golden brown eyes, only inches away. She saw
the pain in them fade, replaced by...well, she blinked her
own eyes, never mind what it was replaced by. The important thing was that he was no longer hurting. "Where's your
brace?" she asked.

"What brace?" Sandor was amused by this, that he was
virtually naked sitting on the side of his bed with his arms
draped about a beautiful young woman's shoulders...a
woman who, though she was covered from neck to toe,
might as well have been naked herself for all the outfit hid
of her shape. And she was in great shape, no mistake about
that. Her breasts, he judged, would just fit the palms of his
hands...

"Your back brace, of course."

...And those long, long legs, covered with shiny silver
fabric, legs that right now were spread wide in a crouch as
she supported all of her own weight, and most of his, on her
thighs... But, ah, she was glaring at him. He asked innocently, "My back brace?"

"You must have one. Even if you did leave the hospital
before they were ready to let you go, you'd never have been
able to move around at all without a back brace. Where is
it?"

Sandor turned his head to look over his shoulder in the
direction of a chest of drawers, and immediately regretted
it. Just that small motion pulled something along his spine
and brought the hot knife cutting into his back again.

"It's okay," said Bruce, understanding what had happened. "Lean on my shoulders, give me your weight. Don't
move anything at all. You shouldn't try to sit unsupported,
not yet. Your back muscles have been torn, you know. Now
where is that brace?"

"Vladimir, get the brace," said Sandor. She was right, and he knew it. He had given up the brace because he couldn't get into it by himself and having Vladimir lace him into the damn thing was more torture than going without it. Once he got into his wheelchair and stayed there, he was pretty much all right. Or so he had been telling himself.

"Sandor," Bruce said in a voice so low he could barely hear. He looked straight into her eyes. They were blue yet gray at the same time, and so very, very clear. She continued when she saw that she had his attention, "When Vladimir brings the brace, ask him to leave."

"Why?" Sandor matched her quiet tone.

From the corner of her eye Bruce saw the man returning with the corsetlike back brace in his hands. "Just do it," she murmured, "trust me."

Still amused, now curious, too, but careful not to move his head, Sandor assumed his most authoritative voice. "Put the brace on the bed, Vladimir, where Bruce can reach it. And then you may leave us."

Vladimir placed the brace next to Sandor, drew himself up so that his spindly height loomed over them both, and prepared to protest. "But, Maestro..."

"I said, leave us!" Sandor commanded.

Bruce had to admire him. That voice could make a stone move. And he had to be very uncomfortable, not just physically, but with her. In spite of the fact that she'd asked him to, there was no way he could trust her yet. She turned her head and visually tracked Vladimir out the door.

"And close the door," Sandor added with the same authority.

Bruce smiled, she couldn't help it. "You're very good at that," she said.

"They don't call me Maestro for nothing." Sandor smiled back. "All except for you, of course."

"Of course," said Bruce briskly, all business now. "We're going to get you into your brace, and then I'll help you dress."

"Oh, really?" His tone was not mocking, but insinuating, sensual. Bruce ignored it, with difficulty. She was all too aware of his body, of the bare chest thickly furred with dark hair along the center line, of legs that had once been fine but were now much in need of strengthening exercises. Someday soon she would begin to work with this body until she knew it as well as her own. But in a purely professional way, she reminded herself.

"Yes, really," she said firmly. "It won't be too hard if you do as I say. I'm going to remove my hand from your back, and when I do that I want you to lean into me and shift all of your weight to your forearms, on my shoulders. Okay, *now!*"

She moved quickly, picking up the brace and wrapping it around his middle with both her hands. "Okay, now we're going to stand up, together. Keep leaning on me. *Now.*" The tempo of Sandor's breathing increased and she knew that he was feeling more than a little discomfort. She felt the strain in her own thighs as she bore both their weights upward. "Good," she said. "Good. Give me all your weight, it will be easier. Good. Now I'm going to move in closer so that I can position the brace properly."

Sandor had done something like this with the nurses at the hospital but it seemed a long, long time ago. None of them had been as deft as Bruce, or half as attractive. Locked in this strange embrace, ignoring the hurts of his body, he filled his nostrils with her scent. The scent of sweet, damp, woman skin. From her clothes he knew that she had been out exercising, probably running. He did not think to envy her that she could run and he could not. He thought instead that if he were to flick his tongue in the curve of her neck, she would taste slightly salty...

While he was occupied with these few thoughts, Bruce had pulled the brace around him and was stepping back. In one hand she held its laces so firmly that already he could feel the support of the steel stays, and her other arm she slipped around him. She anchored her hand under his armpit and turned him so that he was at her side. Somehow in all this she still was holding him up. Now they were glued together from shoulder to hip like lovers out for a walk. Except, of course, for the fact that she still held tightly to the laces of the brace. Sandor grimaced—what he hated most about the thing was that it looked, to him, so much like a woman's old-fashioned undergarment.

"Okay," said Bruce, "now we're going to take two steps and you're going to sit in your wheelchair, and then I'm going to lace you up. That way you'll have the support of the chair while I'm doing it. Ready?"

"Umm," grunted Sandor. He wasn't enjoying this anymore. Just the thought of her lacing him into the damn female-looking brace made him feel emasculated again, as he had so often felt since the accident.

She got him into the chair, laced him up, and then sat on her haunches in front of him. She'd been working hard, and it showed. Her cheeks were flushed, her breathing a little rapid. She untied a sweatshirt she'd had tied around her waist and let it drop to the floor, pulled the sweatband off her head and tossed it away. She shook her head vigorously and her marvelous red hair flew, then fell into place.

God, but she's attractive! Sandor thought, not realizing that once again Bruce had taken him out of melancholy self-absorption. He smiled at her, but she frowned at him and asked, "How long have you been going without that brace?"

"Oh, I don't know," he responded. "Most of the time since I left the hospital, I guess."

"I don't have to ask why. You can't possibly put it on yourself, and no matter how devoted Vladimir is, he obviously isn't trained to do more than keep your clothes in order and go on errands. He's only a . . . a . . . what do you call it, a . . ."

"A valet," Sandor supplied. "You're quite right. He does a good job with clothes, but he's only a passable chauffeur. And as you've no doubt observed, Vladimir can't really cook. I haven't minded, since I seldom feel like eating anyway."

"I'm not talking about cooking! But I guess I'll get to that. You're not going to get any better without plenty of good food."

Sandor narrowed his eyes and suspiciously challenged, "Who says I want to get any better?"

"I do!" Bruce's eyes blazed. There was a passionate caring in her voice, in her whole body, that reached out and touched Sandor as surely as if he'd put his hand in a flame.

He let her fire take him, let it fill him with warmth. But only for a minute. He should not allow this woman to make him feel . . . anything. A hard, bitter lesson he'd learned on his European trip: that for him now, with his deadly inheritance, all feelings were dangerous. All feelings—physical, emotional, even the pure passion of his music—all dangerous. He had learned that lesson, all right, and as if just to be sure he didn't forget, the plane crash had driven it home. So he said more coldly than he felt, "Why should you care so much?"

"It's—" She bit off the words *my job*. "It's just the way I am, that's all." She stood up and went to get Sandor's shirt and trousers from the bed.

She could feel him shutting her out again, and she couldn't bear it. She couldn't bear the thought of another day like yesterday, when she'd tried without success to get Sandor to dictate letters to her, or to let her read to him, or push him in his chair to the river's edge where they could watch the boats go by. She was supposed to be an all-purpose companion, but she couldn't stand the deception. She had professional skills Sandor desperately needed, certainly much more than he needed a secretary; probably more, even, than he needed companionship.

Bruce looked back at him. His head was drooping again and his shoulders slumped, which gave a concavity to that well-furred chest. If she didn't do something, something more than just help him on with his clothes, soon Sandor would surrender again to his depression.

Bruce made a decision. It was a gamble, but she was going to take it. Shirt and trousers in hand, she walked back to him. "Sandor, do you still want to know why I asked you to have Vladimir leave the room?"

"What?" His head came up, his eyes focused on her. "Yes, I guess I do."

"I didn't want him to see how much better I can take care of you than he can. More than that, I can show you how to take care of yourself. You can, you know. With the right kind of help, in no time at all you can do things that are hard for you now, and eventually you'll be able to do things that now seem impossible." The note of passionate caring had crept back into her voice.

Sandor looked at Bruce. She was hard to resist, but he said nothing.

"Will you let me . . ." She was pleading, her eyes all compassion. "Will you let me . . . I need to touch you. Please?"

In spite of himself, Sandor felt a small frisson of anticipated pleasure. He had not changed so much that he was

unwilling to be touched by an attractive woman, even if he
was not at all sure what she wanted. The corners of his lips
curved upward, ever so slightly. "Since I am virtually your
prisoner, my dear Bruce, how can I refuse?"

She did not respond to his amused tone. With a dead serious expression on her face, she ran her fingers all over his
body. Her touch was usually gentle, sometimes probing,
never sensual. She flexed his arms, his legs, she even inspected his feet. She asked him to lean forward, and she
touched the scars on his back, felt along his spine to the
point where the brace began and even traced the line of the
spine through the brace. Her hand went lower, beneath the
waistband of his shorts to his tailbone. Then once more she
sank back on her haunches. Her chin came up, as if to meet
a challenge, but she was nervous. Sandor could see that. Her
tongue came out and moistened her full lips before she
spoke.

"Sandor," she said, "I'm not exactly who you think I
am."

On his guard now, Sandor said gruffly, "That has been
the case ever since you came to my door three days ago. I
suggest, before you take what is likely to be an embarrassing confession—embarrassing for you, I mean—any further, that we put on the rest of my clothes."

"Oh, of course. I'm sorry."

She helped him as efficiently as she had before. Sandor
was amazed how much easier it was for him to move about
with the brace supporting his back. Grudgingly he admitted to himself that he was grateful to her for that. He hoped
whatever she had to confess was not so terrible that he
would have to ask her to leave. He buttoned up his own
shirt, and glancing at Bruce saw that she had backed up to
his bed and perched on its edge. "Well," he said, "I'm
waiting."

"You left the hospital against medical advice."

"And what of it? Don't tell me they've sent you here to take me back!"

"No, of course not. You would have been discharged soon, in any case. But since you left the way you did, you didn't have your discharge plan."

"I didn't need a discharge plan. I'm not interested in a lot of bureaucratic hospital hogwash. I just needed to get out of there, and I did, as soon as I could."

"You're wrong, Sandor," said Bruce with quiet conviction. "You needed physical therapy, and the discharge plan would have set it up for you."

"Physical therapy!" Sandor spat the words as if they were obscene. "My body is ruined. My life is ruined. I'll have this pain as long as I live, which for one reason or another may not be very long. I had some of that so-called therapy when I was in the hospital, and I can tell you it was nothing more than torture dignified with a medical-sounding name! I'm not interested in any more of that, I can tell you, Bruce MacLaren!"

"And I can tell you, Sandor Szelazeny," said Bruce with quiet determination, her calm gray gaze never flinching from his angry and anguished face, "that you do need physical therapy. In the hands of a good physical therapist, it won't be torture." She took a deep breath, stood, and went to him. She held her hands out, palms upward, as if for his inspection. "These hands are good, Sandor. I've helped you this morning, admit it."

"Mmpff," he grunted, narrowing his eyes so that his heavy brows almost came together.

"My hands are good," Bruce persisted, "because I know what I'm doing. I'm a licensed physical therapist. Whether you want to admit it or not, you need me."

The rumble started low in Sandor's throat, ominous as thunder, and burst from his lips in ear-shattering denial. "No!"

Swiftly Bruce knelt beside his wheelchair. "It won't be forever, you'll only need me temporarily. I know how hard this is for you, believe me, I do know. You're used to being in command, in control. You will be again, I promise you."

Sandor sneered. "You sound so virtuous, so self-righteous! You tricked me, you and that manager of mine, Bernie Gross. All he wants is for me to get back on my feet so that I'll conduct again and make more money for him."

"Maybe that's what he wants," Bruce acknowledged, "but it's not what I want."

"And what do you want, Miss Pollyanna Physical Therapist?"

"I want your body to function as well as it possibly can. I don't care what use you put it to, I just want your body to work for you again!"

Sandor believed her. He reached out, tentatively, and touched Bruce's bright hair. His voice dropped to softness, his tone near yearning. "You're so determined to give me hope. You don't realize that for me hope is the most cruel gift."

Sandor's touch sent a ripple of shivers along Bruce's skin. The tone of his voice tore at her heart. She said, "Hope is never cruel. And besides, I'm not talking hope, I'm talking reality! I've just examined you, and I've read your medical records. I know that your spine has healed, that all you need is to strengthen your muscles, and I can show you how to do that. You may never have the flexibility you once had, and there may be times when the pain returns, but you're going to be able to do virtually anything you want to do. A body is a wonderful instrument, Sandor."

"An instrument," he mused, stroking her hair, which felt like rich, heavy silk. "The body, an instrument. An interesting concept for a musician."

Brucé waited. Her skin continued to dance under the stroke of his hand. Neither she nor Sandor saw Vladimir, who had opened the door and stood there like a dark sentinel.

Sandor heaved a deep sigh. He was tired, resigned, no match for her determination. "So, Bruce MacLaren, you would play upon this instrument that is my broken body?"

She grinned. "No, I would teach *you* to play upon the instrument of your own *healed* body. Maestro!"

Finally, reluctantly, Sandor yielded. He smiled. Then he sobered, caught both of Bruce's hands and held them in his own, tightly. He said, "Two days ago I let you into my house, against my better judgment. Today I decide to place my body in your hands, also against my better judgment. I know you will not believe me, Bruce, but I feel I must warn you. There is something far, far more wrong with me than a broken back. Not a physical thing, not something even your skilled hands can heal."

He was so intense. "What?" Bruce asked.

Sandor, his eyes darkening, hands gripping like a vise, said, "I am under a curse."

Vladimir, silent in the doorway, turned away as if satisfied by what he had heard.

Chapter Three

"No, Mr. Gross, I don't think he's teasing me." Bruce groaned silently, made a face at the pay telephone, and wished heartily that she had never asked Bernie Gross what Sandor might have meant about being under a curse. "Well, of course I've asked him to explain, but he won't, and I'm certainly not going to ask Vladimir. Look, forget I brought it up, okay? If you don't know anything about it, I'm going to assume it's just a part of his depression."

Bruce twined one long leg around the other as she listened to Sandor's manager. She was trying to be patient with the man, and not succeeding very well. She explained, "Most people in Sandor's situation are depressed for quite a while, and he's lost more through his injuries than most people have ever had to begin with. It's normal for him to say things like he isn't sure he wants to get well and that he thinks he won't live much longer. This curse thing is probably just part of that."

Once more she paused to listen and then took a deep breath, prepared to be firm. "All right. I promised you that I'd let you know when I told him why I'm really here, and I've done that. He is working with me, he didn't throw me out when I told him, even though I did it sooner than you thought I should. I have to use my own judgment here.

Now, I'm not going to call you again. I expect I'll be here somewhere between three and six months, and as long as you don't hear from me you can consider that no news is good news. Goodbye, Mr. Gross.''

Whew, thought Bruce. *I'm glad that's over!* She turned after hanging up the phone, and to her dismay, found several pairs of eyes watching her. The pay phone was in the downtown corner drugstore, which had an old-fashioned soda fountain with counter and booths. The drugstore was, Bruce would soon find out, a popular gathering place for those who lived and worked in the downtown historic district. It was not a place frequented by the tourists who mostly came to see the Tryon Palace, so Bruce's tall figure and fresh, lovely face aroused interest. Sensing that interest, and hoping no one had overheard her conversation, she walked up to the counter and ordered, just to be friendly.

''Hi,'' she said, ''I'd like a Coke, please.''

''Hey,'' returned the man behind the counter, with a warm smile. ''You visitin' from up north?''

''Well, yes and no. I'm living here for a while, but I'm from New York. How did you know?''

''If you was from around here you wouldn't say 'hi,' you'd say 'hey,' for one thing. For another thing, didn't anybody tell you yet that in New Bern you oughta drink Pepsi instead of Coke?''

''No, but that's fine with me.'' He brought the Pepsi in a tall old-fashioned glass and belatedly Bruce thought to ask, ''Why?''

The man's eyes twinkled. ''You didn't never hear 'bout Pepsi, born in the Carolinas?'' Bruce shook her head. Her nervousness, her concern about eavesdroppers was forgotten in his obvious friendliness. He went on, ''The fella that invented Pepsi did it right here in New Bern.''

''I had no idea.''

"Then you haven't been to the Visitor Center yet. They got a whole room there donated by the Pepsi people, with his portrait in a big frame and everythin'. Got lots of other interestin' stuff, too."

When she finished her drink, Bruce walked over to the Visitor Center, which was down near the water by the new hotel. She returned home laden with brochures and fired with her usual optimism. There was so much to see and do here! And she was determined that Sandor would see and do at least some of these things with her. He seemed to be hiding in his rented house, and that certainly wasn't good for him.

SUCCESS WITH SANDOR came in small increments, but it came. Observing that Sandor was underweight and had very little appetite, Bruce tackled this problem first as it seemed the easiest to solve. Vladimir really was a terrible cook, and she herself couldn't do much better, so she set about to find someone who could. Within a week she had hired a cook, a woman about her own age named Virginia Hassel, who worked part-time at the deli on Pollock Street. Virginia came to the house in the afternoons during the deli's downtime, and prepared a meal that would either cook slowly or could be reheated at the dinner hour. They had almost lost her on her second day, until Bruce realized that Vladimir was hanging around and doing what she privately called his "vulture act" in the kitchen. Vladimir as vulture was enough to give anyone the willies—Virginia had Bruce's complete sympathy. Words alone, even from Sandor, wouldn't keep Vladimir at bay; but Bruce, in self-defence, had adopted a particularly baleful stare that seemed to do the trick.

So Bruce stationed herself in the kitchen when Virginia came to cook, and directed the baleful stare at Vladimir

whenever he put his head into the room. A happy side effect of this arrangement was that Bruce gradually learned to
be a better cook, and she learned, more rapidly, a lot about
the history of New Bern. Virginia's "people," as she called
her family, had been in North Carolina since before the
Revolution. One of her ancestors, James Hasell, had even
been acting governor, appointed by the royal council after
Governor Tryon left in 1770. Virginia explained that Tryon
Palace had originally been called "Tryon's Palace" as a term
of derision by pre-revolutionary Carolinians who thought
the money to build the grand house could have better been
spent in other ways. Bruce learned also that the present
Tryon Palace was a faithful reconstruction, done in the
1950s from the architect's original plans. It sounded fascinating, and Bruce wanted to see it for herself...but not until
she had made much more progress with Sandor than she had
so far. For now, the sight of the imposing brick and iron
gates as she passed by on her morning run would have to do.

Sandor thrived on Virginia's cooking. His face filled out
so that his cheekbones were less pronounced; so were the
hollows above his collarbone. Bruce had made contact with
the Physical Therapy Department at the Craven County
Hospital and through them she rented an exercise table and
ordered the set of graduated weights she needed. When the
weights came Sandor used them grudgingly. One day Bruce
lost patience, and gave vent to her frustration.

"Honestly, Sandor, I know you can do better than that!"

"Why should I?" He lifted one saturnine eyebrow. "I
told you at the beginning that I have no wish to regain my
former strength. You're the one who wants that, not I." As
if to prove his point, Sandor opened his hands and let the
small dumbbells he had been holding drop to the floor from
where he lay on the waist-high exercise table.

Bruce yelped, and bent to pick them up. "You're like a spoiled little boy, do you know that? If you don't care about yourself, you might at least care about this beautiful old house you live in. You could dent the hardwood floor dropping these things!"

"My dear Bruce—"

"Don't my dear Bruce me, Sandor!"

"My dear Bruce," he began again with exaggerated calmness, "I do not care about this house. I do, however, care about the new house I intend to build. And about which you know nothing even though you have been here, I believe, exactly one month today."

"New house?" This was wonderful news, the most hopeful thing she'd heard from him yet. He couldn't be as depressed as he'd seemed if he was planning to build a house, nor could he really think he was going to die soon or believe he was cursed. Such beliefs simply didn't go with building new houses! "Tell me, please." She went to him quickly, zipped off the Velcro tabs of his ankle weights and helped him to sit up, bracing a thick foam wedge at his back.

"I've been waiting for you to ask where I go when I go out in the car with Vladimir. For a woman with your degree of curiosity about most things, I find it amazing that you haven't asked."

"I may be curious, but I respect people's privacy. Where you go in your own car with your own, ah, driver, is your business. That's why I haven't asked." *But oh, my, yes, I've wondered,* Bruce admitted to herself.

"We go to the building site. Perhaps today you would like to come with us, and you can see for yourself."

THE NEXT DAY, Bruce decided that she had to return to the building site on her own, driving her own car. Her car, her first and seldom-driven before she came to North Carolina, was a pre-owned tan Volvo her father had chosen, insisting that it was the safest vehicle on the roads today. She had to return to check out her feelings, to see if she felt the same on her own as she had riding with Sandor in the back seat of his Mercedes with Vladimir at the wheel. Unfortunately, she did; she couldn't blame the bad feelings on Sandor's presence or on Vladimir's driving. She felt just as uneasy, just as threatened, alone today in the ultra-safe Volvo as she had felt yesterday.

The big question was, why? She couldn't blame the uneasy feeling on Sandor's insistence that his new house be kept secret. He hadn't told her that until they were at the site, and she'd felt threatened before, throughout most of the forty-five minute drive.

It was true, though, that Bruce found the secrecy business bizarre. Worse than bizarre, paranoid. Surely it was abnormal to go to the lengths that Sandor had gone: purchasing the land through an intermediary, importing materials and workmen and an architect from Virginia so that no one in New Bern would know that the new house existed. He said he intended that when he left the rented house on East Front Street, he would seem to simply disappear. Bruce knew she should feel encouraged that he trusted her enough to let her in on the secret, but instead she felt a bit dirty, touched by Sandor's paranoia. And she had a lingering, awful feeling of something very, very wrong.

Bruce MacLaren was not a fanciful person, though beneath her efficient exterior she was more emotional, more of a romantic than most people could have guessed. She did not have phobias, wasn't scared of the dark, or of heights, or of closed-in spaces. She didn't believe in ghosts or voodoo or Gypsy curses; as a matter of fact she had a hard time believing in her own religion. Nevertheless, the drive to the place where Sandor had chosen to build his house scared her. It had scared her the first time, with Sandor, and now it scared her again, in her own car, herself at the wheel.

Following the route Vladimir had taken the previous day, Bruce had driven across the Neuse River Bridge and then turned onto a two-lane blacktop road that ran on absolutely flat land through a dense pine forest. Or at least, to her city-bred eyes, it looked like a forest and the trees looked like pines. After the first few miles there was nothing but the road and the trees, not even an occasional house. The isolation was complete. And eerie.

It was not possible to look for landmarks—there were none. She could only drive for what seemed like an appropriate length of time and then begin to look for the unpaved road that, as well as she remembered, came in on the right. Her tension mounted. She felt lost; she felt an edge of panic that reason did little to assuage. Not only was this as bad as it had been before, with Sandor beside her, it was worse.

Finally she saw the unpaved road. Praying it was the right one, she turned onto it. Her big, heavy car bumped and lurched—she hadn't slowed down enough for the rough road surface. The motor died.

Trees were closer here, closing in on the car. Bruce rolled down her window and gulped deep drafts of air to calm her nerves. The silence was absolute. She thought, panic rising, that if she wanted to get out of here she could not—she was trapped, there wasn't enough room to turn the car around! Never in her life had she wanted more to turn tail and run, to race home to familiar surroundings, people who cared about her. Home to Sandor.

Now that really was ridiculous! thought Bruce. The very ridiculousness of it made her feel better. If she wanted to go home to people who cared about her, she would have to go all the way back to New York. Sandor didn't care about her, or if he did, he had a strange way of showing it. And if she was beginning to care about him…well, she always did care more for her patients than she should. She knew that about herself, and she'd learned to compensate, to hide her feelings. Sometimes she could even hide them from herself.

She reached out and turned the key to re-start the motor. The starter made a grinding sound but the motor didn't catch. Now the isolation sank into Bruce like a cold, hard stone. Why did Sandor want to build a house in such a deserted place? If her car would not start, she would have to walk for hours to get help. And Sandor, if he were living out here and had an emergency, what would he do? Of course, Sandor had Vladimir. Small comfort. Bruce couldn't imagine anything much worse than being out here, miles from anyone, in the same house with creepy Vladimir.

Once again she turned the key, and heaved a sigh of relief when this time the motor turned over. She drove carefully, and in a few minutes reached the place where Maestro Sandor Szelazeny had chosen to build his new house.

The site was as quiet and empty as it had been yesterday. The land had been cleared and lines laid out for the foundations, but the actual building had not yet begun. Bruce left the car in a spot wide enough that she could turn around, and walked across the cleared ground to the shoreline.

When she looked out over the water, away from the suffocating density of the tall, scraggly pine tree, this place was beautiful. Sandor owned three acres a few miles northeast of a quaint little harbor town called Oriental. His land was at a point where the Neuse River, having already swallowed up the Trent at New Bern, widened into the vast Pamlico Sound. Eventually, Sandor had explained, the Pamlico ran up against North Carolina's Outer Banks. Its waters were now blue, now gray, changing as tall white columns of clouds sailed majestically overhead. Wide-winged birds mounted the air, then swooped down in graceful arcs. The Sound here was miles and miles across; unless she turned around, it seemed to Bruce that the whole world was made of water.

The silence here was not, after all, silence. Rather the sounds were different. So subtle that at first her city-tuned ears did not hear. Nature sounds. Birds calling, from so high in the air their voices were almost lost on the wind. The water gently lapping at the shoreline. A faint rustle of the breeze she felt fresh and steady in her face. And from the far side of the water, so far away that it looked like a toy, the purr of a boat's motor. Bruce was glad she had come back here on her own, and for the moment she forgot why she had done so. As she stood on the shore and looked out across that vast expanse of water, she understood for the first time in her life how it felt to be truly alone, and not lonely.

Perhaps, she thought, at last turning away, *I do understand now why Sandor has chosen this place. He wants to be alone, and it is beautiful here.*

Nevertheless, she realized as she got into her car once more, the isolation is also a fact. So is his wanting to keep this building project a secret. These things bothered her. Something about Sandor's whole situation bothered her, more and more every day. It wasn't that he was still depressed and more or less uncooperative. That was fairly normal, it was just taking him longer to break out of it than it did most of her patients.

Taking him longer because he didn't yet want to break out of it! Bruce smiled. She knew that the stubbornness with which he clung to his disability was a reflection of Sandor's strength of will. Once he made up his mind to apply that strong will to the improvement of his body, he would make astonishing progress.

So, if that wasn't it, then what was it about Sandor's situation that bothered her so much? She puzzled over the problem, and in her puzzlement didn't notice the narrowness of the road or the closeness of the trees as the miles of her drive back to New Bern clicked by. Nor did she notice the silver-gray car that had driven out of the trees and followed behind her.

Finally Bruce realized that "puzzle" was an apt name for the process she was engaged in, and was also a clue to the solution she sought. What was bothering her was that there was a piece missing, with the result that she felt as frustrated as if she were trying to work a jigsaw puzzle with a missing piece.

What was missing, Bruce realized, what she so desperately wanted to know, was the real reason for Sandor's behavior. There was obviously something very, very wrong in his life. Something more than the fact that he had broken his back. There was a reason he, who had thrived on public attention, had decided to withdraw from the world to such a drastic extent. What was the reason? What was the nature of the missing piece to this puzzle?

At the Neuse River Bridge, Bruce came to a sudden stop because she had to, the drawbridge was up for a boat to pass through. Her thoughts came simultaneously to just as sudden a stop. What if he'd already told her the reason, and she just hadn't wanted to believe it? What if Sandor Szelazeny really believed that he was cursed?

Bruce did not see the silver car pull off and wait at the side of the road so that it would not be directly behind her Volvo at the bridge. She was too occupied with her own thoughts. She could not, would not believe that a curse can be real enough to make bad things happen. Sandor might be a little paranoid, but he couldn't believe such a thing, either. Could he?

The line of cars started up again, Bruce with them. Her mind was in a whirl. Her training had always, before, stood her in good stead. She had been taught that to motivate a difficult patient you have to understand and eliminate the groundless fears such a patient will use to stay stuck in a disability. She had dismissed Sandor's mention of a curse as just such a groundless fear. But what if, what if...? No, she couldn't think like that. If she did she'd be just as paranoid as Sandor, and then she'd be of no help to anyone.

The forbidden thought persisted: what if Sandor's seemingly bizarre actions and decisions were completely justified? What if his belief in a curse had some as-yet-not-understood basis in reality? Her intuition told her that this could be true. Yet her professional training still insisted that anything as irrational-sounding as a "curse" had to be no more than the well-known and well-understood groundless fear.

Suddenly Bruce was confused, at war within herself. Intuition fought against professional knowledge. She pulled into the driveway at the side of the house and for a moment rested her forehead on hands clenched at the top of the steering wheel. The unrelenting confusion exhausted her. Bruce was a straight-arrow sort of person, one who went to the heart of a matter, dealt with it, and then moved on. Confusion was simply not her style; she had to decide what to do.

Her sense of humor came to the rescue. She decided that she did not need to understand, did not need to have the missing puzzle piece. It was no skin off her nose if Sandor wanted to give up a promising career and live in the back of beyond with a Transylvanian vulture. She didn't care if he had been cursed as a baby in his cradle by the Evil Black

Fairy, or whatever. She was getting too involved, and that was *her* problem. She could solve her own problems easily enough!

Bruce got out of her car and resolutely stalked into the house. She would do her job, period. End of discussion. Either Sandor would learn from her how to care for and value his body—which, after all, could so easily have died on him—or he wouldn't. No skin off her nose, no siree. She had never "lost" a patient, never had one who did not, sooner or later, respond to her teaching. Maybe Sandor would be the first. If so, then she didn't care!

Who am I kidding? Bruce asked herself, pausing at the top of the stairs on the way to her room. *I do care. Even if I get too involved, even if when it's all over, I get hurt, I do care. Sandor is the most exasperating, most infuriating, most... fascinating man I have ever known. I want to give him his life back, on a silver platter.*

Silver! Through the round second-story window above the front door, opposite the top of the stairs, came a flash of silver light. Seeing it, Bruce smiled. The silver glint coincided perfectly with her thought. She turned and went on down the hall to her room.

The silvery-gray car, from whose surface the dying afternoon sun had struck the flash of silver, sped away down the street. If Bruce had known what the driver of that car thought of her, then the sight of a silvery light would not have made her smile. Not ever again.

Chapter Four

Bruce's first impulse on seeing what had been done to her room was to scream. Only the knowledge that Sandor should be resting at this hour stopped her; whatever might happen, the patient must not be disturbed! She shoved her fist against her open mouth and felt the hardness of her teeth against her knuckles. Slowly she turned her head to see the full extent of the damage.

Her bed had been ripped apart—pillows thrown on the floor, the crocheted bedspread half on, half off, sheets pulled out from one side of the mattress and the mattress itself shoved to one side, askew atop the matching box spring. All the drawers in the chest were open, their contents of underwear, socks, stockings, panty hose, scarves, sweaters, T-shirts and sweatshirts, leotards and tights, strewn both in and out of the drawers. The little velvet jewel case she kept on top of the chest had been upended, its meager and not very valuable contents dumped in a golden heap. The closet door stood open, the clothes on hangers all awry, as if someone had hastily pawed through them. Her empty luggage had been pulled from the back of the closet and all the bags unzipped; shoes were thrown around every which way. On the low bookcase under the windows the books were sprawled, some left open, dropped face-down with no regard as to crumpling their pages.

And her precious notebooks...! Hesitantly, fearing what she might find, Bruce approached the pile of papers that had once been her notebooks in their three-ring binders. These were her own private notes, a collection of case studies out of which she planned some day to compile a kind of textbook for physical therapists, and jottings of her own ideas on how to handle the particularly difficult patients with whom she excelled. Her progress notes on Sandor were there, as well. All very private material, and irreplaceable. Bruce knelt in the midst of the mess, with shaking hands sorting through pages of her own handwriting. Perhaps everything was still here, it would take hours to find out.

She had been at first too shocked by the sight of such vandalism to think straight. But as Bruce grimly began to sort through her papers, looking automatically first for Sandor's progress notes, her thinking processes began to work again. She realized that from the very moment of seeing all this mess, she had instinctively assumed it was Vladimir's doing.

She sank back into a sitting position on the floor, her eyes a hard stony gray and her mouth pressed into a firm, disapproving line. What an extraordinarily childish thing to do, such stupid destruction! He must have come into her room while she had driven out to the new house site and trashed the place, in a vain and foolish attempt to...to...what? Frighten her into leaving? Harass her? Surely he hadn't wanted to steal anything—she didn't have anything worth stealing. The only thing of any real value that she owned, aside from her car, was the Rolex watch that was her one self-indulgence. She looked at the watch on her wrist, saw that it was almost 4:00 p.m. She always wore the watch, never left it in the jewelry case or lying about. Vladimir would have noticed that, she was sure—he noticed everything with those beady eyes of his, he never missed a thing!

Bruce tossed the hair out of her eyes. She was much calmer now and a new thought occurred to her. Perhaps she had jumped to conclusions. Vladimir, for all that he looked like something out of a thirties black-and-white horror film, did seem a bit too dignified to stoop to the making of this kind of mess. And if he was not the one responsible....

Cursing herself for being so blaming and self-centered, Bruce scrambled to her feet. If not Vladimir, then someone had gotten into the house from outside! The black Mercedes had not been in the driveway when she'd pulled in, had it? No, she didn't think so; she hadn't paid much attention because she knew that Vladimir often took the car to go shopping while Sandor rested in the afternoons. The front door had been locked, though...hadn't it? Surely she had unlocked it, would have noticed if she hadn't needed her key? She was astonished at how hard it was to be certain of details that she normally took so much for granted.

Checking the other rooms on the second floor didn't take long. Nothing seemed to have been disturbed in any of them, including the only other inhabited room, which was Vladimir's. It was not until Bruce rounded the turn of the stairs, one hand gripping the smooth wooden banister, that she realized an outside intruder—if there had been one—could have harmed Sandor. She didn't believe it, didn't seriously think the destruction in her room had been anything but a nasty prank by the Maestro's jealous valet, but her heart began to thump uncomfortably in her chest anyway. Her hands instantly dripped cold sweat, the one on the banister leaving a wet, slippery trail.

Think, dummy! Bruce commanded herself. *Go slow, don't run,* she told her feet. Chances were at least ninety-nine to one that Sandor was perfectly all right, that if she went running down the hall and burst into his room yelling "Are you all right?" she would only alarm him. She forced herself to go into the living room at the bottom of the stairs, and into the library with its half-empty shelves—the furnishings with which the house came supplied did not include many books. Everything, including the books and the desk in the library, was in place in both rooms. The big family kitchen, the room where they spent the most time, looked as warm and welcoming as it always did. Virginia had come and gone, leaving the evidence of her presence in a casserole that cooked slowly in the oven and spread its delicious fragrance through the air.

Only Sandor's room, the former dining room, remained. Taking a deep breath, with her heart still bumping ridiculously in her chest, Bruce rapped softly on the closed door with her knuckles. No answer. She did not know whether or not Sandor really slept when he rested in the afternoons, but she prayed now that he would be in bed, safely asleep. She didn't want to have to talk about this, not yet, not until she'd had a chance to decide what—if anything—to say.

Bruce pushed open the door, slowly. Sandor was not in bed. He sat in the wheelchair facing the window, his head dropped down so that his chin rested on his chest. Surely he was asleep. In the doorway, Bruce hesitated. Her hands were still cold and damp. Perhaps it was foolish, but she had to be certain that he was all right, that he was... breathing. Softly, softly she approached.

Sandor slept. His chest gently rose and fell with the rhythm of his respirations. In Bruce's own chest, her heart stopped its thumping, and melted instead. He looked so totally defenseless, though she knew that he was not. If he were to awaken at this very moment and find her standing a foot away, looking at him, he might glare and bark and practically spit fire at her for interrupting his privacy. She

would like that; she enjoyed their verbal sparring, and she
had known for quite some time that his bark was much,
much worse than his bite. Or, he might rouse and notice her
with a silent scowl, turning his face and his body in the chair
away from her—that she would not like. Refusal, denial,
total rejection. Bruce could not bear Sandor's rejection, and
she was no longer so sure that it was only because in reject-
ing her, he rejected the help he needed for a complete recovery. She suspected that she wanted more from Sandor
than his simple cooperation in getting well. Of course, she
must be sure that he never knew.

Reluctantly, Bruce backed away from the sleeping Sandor. She had an almost uncontrollable desire to smooth the
thick, unruly shock of hair back off his forehead, to tuck the
afghan more securely around his legs, or simply to touch his
hands, which lay open, the fingers half curled, on his lap.
Sandor's hands were wonderful, large and long-fingered,
and he used them in ways that were unconsciously elo-
quent, strong and graceful at the same time. What would it
be like, she wondered, to feel those hands on her own body?
He never touched her, though she so often, of necessity,
touched him.

A hot flush rose in Bruce's cheeks as she realized what she
had been thinking, and she hastened the last steps through
the door and closed it behind her. How could she let herself
do that? She gave herself a stern lecture as she went quickly
back through the hall, suddenly concerned that Vladimir
might return and find her outside the Maestro's door. The
one thing a physical therapist must never, never do was to
even think of touching her patient in a way that might possibly feel sensual, arousing. Never! And to want the patient
to touch her in such a way...no, it would never, never do!

Bruce was ashamed of herself. Her face burned all the
way back to her room. She shut the door and began to clean

up the mess with a vengeance. The self-discipline that had always been one of her strong points came to her aid, and by the time she had restored order to the room she had restored order to her thoughts and feelings, as well.

To keep silent about what had happened in her room seemed to be the only reasonable choice. Nothing had been taken, someone had just come in and made a big, disturbing mess. But who was responsible, Vladimir, or an outsider?

Bruce knew Vladimir disliked her, it was perfectly obvious, and the reason was equally obvious: he saw her as an intruder, an invader of his turf. However, it was also obvious that Vladimir was devoted to Sandor, and Sandor was making steady improvement under Bruce's guidance, and Vladimir knew it. If she accused Vladimir, fairly or unfairly, there would be an argument and it might very well come down to one of those ''If she stays, I go'' things, in which case Bruce would surely lose and have to leave.

On the other hand, if Sandor were told that someone had broken into the house and vandalized Bruce's room.... That alternative didn't bear thinking about, not with Sandor already so paranoid. If anything had been taken, or property destroyed, it might be different. Aside from the assault on Bruce's nerves, no harm had been done.

She herself could not have been a target of anyone other than Vladimir—she didn't know a soul in New Bern outside this house, and didn't have an enemy in the world that she knew of. It was remotely possible that a burglar had gotten into the house after seeing that both cars were gone, someone who didn't know that Sandor stayed in a room on the first floor; and the burglar had just happened to start in Bruce's room where he found nothing. Then, Virginia had come and startled the criminal in mid-burglary, and he'd run out of the house undetected. The more Bruce thought about that alternative, the more plausible it seemed. By dinner-time, when she had to go downstairs and face Vladimir and Sandor, Bruce felt quite serene in her decision to say nothing of the incident.

BRUCE'S SERENITY did not last long. In fact, less than a full twenty-four hours. The day had started out beautifully, as most days did in New Bern. More and more, Bruce enjoyed her morning run. It was the air, she had decided, so clear and clean, fresh with moisture from overnight dew and the two unpolluted rivers flowing around the town. After her run, she decided that she would take Sandor to the little park located at the point where the two rivers met and flowed together in water so wide that it looked almost like open sea.

He protested, of course, but Bruce was adamant.

"You never go out, Sandor," she said, "anywhere except to your building site. It simply isn't good for you to stay cooped up all the time."

"I like being cooped up. I prefer it," Sandor grumbled.

"It's bad for your mental health—"

He interrupted, now growling, "My mental health isn't your concern, Bruce MacLaren. You stick with the physical stuff, and leave my mind alone!"

"Uh-uh," Bruce shook her head, making her heavy coppery hair swing. "I'm going to get tough with you, Sandor Szelazeny!"

"You mean you haven't been tough before?" Sandor's bushy eyebrows arched upward in mock astonishment, but Bruce could see the light of enjoyment in his eyes. He loved the bantering every bit as much as she did.

"Not nearly tough enough." Decisively, Bruce went behind the wheelchair and pushed it toward his room. "For example, I haven't said a word to you about being depressed, now have I?"

"I'm not depressed!"

"Really. Then I wonder what you call it when you don't eat right and you spend at least half your time off in some gloomy place in your head." She pushed him toward the armoire that served as his closet and opened the doors. "Now, which sweater do you want? It isn't at all cold outside, so you don't need a heavy one. A bright color would be nice—"

"I'm not going out!"

"Yes, you are. We both are. How about this yellow one?" She tossed it to him with a grin. "You put it on while I get your canes."

Sandor, mumbling in a rumble to himself, pulled the sweater over his head and worked it down around his middle. He winced once with the pain of motion and said to cover it, "Surely you don't think I'm going to *walk* wherever this is that you've decided you're taking me."

"Not entirely, no." Bruce was pleased that he'd given up fighting the idea of going out. She'd never before been able to entice him anywhere outside with her except on the lawn behind the house. "I'm going to push you in the wheelchair down to the park at the end of Front Street. But once we get there, you might like to get out of the chair and walk around a little. I think you're ready, as long as you have a cane in each hand." She tucked the canes in by his side and pushed him smartly through the door and down the hall.

Vladimir, dressed in his usual black, came down the stairs. "Maestro—" he began.

To Bruce's happy surprise, Sandor himself cut him off. "Bruce and I are going for a walk, Vladimir. Open the door, if you please."

"Certainly, Maestro," said Vladimir stiffly, complying. "And how long will you be gone?"

"An hour or so," said Bruce, maneuvering the wheel-chair through the door and down the wooden ramp that covered half of the three steps down to the sidewalk.

Vladimir cleared his throat, and both Bruce and Sandor turned to look at him. In tones slightly less sepulchral than usual, Vladimir said, "If I may say so, sir, it's good to see you getting out again."

Well, thought Bruce, astonished, *wonders will never cease.*

"Humph!" said Sandor. He made one last protest as they started along the sidewalk. "People are going to see me in this . . . this despicable condition!"

"So what?" said Bruce brightly. "You don't know any-body here, and why should a famous person like you have to care what people think of him anyway?" She stopped at the corner, looked up and down the street, then negotiated the chair down the curb with no problem. "The point, San-dor, is not whether or not people see you. The point is for you to see something of this lovely little town you're living in. Just look around you—the daffodils blooming, all the new grass coming up, and all these wonderful trees begin-ning to show their blossoms! Smell the air! It's wonderful, isn't it?"

Sandor looked; he sniffed at the air. Then cautiously he took a deep breath. She was right, the air was wonderful. And there seemed to be flowers everywhere. It was spring, and he had forgotten how beautiful spring could be. He turned his head as they crossed a wide street that led onto a bridge, and saw the blue of the river beneath a cloudless sky of an even deeper blue. He felt the hard knot that had been in his chest for so long now—a knot made of equal parts bitterness, anger and fear—loosen, break up and dissolve completely away.

Later, when he had left his wheelchair, walked across the grass unassisted except by the two canes and sat next to Bruce on a picnic bench with only his back brace for support, Sandor said grudgingly, "I guess the exercises have helped. I couldn't have done this much before. Thank you."

"You're welcome." Bruce's eyes were bright with a glaze of unshed tears; she was so proud of him that she wanted to weep. He had, indeed, done much more than she'd dared hope. She asked, "How's the pain?"

"Not too bad." He looked around with interest. "You're right, this is a beautiful place." He raised a cane and pointed with it. "Look, sailboats."

"Mmm-hmm. Do you sail, Sandor?"

"No. I have friends, acquaintances, who sail and I've been out with them on their boats. But I was always too busy doing other things to learn. How about you?"

"I wish! Sailing is a little out of my league."

He raised a busy eyebrow inquiringly. "I shouldn't have thought that anything you might decide to do, my dear Bruce, would be out of your league."

She accepted the compliment, ducking her head in a fleeting moment of shyness. "Professionally, maybe. But socially, that's a different story. Girls who grow up in a working-class neighborhood in Brooklyn, like I did, don't much aspire to sailing. I can't even swim."

Sandor looked at Bruce, suddenly aware of her as a whole person, with a background and a family, brothers and sisters probably, friends . . . a man in her life, surely. They had come from worlds apart. He was maybe ten years older than she, yet in a flash of certainty he knew that he did not want her to go back to her own world and leave him in his. Not for a long, long time, and perhaps not even then. "Ah, do you still live in Brooklyn? When you're not living here with me, that is?"

"No." Bruce shifted on the bench. She looked not at Sandor, but out across the water. This was getting to be too much like one of the social situations that made her so uncomfortable. "I have an apartment in Greenwich Village. And a cat. My little sister, who's not so little anymore, is staying there and cat-sitting while I'm down here with you."

A silence fell between them while Sandor discovered that his mind still worked. The sudden awareness that he wanted Bruce MacLaren—*wanted* her, man-to-woman—acted on his gray-shrouded mental processes like jump-starting a battery sluggish from long disuse. All the obstacles he knew were between them, all the problems, were swiftly noted and disregarded. He forged ahead. "You're not married, then." He hadn't thought she was, but best to be sure.

Bruce darted a glance his way, then returned her steady, increasingly uneasy, gaze to the water. "No, of course not. I—I mean, I wouldn't very well have left a husband to come here, knowing I was likely to be here for months."

"But you did leave someone behind? A man, important to you?"

"Not really." The face of a doctor she'd been dating came to mind; with a bit of a jolt she realized she hadn't thought of him once until now. For a long, potentially dangerous moment during which she could feel Sandor watching her, could feel his eyes warmer than the sun on her skin, Bruce allowed herself the luxury of thinking that perhaps, just perhaps, Sandor was becoming as attracted to her as she knew she was to him. For just a moment she put aside the physical therapist and let herself be a woman.

And in that moment Sandor said, "I'm glad." The acute emotional sensitivity that was so much a part of him, which had for so long been stifled, swelled and surfaced and flowed into the two words. He reached out; with long, sensitive fingers he stroked her cheek.

Bruce drew a ragged breath. He had melted something inside her with his words. The touch of his hand, which secretly she had long desired, was almost more than she could bear. She did not dare to look at Sandor. She closed her eyes and trapped his stroking hand in her own, holding it firmly, moving the hand inexorably away from the vulnerable softness of her face. She felt his fingers curl beneath her own, as if in question, but still forced both their hands down, down, until she pressed his hand to the rough surface of the bench. "Don't touch me," she said with a catch in her voice. It seemed the hardest thing she had ever had to say or do.

Sandor was not easily discouraged, nor did he guess how much Bruce's refusal had cost her. He teased, "Oh, that's hardly fair! You're always—"

But Bruce didn't, couldn't, stay to hear more. She opened her eyes but still did not dare look at him. Instead she stood up and moved behind the bench, interrupting him to say, "You've been sitting on this bench for longer than is good for you. I'll get the wheelchair."

All the way home, she silently repeated lessons she'd learned in training, lessons whose rightness had been borne out later in her practice over and over again: the relationship between physical therapist and patient is similar to that between psychotherapist and patient. There comes a time in recovery from a very serious injury, usually when the patient is beginning to feel significantly better and stronger, when feelings of profound appreciation and gratitude can be misinterpreted as "falling in love." The psychotherapists call this "transference." In physical therapy there was no real name for it, nor were there any helpful guidelines for handling it. The only thing the therapist could do was hang on to her head. And her heart. If she didn't, she was the one likely to be hurt.

Bruce knew all about that first-hand; it had happened to her once and she'd almost left the profession because of it. She would never allow it to happen again. Especially not with Maestro Sandor Szelazeny. A fully recovered Sandor would have no need of her and would forget her in the bat of an eyelash. But she, even as it was now, would never forget him. How many thousand times worse would it be if she allowed herself to really, completely love him?

And besides, thought Bruce, squaring her shoulders, *falling in love with a patient is unethical. So that takes care of that.* Her chin came up, defiantly. She pushed Sandor's chair with such vigor that she bumped a curb and almost spilled him out.

"God, woman!" he protested, "Watch where you're going!"

"Oh," Bruce gasped, shocked that she could have been so preoccupied. "I'm sorry! Are you all right! Did I hurt you?"

"No," grumbled Sandor, "just another gut-wrenching pain. I'm used to them." He returned to his own thoughts as Bruce promised to be more careful.

He had been thinking that she might have been right, when she told him not to touch her. All the obstacles and problems he'd so casually brushed aside earlier now loomed before him big as boulders. What right had he to be seriously interested in a woman now, even a woman as unusual as Bruce MacLaren? He fully intended to lead the life of a recluse and an exile; only if they couldn't find him—whoever *they* were—would he be safe. He couldn't ask any woman to share that kind of life. Could he?

He looked around again as Bruce pushed him along, and to his own surprise liked what he saw. He had chosen New Bern as his hiding place by consulting a map; he'd heard of the remoteness of North Carolina's Outer Banks, and one glance at the map confirmed it, but he didn't think he could handle being quite that cut off. New Bern had just looked like a reasonable compromise, and driving around and locating the land he'd bought less than an hour away from the town had confirmed his choice. But he hadn't expected to actually like the place. Now, it seemed, he might. He and Bruce could work an hour or two of daily exploration into their routine—that would please her, he was sure.

Thank God he didn't have to worry about money. He didn't have to return to conducting. The thought of never again holding a baton in his hand, never again commanding an orchestra, never again creating the music that gave him pleasure so deep it was truly sensual, caused Sandor pain that was in its way worse than physical pain—as it always did. He seldom allowed himself to think of that, and resolutely pushed it from his mind. He was fortunate that he didn't have to work in order to live, and he was grateful for that, at least.

But what about his ruined body? Could he offer any woman a relationship with this body? Was he even capable of having sex? Oh, he had erections still, occasionally, but the whole process of making love was much more than that, and a rather athletic affair, the way he'd always done it....

He mused on that until he saw his rented house ahead, and then quickly decided that he would simply believe Bruce. He hadn't before. She said he would be able to do all the things he used to do, that if he did the exercises she set for him he could regain all his former strength. He'd thought she was just trying to raise his spirits, but what if she'd been telling him the truth? He would stop being half-hearted about the physical therapy. He would go ahead and seize the hope she was always holding out to him.

Seeing the house ahead, Bruce put her mind back on her work; she wanted to be sure the lessons of this first outing had not been lost on her patient. "Almost home," she said. "How are you feeling? That's a clinical question, Sandor. I want you to really think about it before you answer."

"I feel great," he answered promptly, disregarding her instructions. Bruce rolled her eyes—how typical!—but she said nothing because he continued with an enthusiasm that was more than she could possibly have hoped for. "I've actually enjoyed myself! I insist that we do this every day. You know, I hadn't thought about it until right now, but this is the first time I've been anywhere without Vladimir since…since the hospital. It's high time we had a break from each other."

"I agree." Bruce stopped at the foot of the ramp and moved around so that she could look critically at Sandor. She couldn't help but be pleased by what she saw. His face was alight, and smiling. A soft breeze ruffled his hair. His posture was erect. He looked years younger. A little thrill of success went through her. "I'm glad you had a good time. One last thing, though. How does your body feel? Pay attention to your body, Sandor, let it speak to you. Let it tell you before you tell me."

Sandor had grown accustomed to denying pain; he had continued to ignore his body, though Bruce had given him similar instructions before. This time he did as she asked. He let his body speak to him, and was amazed at what he learned. "My back feels…okay. About like it usually does. No real pain. No, wait. It aches, but maybe not as much as usual."

That's very, very good, thought Bruce, considering how long he sat on that hard, backless bench. She waited, as Sandor's expression told her that he was continuing his physical self-assessment. Maybe, after all the weeks of grudging half cooperation, he was going to turn out to be a good patient after all.

"Ah," ventured Sandor, moving his legs experimentally, "ah, there is something new, though. My legs feel strange."

Bruce smiled—a big, wide smile that included her eyes and made her whole face luminous. "That's wonderful! That's exactly what I wanted to hear!"

Sandor tried to scowl, and couldn't. When she smiled like that, he wanted to give her the world. He felt the curving of his own lips as he asked playfully, "What kind of woman are you, anyway, to get so turned on because my legs feel strange?"

"I am what I told you I was a long time ago—a good physical therapist! Your legs feel strange because you walked farther today than you have walked before. Don't you see what this means? It isn't your legs that keep you in that wheelchair, it's your back. Your spine itself has healed. What has been giving you the kind of pain that keeps you in that wheelchair is the damage to nerves and soft tissue. When those things have healed sufficiently that you can stay on your feet long enough for your weak leg muscles to feel 'strange,' that's real progress!"

"Well, I'll be damned!" gloated Sandor.

"And just think," declared Bruce, seizing the wheel-chair and propelling it vigorously up the ramp, "how easy it will be to make your legs stronger! There are all sorts of exercises, and Velcro ankle weights...."

"I can hardly wait," muttered Sandor, but his spirits were as high as Bruce's.

However, just inside the front door their high spirits crashed. It was a disaster.

Chapter Five

Vladimir sat on the stairs, halfway up. His bony, black-clad knees and arms stuck up and out like a spider. From this perch he surveyed the chaos on the floor below with a funereal expression on his long, pale face.

Sandor's voice was heavy as lead. "So, it begins again!" he said, and looked up at Vladimir. "Or should I say, it continues?"

Bruce leaned against the open door for support. The degree of disruption here was far, far worse than in her own room. The stairway was littered, the hall floor all but impassable. She didn't like to think what the rooms on either side would look like. But this time she wasn't shocked, she was angry. "I'd like to get my hands on the S.O.B. who did this," she said loudly, striding into the clutter. She glared up the stairs. "Well, Vladimir, get off your duff and get down here and help me clear a path through this mess! We can't leave Sandor sitting out here in the hall all day!"

Startled out of his usual dignity, the valet assembled his arms and legs and hastened to help. "Maestro," he pleaded as he bobbed about picking things up. "I'm sorry. I hope you will forgive me. I went for a walk, also. Ah—" he glanced at Bruce "—in the opposite direction. And when I returned a few minutes ago I found the house in this condition. I was so distressed that I didn't know where to begin...."

"*You're* sorry!" said Bruce, kicking at sofa pillows that had been thrown out into the hall. "I'm the one who should be sorry. If I'd told Sandor what happened in my room yesterday we could have called the police then, and maybe cut the bastard off before he tore up the whole house!" She stopped the hectic, angry pace of her activity long enough to catch and hold Vladimir's eye. "I owe you an apology, Vladimir."

"Beg pardon, miss?" he asked, straightening to his spindly height and looking down at her.

"I thought it was you who trashed my room while I was out yesterday afternoon." An expression of such extreme distaste came over Vladimir's face that Bruce involuntarily shrank back. "I—I know you don't like me, so when I found my room all torn up I thought you'd done it. To give me a hard time. You know, to harass me," she explained rather lamely, then rushed to add, "but by the time I got it all cleaned up I realized it wasn't really your style."

The sour expression on Vladimir's face had not changed a bit. *Nuts,* thought Bruce, *I haven't got the patience for this guy's delicate sensibilities, not now.* She bent once more to her task of clearing a path for Sandor. "Anyway, I do apologize. Obviously whoever trashed my room yesterday was interrupted before he could finish the job, and came back this morning."

"I assure you, Miss MacLaren," said Vladimir coolly, "that whether I like you or not, I would never do anything one might call 'trashing'!"

"Yeah, I figured that out," Bruce muttered. Well, at least she had tried to be nice.

Through all this, Sandor said nothing. He remembered telling Bruce, weeks ago, that hope was the most cruel gift she could give him. He had just found out how cruel. If they had found him here, they could find him anywhere; they would hound him to the end of the earth. All the morning's bright promise turned to dust inside him.

Bruce still burned with anger, and when she was angry she wanted action. She kicked a few remaining objects out of the way and came for Sandor's wheelchair. "Come on," she said through clenched teeth, "we've got a phone call to make."

She wheeled him to the kitchen and stopped. "Oh, God," she said. Pots and pans were everywhere. All the dishes and glasses had been taken out of the cabinets; fortunately, they had been piled rather neatly on the counters and nothing was broken. Bruce did not find this odd, at the time.

"Just stay there," she said to Sandor determinedly. The kitchen telephone was a wall phone and had a long cord. She thought it would reach, and it did. She held out the handset with its pushbuttons in the receiver to Sandor. He paid no attention, he stared at a point somewhere beyond her.

"Sandor," said Bruce, dropping in a crouch beside him, "you have to call the police." He didn't move, not so much as to blink an eye. "If we'd done it yesterday, this might not have happened." Still no response. Bruce took a deep breath. "All right, if you won't do it, I will!" She started to push 911.

Sandor knocked the receiver out of her hand. It clattered on the floor. "No police!" he said through clenched teeth.

"The Maestro does not want the police called," said Vladimir. He had come up so quietly Bruce hadn't known he was there. He was always doing that, it gave her the willies.

"He made his point," said Bruce, retrieving the phone and checking to see that it still worked before she hung it up. Then she leaned for a minute against the wall, her head turned away from Sandor and the faithful retainer. Sandor's swift, violent swat at her hand had not hurt, but it had shocked the anger out of her.

She took a deep breath, calming herself. Then she turned to face them. Vladimir stood behind the Maestro, his hands protectively on the back of the wheelchair at Sandor's shoulders, as if he were guarding him. "Okay," Bruce said. "Now maybe one of you would care to tell me why in the world we shouldn't call the police."

"Vladimir and I have been through these things before."

Dimly now, Bruce recalled Sandor's saying, "So, it begins again!"

Vladimir bent over his Maestro. "Sir, perhaps now you will believe that we should go back."

With infinite weariness, Sandor raised the back of his hand and rubbed it, hard, across his eyes. Then, eyes closed, he shook his head from side to side so that his shaggy dark hair caught the motion. There was a sadness on his face so deep, so tragic, that Bruce ached with empathy. She couldn't help herself; she went to him, Vladimir or no Vladimir, and knelt by his feet, putting her hand on his knee, her cheek on that hand.

When he spoke, his voice seemed to come from an empty, hollow place. "No, we will not go back. *I will never go back!*"

"But, Maestro...." Vladimir was ignored; if he finished the sentence neither Bruce nor Sandor heard him.

Sandor stroked Bruce's hair, thinking this might be the last time he would touch that silky brightness. He said, "But, Bruce, you should go back. Back to New York. Back to your home, where you belong. There is no point to you being here longer."

Bruce raised her head to look at him. In a voice scarcely above a whisper she said, "I don't understand. Something is happening here, something more than just that the house was broken into, and I don't understand."

Sandor had been close, so very close to wrapping himself once again in his cloak of gray dullness where no thought and no feeling could intrude. In a way he wanted, even welcomed it, a place if not truly comfortable then at least familiar. But he could not deny the honest yearning in those clear gray eyes; nor could he help but feel the caring that poured out of her and over him like a soft embrace. He brushed Bruce's smooth brow with his fingertips. He was also very much aware of Vladimir, who stood behind him like a dark shadow.

From some reservoir deep within, Sandor summoned strength and put it into his voice. "Vladimir, start cleaning up. Start in the living room. Now."

"Yes, Maestro." As always, Vladimir was obedient.

When he had gone, Sandor gestured toward the row of windows. Though the seating area was as disarranged as everything else, he longed to be in the sunlight. "Let us go over there."

Bruce nodded. She quickly gathered magazines and set potted plants back in their places, plumped the pillows onto the couch. "Would you like to get out of your chair and sit on the couch? I'll help you."

"Yes, I'd like that," said Sandor. He wheeled himself over to her. "I still have the canes, perhaps I can do it myself."

Bruce bent to release the wheelchair's footrests. "Remember how I showed you...."

"Yes, I remember. Put the canes out first, shift weight to the canes, then stand... Ah!" Sandor suited actions to words and did quite well. Even so, when it came time to sit, the couch seemed a long way down and he was glad of

Bruce's supporting hand at the small of his back as he sank into the cushions.

For a few moments he said nothing. He appeared to be relaxing, soaking up the sun's warmth; but in reality he was trying to decide how much he should tell Bruce. It was difficult, especially since there was so much that he himself did not understand.

Finally he said, "Do you remember when you first came here, I told you that I was under a curse?"

Bruce nodded. Her eyes were wide.

"You didn't believe me."

"It was a strange thing to say. I was willing to believe that you believed it, but really, Sandor...."

Sandor's lips curved up on one side in an ironic sort of grin. "In this day and age, who would believe such a thing? I won't bother to tell you the whole story—it's too fantastic, and you don't need to know all the details to have the understanding for which you asked. You must remember that I am of Hungarian ancestry. I myself often forgot. In America such things do not seem important. But on that last European tour of mine I discovered that I had a grandfather I hadn't known about—my mother's father. He died—now I really am the last of the line. The people handling his estate got in touch with me when I had just begun the tour, and when I could take a break, I went to meet with them. Vladimir went with me. I didn't tell anyone else where I was going, just that I needed a break for a few days.

"That was when I learned many things I had not known before." Sandor looked away; the horrors came rushing back at him. There was no way he could speak to Bruce, or to anyone, about such things. When he had himself again in hand, he continued. "I did what I thought necessary, and of course I dismissed the very idea of a family curse. I resumed the tour. But soon . . . accidents began to happen."

Sandor gestured to the wrecked room, and expanded the gesture to include the house beyond. "Things similar to this. And other things, perhaps less destructive but still disturbing. Suddenly our whole party was plagued by inconveniences, and seemed on the brink of disaster. And I knew it was my fault, somehow."

"But how? And why, Sandor?"

He shrugged. "I began to consider that it might be the curse. But let me continue. We went on with our commitments, though our nerves were all in tatters. Finally I removed myself from the others. Our last concert was in Brussels. I chartered a plane for myself alone—not even Vladimir accompanied me because I forbade it." He closed his eyes and clenched his teeth; his hand tightened on the head of the cane, which he still gripped, until his knuckles were white.

This silent suffering Bruce understood. Softly she said, to move him along out of the awful memory, "That was the plane that crashed, and your back was broken."

"Yes. And the pilot died—though it was a long time before anyone would tell me that. That plane crash made a believer of me, Bruce. The curse is real. The only—how should I say?—redeeming thing about it is that the curse is on me alone, since I am the last of the line. I'm responsible for that pilot's death. I will not be responsible for anything happening to you. Or to anyone else. That is why I must be alone. Vladimir will probably be all right—his family have served my family in this . . . this situation, for centuries. In fact, he accepts all of this much better than I do. You must leave, Bruce. Go back to New York where you will be safe."

Her mind spinning with thoughts and questions, Bruce seized on the two words that seemed to echo in her head. "Go back? Vladimir said something to you about going back. What did he mean?"

Sandor heaved a heavy sigh. He feared he had told her too much already. "He wants me to go back to the old place, to continue the family tradition. I will not. The tradition is evil, and must be broken. If my death is the only thing that will make a final end to it, then *selah.* So be it."

Bruce was deeply troubled. She got up from the couch, saying, "I need to think about what you've said, Sandor, and I think better when I'm doing something that I don't have to think about," she smiled wanly, "if you see what I mean."

He nodded.

"Stay there in the sun. I'll think while I straighten up the kitchen." She suited her actions to her words. When she came across the coffee-maker on the counter, she brewed a pot and took a cup to Sandor. He accepted it and thanked her with an expressionless face. She saw that he was hovering once more on the brink of deep depression. She did not intend to allow that to happen; she couldn't bear to see him lose so much ground in so short a time. Regardless of the fact that her own thoughts were still far from organized, she got herself a cup of coffee and sat down with him again.

"I decided to join you."

He didn't seem to hear.

"Drink your coffee, Sandor," said Bruce firmly. The tone of her voice reached him. He blinked, and drank. Better, she thought. Moistening her lips with the tip of her tongue, she began to speak. "I respect your beliefs, Sandor, whatever they may be. Look at me, please!" She waited until he did, then continued, "I do understand how, with all that has happened to you in the past year, you could come to believe in this curse. But I want you to admit that there could be other explanations. If I give you a couple of examples, will you at least consider them?"

She was doing it to him again, drawing him out of the folds of that dull gray cloak, pulling him to her with her brightness. The sun struck her red hair to a fiery halo. With effort, he said, "All right."

"First off, the plane crash was a straightforward accident. The pilot's death and your serious injury were accidents!"

"No," Sandor shook his head. "I am pursued because of the curse. I don't know if they are demons or real human beings who pursue me, but they arranged the crash. It was no accident."

"I read the reports. Your manager gave me a file and I sat in his office and read every word—newspapers, insurance company, F.A.A., everything. Accidents do happen! You are not responsible for that pilot's death! Please, you must admit that an accident is a much more likely explanation than a curse."

Sandor raised both his great eyebrows and stared at her, but he said nothing.

She went on. "And anyone could have gotten into this house. We don't even know yet if anything has been stolen, or broken. It's probably just simple burglary. Don't tell me they don't have burglars in New Bern, North Carolina! Or people looking for drugs. Come to think of it, that's the most likely explanation of all. If a druggie heard there was a man in this house recovering from a broken back, he'd probably guess that you were on some pretty heavy pain-killers. Come on, Sandor—a curse is the very last explanation you should think of, not the first!"

"There have been too many coincidences," said Sandor stolidly.

In exasperation, Bruce jumped to her feet and planted her fists on her hips. She shook back her hair. "All right," she practically shouted, "bad things have happened, but there's a reason for them." She swept one arm through the air. "In fact, there could be a whole slew of different reasons. I refuse—do you hear me, Sandor Szelazeny—absolutely, categorically *refuse* to accept a superstitious or a supernatural reason until we've explored every single other reason there could possibly be! And I'll be damned if I'm going to let one incident of a trashed house be a setback in the course of a perfectly beautiful recovery. *Your* recovery, Sandor! Remember this morning, how you felt, the things you were saying just before we came in the front door?"

Bruce brought her face close to his and nailed his eyes to hers in challenge. "I am not going away, and you can't make me. If you fire me I'll just stay here and work for nothing. You'll have to call the police and declare me a trespasser and make them haul me away. And we already know how you feel about calling the police, don't we?"

She was an irresistible force. Her cleansing fury brightened the entire room. No, more than the room: his entire world. Sandor's spirits rose, and he laughed. Laughing caused a brief spasm of pain in his back muscles, but it was easy to ignore. He caught Bruce's shining face in his hands and kissed her, hard.

"Yes," he said when he released her. "Yes!"

At that point Vladimir entered the room, but they didn't see him, and he went away again.

TWO DAYS LATER there was a small article in the local paper that said that two other houses on East Front Street had been broken into, but nothing had been reported missing in either incident. The police had no suspects. Bruce shoved the newspaper under Sandor's nose triumphantly. "There," she said, "you see? We were not the only ones."

"Mmpff," was Sandor's only response, but he smiled.

We've just weathered a tempest in a teapot, thought Bruce, *but what a teapot!*

She gave no more attention to Sandor's curse, but decided instead to do something to expand his social circle. He was quickly becoming too dependent on her, not just for his physical progress but for a level of companionship that could easily become unhealthy for both of them. She had an idea that she proposed to Virginia one afternoon.

"What do you think about you and me cooking up a little dinner party, Virginia?" she asked.

"What did you have in mind?" Virginia responded. She was peeling shrimp for a jambalaya, and her efficient hands didn't miss a beat.

"Well, I don't know very many people. I'd like you to be a guest, and for once I'd ask Vladimir to sit down and eat with us. He never does, you know."

Virginia wrinkled her pert nose. She was a few years younger than Bruce, not pretty but pleasant-looking, with an apple-cheeked round face, warm brown eyes, and long honey-colored hair that she wore pulled back from a center part. Whereas Bruce's daily uniform was jeans and a long shirt or sweater, Virginia favored full skirts almost down to her ankles—perhaps to hide a rounded figure that reflected love of her own cooking. Her lack of pretentiousness was underscored by the knee socks and Birkenstock sandals that she wore with everything.

"That man!" exclaimed Virginia. Looking around, she lowered her voice, "Are you sure he actually eats? He looks more as if he might drink blood, or something."

"Don't worry," Bruce said with a laugh, "he can't hear you. He and Sandor went somewhere. And he isn't a vampire. I've really been trying to be nice to him lately. I think I may have been too harsh in my opinion of him before.

Anyway, I thought I'd also ask Celeste, you know, the woman who lives across the street.''

"Oh, everybody knows Celeste," said Virginia, throwing a large handful of shrimp into the pot. Then she washed her hands in the sink and leaned back against the counter, casually wiping them dry on her apron. "You, uh, you have to be sort of careful of Celeste, Bruce."

Bruce was folding pocket rolls. She'd discovered under Virginia's tutelage that she had a facility for bread-making, and she enjoyed it. She glanced up, grinning. "You mean because she's a man killer? I picked up on that. I think that's just exactly what Sandor needs. She'll flirt with him and call him 'Maestro,' and he'll eat it up."

"Oh, I'm not really sure what I mean. She's harmless enough that way. I mean, with men. I don't know, maybe I'm just jealous."

Bruce looked askance. "You, Virginia, jealous? Forgive me if I seriously doubt that. I also know you're not a gossip—if you were I'd know every juicy thing there is to know about this little town by now, and instead all I know is a lot of history! So, what is it? What's bothering you?"

Virginia folded her arms across her ample breasts. "Well, maybe you know Celeste grew up here."

"She told me she's a native, that she knows everybody."

"That's true. You know, Bruce, I'm not a snob—" unconsciously Virginia looked down at her feet in the clunky Birkenstocks, as if for confirmation "—but Celeste more or less came from the wrong side of the tracks. She kind of clawed her way up. She's a lot older than I am, older than she looks. In fact, I was in grade school when she was in high school, but I heard about her. It was hard not to."

"Whatever she did then, it's ancient history now," said Bruce. It was a good thing she'd come to know Virginia so well, or else she really would have thought her a snob.

"Anyway, that's all the more reason for you not to be jealous, isn't it?"

Virginia shook her head. She went over and stirred the pot of jambalaya, sniffed it critically, added rice and turned the heat down. "No. There's more. I've told you that I want to start my own restaurant here. What I'd really, really like to do is have my own variation on a bed and breakfast—it would be a bed, breakfast and supper."

"You'd be wonderful at it, too. What a great idea!"

Virginia smiled. She leaned over and inspected the pan of rolls as Bruce folded over the last one. "Yeah, and you could come and be my bread-maker. How about it? You have a real gift for this!"

"I appreciate the compliment, but I wish you'd get on with your story." Bruce covered the rolls with a fluffy, terry kitchen towel and set them aside to rise.

"Okay. The reason I might be jealous of Celeste is that even though my family has been here in New Bern since the year zero, and we have what passes for a pedigree a mile long, I can't scrape up the money to do what I want to do, and the family can't afford to help me. I have an Associate degree in business, so I can handle the business side. I went to cooking school for six months in Boston, but I'm still little more than an apprentice at the deli—mostly for lack of money. I can't even buy into a business, much less start one of my own. Whereas Celeste...."

Virginia's apple-cheeks had turned bright red. "I'm embarrassing myself talking about this," she said softly.

"I didn't want that," said Bruce. "If you'd rather not go on...."

"No, I started it, I may as well finish. A few years after high school, Celeste left town. I think she got married a couple of times, whatever, she came back three years ago with her maiden name... and a lot of money! She bought that big house across the street and—get this!—soon after she came back, her parents moved away to some retirement place in Florida.''

"There's nothing too unusual about that, surely.''

"No, unless you realize that the Stanhopes couldn't have afforded that sort of thing without Celeste's newfound money paying for it. To tell you the truth, it did look as if she were trying to get rid of them. You know, so people wouldn't remember where she came from.'' Virginia ducked her head again, as if ashamed of what she'd said. But she went on.

"Then the next thing you know, Celeste has opened this antique shop and she's always traveling all over the world buying things for it. She's up to her old tricks, too, clawing her way up socially. The difference is, she has money now, so it works. People accept her, but they do talk about her behind her back. And I don't think anyone likes her. She's really, really hard to like! So it isn't too good an idea to choose Celeste as your main contact when you're getting to know people. But you see what I mean, don't you, about why I could just be jealous?''

"Yes, I see, but I don't think it's jealousy. I think there's still something you haven't said.'' Bruce looked at her new friend critically, and decided to ask outright, "What is it?''

"You're going to think I'm the world's most horrible person, if you don't already.''

"No, I won't.''

"Okay.'' Virginia took a deep breath. "I don't trust Celeste. I can't tell you exactly why. Her shop is right up the street from the deli, I see her every day and she always makes a big effort to be nice. But I just don't trust her! God, Bruce—'' Virginia turned away, busily removing her apron, smoothing her skirt and her hair ''—I wish I'd never said anything, really! Please try to forget it, all of it. I'd be delighted to help you with your dinner party, and to be a guest, too, if you still want me to. You be thinking overnight about what you want to serve, and we'll talk about it tomorrow. Okay?''

"Okay," Bruce agreed. And because she was by nature both charitable and honest, she did forget what Virginia had said.

LATER IN THE AFTERNOON, Bruce went up Pollock Street to see Celeste in her shop, Celestial Antiquities. The shop, like so many in the historic section of town, was on the first floor of a restored house. Bruce had no idea what was on the upper floors; storage, she supposed. Though she had no real knowledge of antiques, it seemed to Bruce that Celeste kept a rather odd assortment. Still, she always enjoyed coming here; except that Celeste usually followed her around chattering, when Bruce would have preferred to browse, alone.

A bell—Celeste said it was a Swiss cowbell—attached to the top of the door clanked as Bruce entered. Bruce waved at the owner in the next room, where she was occupied with a couple who looked like tourists. Glad that she might have a chance to look around on her own for a change, Bruce threaded her way through some spindly legged chairs toward a wall filled with bric-a-brac. Perhaps she might find some little present for her mother. . . .

The doorbell clanked again, and Bruce glanced over her shoulder at the newcomers—two men, so similar in appearance they might have been twins except that one was a bit shorter and stouter than the other, and had a mustache. They wore three-piece tweed suits and hats of a kind Bruce hadn't seen in real life but only in movies—homburgs, she thought they were called. More tourists, she thought, and turned back to her perusal of the bric-a-brac.

A minute later there was a sharp crack, and an exclamation, "Oh, I say, Reggie! Did y' see that? The demmed thing leapt straight into m' path."

The accent was quite distinctly British, and Bruce hid a smile as she glanced once again over her shoulder. The mustached man, looking at one of the spindly legged chairs as if it had deeply offended him, was vigorously rubbing his shin.

The other man unperturbedly plucked his brother—with so much physical resemblance between them they had to be brothers—by the collar and led him onward. "Come along, Ronnie, and do try to be more careful. There's Celeste. Hallo, dear! As y' can see, we've arrived." They disappeared into the next room.

Bruce, left more to her own devices than ever before in the times she'd visited Celestial Antiquities, didn't find a gift for her mother, but she did find something that at first astonished her so much it nearly took her breath away. In a little alcove, which she had seen but never entered, a huge old armoire had been left open. Its shelves were packed to bursting with objects of silver: many-branched candelabra, vases of all heights and shapes, pitchers, goblets, trays round and rectangular, teapots, coffeepots, boxes of every size imaginable, bowls, bells, porringers and picture frames. Many were intricately twisted, scrolled, and ornamented, chased and engraved, and all were polished to a blinding luster. It was a dazzling collection that looked more as if it belonged in a museum than in a shop like this, where a few good things mixed with many of indifferent quality. Or so, at least, it seemed to Bruce's unpracticed eye.

Bruce was still staring when Celeste came into the alcove with a swish of skirts. "There you are, Bruce," she said. Her high heels clicked rapidly across the polished hardwood floor as she hastened to the armoire and closed its doors, locking them with a little key she pocketed. The effect was as if the sun had suddenly gone behind a cloud.

Bruce blinked. She said, "That's an impressive collection."

Celeste frowned, raising her hand to her hair in a fussy gesture, though her well-lacquered coiffure was perfect. "Yes, well, I usually keep it locked. I can't imagine how I could have been so distracted...." As if she suddenly realized how strangely agitated she looked and sounded, she put on a bright smile and said, "Those things aren't really for sale, you see." She advanced on Bruce with that smile pasted in place. "I'm so glad you're here, you couldn't have come at a better time. I want you to meet two very dear friends of mine who have just this moment arrived from England..."

Which was how Bruce met Reginald and Ronald Ramsay. She was immediately so delighted with them that she invited them both—along with Celeste, of course—to the dinner party.

Chapter Six

Virginia did not wear her Birkenstocks to the dinner party. In fact, she came dressed in a lovely Old World style that charmed everyone. She wore black Victorian-looking boots with small heels and tiny buttons; they were so intriguing, as they disappeared under her long skirt, that Bruce suddenly understood why men of that era had found ankles a thrill. The skirt was cut full, in a fabric of brilliant gypsy-colored stripes: red, purple, gold, and a beautiful teal green. Her blouse was white, gauzy, full-sleeved, with a wide lace-bordered collar. She wore her hair in the usual way, pulled back from a center part; but it was caught at her nape with a purple ribbon whose streamers fluttered gracefully when she moved. Long earrings of delicate gold filigree brushed her shoulders.

Next to Virginia, Celeste looked as if she were an actress who had somehow gotten onto the wrong movie set. However, her first long critical glance at the younger woman seemed to suggest that as far as Celeste was concerned, it was Virginia who was out of place. Fortunately, this bothered Virginia not at all; she wouldn't have been caught dead in what Celeste was wearing: a pale pink georgette, with a handkerchief-point hem and a long scarf attached at the neckline. Her stiletto-heeled shoes had been dyed to match.

Nevertheless, Sandor seemed as taken by Celeste as Bruce had thought he might be. He looked very elegant himself; he had dressed with care, even though he protested until the last minute that he didn't like the idea of this party and would endure it only because Bruce insisted. Sandor wore a smoky gray velvet blazer, which brought out the streaks of silver in his hair, over a white silk turtleneck and darker gray slacks.

Vladimir had seemed appalled when Bruce suggested that he be a guest and sit with them at the table they'd set up in the library, since Sandor now occupied the dining room. Sandor had intervened, taking Bruce aside and explaining that although she meant to do the man a kindness, Vladimir would enjoy the evening far more if he were allowed to act as butler. So Vladimir, dressed in formal black attire, greeted the guests at the door, served drinks and the meal that Virginia and Bruce had prepared in the afternoon.

And Bruce wished she had thought to go out and buy herself a new dress. She felt like an ugly duckling next to Virginia and Celeste, in the one good dress she had brought with her. It was a narrow column of plain black silk and she wore it unadorned, because she hadn't brought to North Carolina the long pearls she usually wore with it.

The Ramsays arrived late. Bruce was afraid they'd forgotten to come, especially when Celeste began to watch the door and fiddle nervously with her diamond tennis bracelet. When they did arrive, Ronnie Ramsay entered in his usual fashion: he tripped over the threshold just as Vladimir, in proper English butler fashion, was announcing them. "Mr. Ronald and Mr. Reginald Ramsay."

Both Ramsays had hair of the sandy color that is neither precisely brown or blond nor red, but somewhere in between. Both appeared to be in their forties, at least—older than Sandor, younger by far than Vladimir. The Ramsays were somewhat shorter than Bruce, square and solidly built, Ronnie with the addition of a little paunch. Their faces, too, were square, blue-eyed, prominently nosed, and floridly complected. Again, in Ronnie's case, there was that little bit extra—his mustache. Neither was handsome but both managed, especially when speaking in their cultured upper-class accents, to seem rather distinguished.

As the evening progressed, Bruce was enormously glad the Ramsays had come on the scene. They were amusing, and gradually their conversation revealed that both, even the clumsy Ronnie—at the dinner table he managed somehow to get his tie caught under his plate—were intelligent men. And without them, no matter how good her intentions, Bruce would have found Celeste's unrelenting attentions to Sandor, and his to her, too much to bear. Occasionally Virginia would catch Bruce's eye with a wise look that seemed to say, I told you so!

Over dessert, after Celeste had none too delicately pointed out to Ronnie that he had chocolate mousse on his nose, Sandor said to the brothers, who were seated across the table from each other, "You mentioned that you met Celeste in the course of your work. Are you also antique dealers?"

"Oh, my no!" said Reggie.

"Not quite," said Ronnie.

Sandor raised one thick eyebrow in inquiry.

"We deal in antiquities, not antiques."

"That is, y' see, it's like we go to the antique shows and auctions, and of course we do buy, but . . ." Ronnie looked to his brother for help.

Reggie carried on. "If, for example, the item on auction is a lovely old box, the antique dealer will want the box. We want what's *in* the box. As it were."

"Quite," said Ronnie. "That is, presuming that there is anything in the box."

"We met Celeste several years ago at an auction in... where exactly was that, luv?"

"Chichester, I believe," she said, with a little trill of laughter. "Of course, it's hard to be certain when one goes to so many."

"Oh, my yes," said Ronnie, "and Celeste does come up with the most scrumptious things out of old boxes and trunks and such. And where we luck out, don't y' see, is she wants the boxes and trunks and we get the scrumptious bits! At a price, o' course. A real treasure hound, is our Celeste."

For some reason, this did not please Celeste. If Bruce hadn't been looking right at her, she might have missed it, but she could have sworn that Celeste kicked Ronnie under the table.

Virginia, who had maintained a composed silence through most of the evening, now said directly to Sandor at her right hand, "But Celeste's main interest is silver. Isn't it? She has quite a collection, I understand, though I've never seen it myself."

Bruce, who had told Virginia about the silver, with elaborate casualness reached for her water glass and drank as she watched Celeste's reaction and wondered what Virginia was up to.

Celeste's little pointed chin came up and she gave Virginia ever-so-swift a dirty look before she turned her violet eyes on Sandor and said in her soft drawl, "It's a *private* collection—I would *never* sell my silver. But I'll show it to *you* sometime, Maestro, if you like."

"Private collection?" asked Reggie.

"We've never seen it!" declared Ronnie, sounding offended.

Sandor smiled, a slow, very sexy smile at no one in particular. He was good at social nuances, and he was enjoying this.

Forthright Bruce, who was definitely not good at social nuances, asked, "If it's private, why do you have it in your store? I should think you'd keep a private collection in your home. Lord knows, you must have room enough in that big house."

Deftly, with venomously polite skill, Celeste turned the conversation and left the question unanswered. "That reminds me. I've brought something for you all—you Bruce, and the Maestro, and your excellent man Vladimir." She took her purse, an envelope of pink satin, from her lap and opened it. Ronnie trailed his tie in what was left of his chocolate mousse, trying to peer across the table.

"Here we are, three tickets to next week's Spring Historic House and Garden Tour."

"It's why we're here at this particular time, y' know. Come to do it again. Smashing tour, absolutely smashing!" said Ronnie.

"Quite," said Reggie.

Celeste inclined her head graciously, as if the compliment were for her personally, and continued, "My house will be on the tour, and I'd like you three to be my guests. Of course, I would have invited you to my home socially before now, but until tonight..." She looked pointedly at Bruce, as if tonight had not been Bruce's idea and everything wrong in the world were Bruce's fault. "Well, I just wasn't sure you all wanted to be sociable."

Now Celeste turned a dazzling smile on Sandor as she offered the tickets to him. She sat on Sandor's right, directly across the table from Virginia. "I do hope you'll come. I'm having a little cocktail party the night before the tour opens. You simply must come. We have these tours twice a year, and absolutely *everybody* who's *anybody* in New Bern participates!''

That, thought Bruce with satisfaction, *is exactly the wrong thing to say to Sandor. He's about as likely to want to meet everybody who's anybody as I am to put my head in an oven!*

Her satisfaction didn't last long, however. Sandor curled his fingers around Celeste's hand for a much-too-long moment before he extracted the tickets. He thanked her in a murmur like a velvet rumble.

LATER, WHILE THE GUESTS were having liqueurs in the living room, Bruce invaded the kitchen and ordered Vladimir out, saying that she didn't drink liqueurs and was going to do the dishes whether he liked it or not. There was so much fire in her eyes that her hair looked pale by comparison, and Vladimir went without a peep of protest. She whipped one of the man's long white aprons over her black dress and was wrist-deep in suds when Virginia came up quietly and observed, "You do have a dishwasher, you know. You don't have to do them by hand."

Bruce blew upward at a strand of hair that kept falling in her eyes. "I get more out of it this way."

Virginia chuckled, and without further comment picked up a dishtowel and began to dry.

After a while Bruce looked over at her. "You don't have to help. You should be out there enjoying yourself with Tweedledum and Tweedledee and the Pink Fairy Princess."

"Actually, I have enjoyed this much more than I thought I would. It's more fun than *Family Feud!*"

"Yeah. Well, I have no right to complain. After all, it was my idea, wasn't it, to get Sandor interested in Celeste?"

"Mmm-hmm. The Ramsays are cute. Especially that Ronnie. I expect he will have fallen over, or gotten himself tangled up in half of New Bern by the time they leave."

"You've never met them before?"

"Never seen them before in my life."

"But, if they're such good friends of hers...and they gave the impression that they've done the house and garden tour...."

"That is a little odd, isn't it?" Virginia stopped wiping and looked at Bruce. "I don't pretend to know everyone or everything in town, but the deli is pretty central, most visitors come through there at one time or another, and the Ramsay brothers are so distinctive. I'm sure if I'd ever seen them before I'd remember."

"Especially since Celestial Antiquities is practically next door, and Celeste is their dear friend."

"Oh well." Virginia shrugged and resumed her wiping. "It couldn't possibly be important. I probably just missed them somehow. You know, Bruce, I was surprised when you left the living room and didn't come back. It took me a while to figure out what you must be doing. I suppose I shouldn't say this, but I hope we're good enough friends..."

"Of course." Bruce paused, hands still submerged in sudsy water.

"It isn't really polite to leave your guests like that."

Now Bruce resumed scrubbing pots with considerably more vigor than required. She grumbled. "I'm just the hired help around here, of considerably less importance than that old family retainer, Vladimir. Of course, part of what I'm supposed to do is play companion—but I'd had just about all the companionship I could stand for one evening!"

Virginia chuckled again. "Why, Bruce, I didn't realize you had a temper to match your red hair!"

"Well, now you know. Besides, I've never been one to set much store by surface politeness."

"Unlike the Pink Fairy Princess."

"Yeah. Who the hell cares, anyway?"

"I know the answer to that one."

"It was a rhetorical question."

"*You* care, Bruce," said Virginia seriously, putting aside her towel. The dishes were done. She faced her friend. "Are you in love with Sandor?"

"No!" said Bruce too loudly; but the sound of water rinsing the sink covered it.

"That's too bad," said Virginia slowly, carefully, "because I think he's in love with you."

Bruce leaned her hands on the rim of the sink, head bent forward so that her hair curtained her face. She felt a ridiculous, hopeless rush of warmth at Virginia's words. Slowly she turned and faced her. "Why do you say that?"

"I don't talk much when I'm in company, but I'm a good listener and a good observer. I saw how he looks at you when you aren't looking, and I saw how he watched the door when you left the room. I could tell the very moment when he figured out you weren't coming back—his face fell. That was when I decided to come after you."

"You're just on my side, that's all. Otherwise you'd also have seen how he's been looking at Celeste. And did you catch that bit when he thanked her for the tickets? God, I felt like something inside me curled up and died!"

"So you are in love with him."

Bruce's mouth fell open as she realized she'd given herself away. It took a couple of tries before she found her voice. "I—I'm more attracted to him than I have been to...well to be honest, to anyone in a long time. But it doesn't matter, because it's against the rules. I can't let it happen, even if he should happen to feel the same way about me—''

"What rules?"

"I'm a physical therapist," Bruce squared her shoulders, "and he's my patient. At his stage of recovery, many patients think they're in love with their therapists. For me and Sandor it's just worse, more intense, because we're always working one-on-one and I'm living in. And that's *all* it is!" She whipped the apron off, shook her hair in place, and smoothed her dress. "Now, I guess we'd better go back and join the menagerie."

Virginia lagged behind, and before Bruce reached the door, she reached out and touched her arm. "Wait, please. There's something I want to say, and then I promise I'll never mention it again unless you bring it up." Bruce waited. Virginia said, "Sandor is an unusual person, really special. But so are you, Bruce. Seeing the two of you together tonight...well, rules can be broken, if the reason is good enough. Just don't forget that."

IN SOME WAYS, Celeste Stanhope was the kind of woman that had always appealed to Sandor. She was more than pretty, she was beautiful, with her dark hair and incredible violet eyes. She had the kind of figure he'd always enjoyed on a woman, petite yet large-breasted. If her face was beginning to show signs of age...well, Sandor reminded himself that he was only a couple of years away from forty, and so, probably, was she.

Celeste had traveled a lot, she was familiar with the major cities in this country and in Europe. She lacked a certain cosmopolitan sophistication in spite of all the traveling, but made up for it by her obvious interest in him. And she was certainly interested! She knew how to get, and hold, a man's attention.

Whereas Bruce.... Bruce did not seem to want his attention; at least, not that kind. He spun his wheelchair around,
wheeled himself to the windows of the big kitchen, and
looked out over the back lawn, down to the river.

He'd made a commitment, both to himself and to Bruce,
that he would forget about the curse and try to develop a
more normal life-style. The depression was gone now; the
fear was at least quiescent. Since he wasn't by nature a her-
mit, Sandor enjoyed getting out more, being with people.
Being with people made Sandor want a woman. A normal
life, for him, always had at least one woman in it.

He felt agitated, and frustrated. If he had any sense, he
knew he would start a flirtation with Celeste. Maybe it
would turn into a full-blown affair; he didn't doubt for a
minute that the woman was willing. Since the dinner party,
she made excuses to come over at the drop of a hat, and
Bruce always tactfully left them alone. Bruce was teaching
him to climb steps again, they were working hard at it, spe-
cifically so that Sandor could get up the steps into Celeste's
house for the pre-tour party. He was looking forward to that
party... but oddly enough, the people he was most looking
forward to seeing were the Ramsay brothers. Not Celeste.

Also, Sandor realized with surprise, he was looking forward to seeing what Bruce would wear to Celeste's party.
Having seen her at their own dinner party in that elegant
black dress, when she always wore jeans, had been something of a revelation. Celeste might be conventionally
beautiful, but Bruce was something else, something...
better. Bruce was so unique in Sandor's experience that he
truly had no words to describe her.

Quite naturally, as if the music had not died out of his
soul months ago, the theme of Mendelssohn's *Scottish
Symphony* flowed into Sandor, filling him completely. He
closed his eyes in bliss, heard the soaring, yearning strength

of the violins...and with it her name: Bruce. Bruce was like a symphony, full, rich, strong, with a beauty so sumptuous and deep that it seemed to go on forever. Sandor heard every note, saw every line of his conductor's score behind his closed eyelids. Music, beautiful music, the instruments blending together, merging with harmonies so perfect, so exquisite...to surge to the heights on a piercing cry of trumpets, to spiral downward on a curve of woodwinds, to end in the softest pianissimo, like a kiss. Pianissimo, the softest kiss....

There were tears in his eyes when at last he opened them. The music had returned to his soul! He looked down at his hands. Opened them, flexed his fingers, raised his arms...and let them fall. But there was the hint of a smile on his face. He might never conduct again, but still he had his music back, inside. Again he heard the theme of the *Scottish Symphony* and with it, her name: Bruce. Bruce had done this. Somehow, loving her had given him back his music.

So that was it! Sandor's smile widened as he thought, *I love her! I'm not just attracted to her, I don't just want her as I've wanted other women. I love her!*

The realization gave him a sense of tremendous well-being. It gave him a new reason to live, and strength and courage to do it. The only trouble was...Bruce herself. She cared for him, he knew she did, but with a kind of single-minded devotion that was somehow detached. And so far, she had resisted his efforts to arouse a more personal interest.

I can change that, Sandor thought, *and I will. I'll make her love me.*

Determined to begin on this most essential project immediately, he wheeled himself to the foot of the stairs and called for her. "Bruce! Bruce!"

Her head, wrapped turban-style in a towel, appeared upside-down leaning over the banister. "What, Sandor? I just washed my hair and I was about to dry it."

He smiled. If he'd been able to climb more than three steps, he would have run up the whole flight of stairs and crushed her in his arms. He said, "Hurry, please. You and I have somewhere to go. And I won't take no for an answer!"

BRUCE WAS DRIVING her own car. Sandor sat in the front seat beside her. At his request—demand was more like it— she was taking him to the building site. She didn't really want to be doing this. She hadn't been out here since the day she'd come alone. This was something he always did with Vladimir, and she would have preferred to keep it that way, but he'd been very insistent.

She glanced over at him. Close up, his face in profile always got to her—those high cheekbones, the well-defined line of his chin, the way his hair waved back at the temples but fell over his forehead. Because he moved her more than she wanted to be moved, she grumbled, "I wish you'd tell me what's so important that I had to bring you out here this morning. Why couldn't Vladimir do it?"

"Because, my dear Bruce—"

She hated for him to call her his dear Bruce; the caressing way he said it made her heart do an unwelcome little flip-flop...

"—I want to be with you this morning. Not with Vladimir. His company doesn't hold a candle to yours." He turned and looked at her with a smile whose warmth nearly took her breath away.

She smiled back uneasily, and then concentrated on her driving.

Bruce couldn't help it, she didn't like this road. She tightened her grip on the steering wheel. If she believed in foreboding, she'd have thought that this particular stretch of narrow road, with its desolate-looking pine trees, held some particularly nasty fate for her in the not too distant future. *Fortunately,* she thought, *I don't believe in such things.*

But when she had driven on another couple of miles and they hadn't seen a single other car, she said to Sandor, "I really wish you hadn't chosen to build your house so far away from everything!"

"If you came out here with me every day, you'd get used to it," said Sandor reasonably. He fully intended that as often as possible from now on he would make these visits with Bruce rather than Vladimir. One way or another, he'd persuade her. "After all, if this were Long Island, you'd think nothing of a forty-five minute drive. Would you?"

"Well, this isn't Long Island. Long Island isn't so isolated, nor so desolate-looking."

"It probably was before it was developed. In fact, it probably looked very much like this."

Bruce glanced at Sandor again. He looked happy, more happy than she'd seen him. Pleased with himself. Perhaps the builders had made a significant amount of progress and that was why, all of a sudden, it was so important for her to see it.

Nevertheless she said, "I worry about you being all by yourself out here, Sandor. I'm not going to leave until you're able to do all the normal things like walking and climbing a whole flight of stairs and driving a car, not to mention getting in and out of the bathtub and stuff like that. But I doubt you'll have your full strength back for as much as a year from when I started therapy with you. And if anything happened to you way out here all alone—"

"I don't intend to be alone," said Sandor with a special edge of meaning in his voice, which Bruce missed. Something behind the car distracted her; she wasn't sure what. It was as if there had been something in the rearview mirror that disappeared, like smoke.

Then his words, if not the tone, registered and Bruce said, "That's something else that bothers me. Exactly how old is Vladimir, anyway?"

"Vladimir?" Sandor hadn't been thinking of his valet when he'd said he didn't intend to be alone. He considered her question. "I really don't know." He shrugged, and chuckled. "Maybe he's immortal."

"That's not really funny, Sandor." Bruce spied the turn-off and aimed the car into it, remembering to slow down. "As much as I've tried to like him, and I've really made an effort, Vladimir still gives me the creeps sometimes. He looks so, so *Transylvanian.*"

Bruce's description chilled Sandor, for reasons she could not know. He tried to make light of it. "That's not surprising. Vladimir *is* Transylvanian."

The car bumped and lurched. Bruce hung onto the steering wheel. She shot a glance at Sandor and saw him grimace—probably the rough ride was jarring his back. The Volvo didn't have the smooth suspension of his Mercedes. She slowed her pace to a mere crawl, then asked, "What do you mean by that?"

Reluctantly Sandor replied, "Transylvania is a real place, not just some fictional spot in the horror movies you no doubt were thinking of. It's in the mountains between Hungary and Romania. The family home is there, near the Hungarian border. That's where Vladimir comes from."

"And where the Szelazenys come from?"

"No, not the Szelazenys. The, ah...my mother's family. His family has long been in service to my mother's family, and he came to the United States with her and my father before I was born. I was born rather late in their lives, and Vladimir must be at least as old as they would be, if they were still living. So..." Sandor calculated, "if he isn't immortal, he'd be close to eighty. My God, I hadn't ever thought of him being that old!"

"Well, I have. So in about six or seven months you're going to be moving out here to the back of beyond with a man so old that he not only may not be able to take care of you in an emergency, but you could end up taking care of him! Now tell me that makes sense."

But at that moment the car bumped onto the last of the sandy track, and the vista of blue sky and the wide blue waters of the Pamlico Sound opened up before them. Sandor said, "Look at that, Bruce, and you tell me. Would it make sense to deny me so much beauty?" His words held a double meaning, for as he said them he was looking not at the view, but at her.

Bruce sighed. She said, "I give up."

The site was busy, full of workmen. She was astonished at how much progress had been made in so short a time. Sandor introduced her to the foreman. Then he made his way slowly with his canes to a grassy rise away from the construction, where he could sit in a folding chair and contemplate the view. Instead he contemplated Bruce as the foreman showed her around.

Bruce followed the foreman, whose name was George. He kept telling her to watch her step; the construction site at this stage of the building was a dangerous place for the uninitiated. She had some trouble watching where she put her feet and, at the same time, paying attention to his explanations. Even so, she could see that the house would be wonderful when it was finished. Large, low, and rambling. All the foundation was now in, George explained, and some of the flooring was laid. The framework for the walls was going up; the walls on the side facing the Pamlico Sound would be all cedar beams and glass. There would be a deck here, where the ground sloped to an abrupt drop into the water. If Maestro Szelazeny—George had trouble with the name and said "Master Zelazzy"—changed his mind and wanted a boat dock, they would put it "over yonder." He scratched his head, adding, "Don't hardly seem right to have a place out here and not have a boat."

"I have to agree with you on that," said Bruce. She thanked the foreman for the tour and picked her way back through the site, glad to reach grassy ground that was clear of construction hazards. When she mounted the little rise, she saw that Sandor was beaming at her. His face was positively glowing. It made her happy to see him so happy.

"I suppose," she said with a smile of her own, "you wanted me to see how much progress they've made. Well, I'm impressed, I admit it."

Sandor indicated the other chair, where Vladimir usually sat. "Here, sit with me." He had calculatedly moved it very close to his own.

Bruce stretched before she sat, raising her arms and breathing in deeply. "The air here is so wonderful. It almost tastes good, like fresh spring water."

"I would have said like fine wine, but essentially I agree with you. Do you really like it, Bruce?"

She considered the question, looking over at the rambling wooden skeleton of the house, then out at the water, and finally up at the sky. Clouds were building in the west, but directly above, the sun shone. A small flock of gulls winged by, their cries were interrupted by the whine of a power saw. She did not know what to say, because the truth was that she both liked and disliked it. Being the practical person that she was, Bruce realized that Sandor had invested a small fortune here, so she said, "It's going to be a fine house, Sandor."

"Yes," he agreed. When he looked at the building in progress he superimposed the design as it appeared in the architect's rendering: exterior walls of rich warm cedar, contrasted with smooth expanses of glass; vaulted beamed ceilings inside, fieldstone fireplaces, and gleaming floors; all would make a fitting background for his mixture of fine antique and good contemporary furniture, his paintings, his Oriental rugs.

He wanted Bruce there, in that setting. In his mind's eye he saw her, sitting on a Persian rug in front of the fireplace, the fire making rosy glints in her hair, one of her long legs folded beneath her and the other stretched out.... It was too soon to tell her anything like that, of course, but perhaps he could think of something meaningful to say.

Sandor cleared his throat. "I began this place as a hide-away. Now, since you have made me see reason, I think of it as a refuge. I have always loved being by the water, Bruce. Aside from my Manhattan apartment, I do have a house on Long Island. Did you know that?"

"No, I didn't. I don't really know very much about you, Sandor. Except for your medical condition." She looked over at him and added hastily, "Of course, that's all I need to know."

"I will sell the Long Island house when this one is completed. My parents had a summer place in Maine, which has been closed up for a long time. I suppose I'll sell that, too. It doesn't matter. I don't want to try to think too far ahead yet."

Bruce nodded. She knew it was still hard for him to think or talk of the future. At least he now seemed willing to consider that he might *have* a future! She reached across, intending to give his hand an encouraging squeeze. "That's good," she said.

Sandor held onto her hand. When she would have pulled away, he rubbed her knuckles with his thumb. He felt as awkward with her as if he were eighteen again. He was finding out that all his years of experience with women had taught him only flirtation and seduction; he had almost no idea how to proceed when what he wanted was something so much more deeper, finer. He could not even speak when he tried. "I—I . . ." he stammered.

"What is it, Sandor?" Bruce whispered. A sudden gust of wind lifted her hair out around her face like a coppery fan.

He could only look at her, with his heart in his eyes. Not knowing what else to do, he raised the hand he held to his lips, intending to kiss it.

But Bruce, who, ever since they had crossed the Neuse River Bridge, had been suppressing her uneasiness, was suddenly blinded by a silvery flash. She snatched her hand away from Sandor and used it to shade her eyes. "What was that?" she asked, alarmed.

"What?" He was disappointed, but responded to the alarm in her voice.

"It's gone," she said, frowning. "I—I don't know. It's gone now, but it was like...like quicksilver. You know, like on a mirror. Like suddenly having someone shine light from a mirror in your eyes."

Then she realized that the last thing she wanted was to have Sandor think someone was spying on them. He hadn't seemed to have a trace of his old paranoia for quite some time, and she certainly didn't want to get him started again now. So she combed her fingers through her windblown hair and smiled. "Never mind. I think it's time we were going.

Can you walk back, or do you want me to get your wheel-chair out of the trunk?''

Desperate for physical contact with her, Sandor thought of a way that was better than nothing. "I can make it, I think, if you'll help. Give me a little support."

"Glad to." In her most businesslike manner, Bruce wrapped her arm around him and anchored herself at his side. "Okay. Here we go."

Sandor let himself lean against her. At one point he stumbled, not on purpose, and swore. "Damn, I'm not as strong as I think I am!"

"Yes, you are," Bruce grinned, but she tightened her hold. "In fact, most of the time you're a lot stronger than you think you are. But walking around here is tricky, even I have to be careful. Whatever you do, Sandor, don't go around where there are all those ropes and wires and things all over the ground."

"I won't," he promised, concentrating now on each step.

When they reached the car, Bruce looked back. Something she had not noticed before caught her eye. It seemed to be sort of a construction shed, which she didn't understand because the workmen had a trailer they used for their headquarters. She pointed. "What's in there?"

Sandor shrugged, more interested now in getting into the car where he could sit down. Though he didn't want to admit it, his legs felt like water and he was hurting. "I don't know. Equipment, I suppose. All I know is they keep it locked. I have a set of extra keys to that and the trailer. Come on, Bruce, let's go home."

Chapter Seven

Bruce got sick at Celeste's party. The first stabbing pain in her gut startled her so much that she sloshed the fruit punch in its cup and spattered the front of her new dress. Celeste, ever the solicitous hostess, came running over and, with little graceful cluckings of dismay, offered to take Bruce back to the kitchen to sponge it off.

Even as Celeste took her arm to guide the way, another pain hit Bruce. This one was stronger; it not only stabbed but tore upward through her insides. Only self-discipline kept Bruce upright and unflinching. She merely drew in a sharp breath and said, "No thanks. I'll just pop across the street and change." Then she hurried through the room and out the door as quickly as possible without calling attention to herself. She saw Sandor, but he didn't see her for the little crowd of admirers clustered around his wheelchair. Wisely, he had allowed Vladimir to bring the wheelchair, though he had climbed the steps quite well on his own.

A third time the pains gripped her; she was in the middle of the street and for an instant feared their severity would force her to her knees right there. But she went on, doggedly, her face now bathed in sweat. She burst through the front door, which they had left unlocked, and like a sick animal seeking its lair forced herself up the stairs to her room. There she threw herself down on the bed, writhing and clutching her stomach.

"Oh, God!" Bruce moaned. Her mind, seemingly at work independent of her tormented body, told her to get up. To go into the bathroom, to force her stomach to rid itself of whatever poison was causing the pain.

She tried. She stumbled, bent over and clutching her middle, to the bathroom. But no matter how she tried, she couldn't make herself throw up. She was alone in the house; Vladimir was with Sandor. She thought of calling Emergency for an ambulance to take her to the hospital, but even as a new cluster of cramping pains seized her, that seemed unnecessarily dramatic a solution. Either she was coming down with a virus that had an unusually severe onset, she thought, or else it must be food poisoning. Whatever it was, the need to empty her stomach had become a compulsion.

What is it that first-aid courses tell you to do to make a person vomit? Bruce tried to remember, and couldn't. But she couldn't go back to rolling around on the bed clutching at her tummy, either. She hauled her protesting body down the stairs to the kitchen.

Frantically Bruce searched the shelves of the kitchen cabinets. At last her hand closed over something she thought might work. It had better; she was getting spots in front of her eyes now. She knew she wasn't far from blacking out. Bruce dumped the contents of a small can of dry mustard into half a glass of water, and poured it down her throat. It burned, it tasted terrible. Her stomach roiled.

And just when Bruce thought she was going to pass out, in a rush of nausea it worked. She heaved and retched, clinging half conscious to the edge of the kitchen sink. She heaved until her sides ached and her stomach was empty. Then came dry heaves, until she brought up her own bile. Her whole body was drenched in the sweat of her physical agony, her hair plastered to her forehead and cheeks. She was shaking, freezing, exhausted.

Bruce washed her hands, her face, the sink; finally, she rinsed her mouth. More than anything else now she wanted to rest and get warm. Later she would try to understand what had happened, how she could have gotten so sick so fast. Lie down, that's what she had to do. Her room seemed too far away, climbing the stairs an impossibility. She staggered awkwardly around the counter divider into the living area of the big kitchen, and collapsed on the sofa with a little squeak of relief.

"BRUCE?" The voice was Sandor's. She recognized it and knew she loved the sound of that voice, but she didn't want to leave this nice, soft, velvety black place she was in. She didn't stir, she slept on.

Vladimir moved to shake the woman awake, but Sandor stopped him. Sandor hissed, his voice a whisper but no less threatening for that, "Can't you see that she's ill? Leave her alone, man!" And Vladimir, his face unnaturally pale even for him, backed away.

Much later Bruce turned over onto her side, instinctively snuggling deeper into the couch and pulling the soft knitted afghan up under her chin.

Afghan? I don't own an afghan, what am I doing with Sandor's afghan? Bruce thought, and her eyes flew open.

Sandor sat at the end of the couch; her feet were tucked up against his thigh. Head down, chin on chest, Sandor dozed. His wheelchair was nearby, his canes were on the floor at his feet. He had come while she slept, stayed with her, covered her.

Bruce clutched the afghan, *Sandor's* afghan, and remembered being sick. Her sides were sore. Gingerly she moved, mentally testing and probing her body for its reactions, as she taught her patients to do. She was okay. Sore and light-headed, but okay.

I'm lucky I didn't break a rib, vomiting so violently like that, she thought. As she lay there considering possible reasons that she might have become so suddenly and severely ill, Sandor started, turned his head, opened his eyes, and saw that Bruce was awake.

He smiled, his expressive lips slowly stretching, curving, the smile spreading until its warmth reached his cheeks, crinkled the corners of his eyes and entered their depths. Within the depths of Sandor's eyes, the warmth of his smile became a bright spark that leapt from them to Bruce and fell into the dry tinder of her heart, and set her on fire.

"Oo-oh," she sighed. And because she was weak, for the moment with no more defenses than a child, she reached out to him. She reached for his warmth, and the smile's promise.

Sandor opened his arms, and Bruce came to him. She came to him! She curled her long self into his embrace as over and over again he murmured against her silky hair every endearment he had ever known. She was soft, warm with sleep, so vulnerable.... He kissed her temples, brushed the curve of her ear with his lips, murmuring all the while. He'd had unbearable thoughts as he'd watched her lost in her heavy slumber. What had happened? What if she were seriously ill? How could his Bruce, that strong, invincible woman, be lying there so helpless? What if she died? How could he live without her?

"I love you," Sandor murmured, his lips so sweetly, so sensuously at her ear. "I love you. I don't want to live without you."

"Hush," Bruce said, but softly. She moved her head against his chest so that she could look up into the face so close to hers. He was not smiling now, but serious. His golden brown eyes compelled, commanded, as he lowered his mouth to hers.

She longed for the coming kiss, her lips opened of their own volition, but her hand obeyed her mind. She slipped gentle fingers up to stop his mouth, whispering, "This is wrong. I'm sorry, I was weak for a moment, I needed you...."

"This is *not* wrong," said Sandor with quiet conviction. "I also need you." Then an urgent note crept into his voice. He tightened his grip around her. "While you were sleeping I realized that I can no longer even think what my life would be like without you, Bruce. I became suddenly, irrationally afraid that something would happen, that I'd lose you."

Bruce reached up, allowed herself the pleasure of touching the side of Sandor's face, feeling the hardness of cheekbone and the softness of cheek beneath, and the faint prickle of beard along the firm line of his chin. She sighed. The house around them was wrapped in the deep somnolent silence of night's small hours. She was so reluctant to break the spell....

Sandor would have given anything for the physical strength to pick Bruce up in his arms and carry her to his bed. Once, not so long ago, he would have been strong enough. He ached, he burned with wanting her. He turned his face into her hand that touched his cheek and pressed his open mouth against her palm.

Bruce's breath caught in her throat and she snatched her hand away. The moisture of Sandor's lips against her palm was searing hot, as if he had branded her.

"I want you," he said simply. "Come with me, to my room, to my bed. Help me to make love to you."

"Hush, Sandor. Don't say such things," said Bruce. She burned with her own desires, which she must ignore, and her heart was breaking. That this man, with the visage and the pride of an eagle, should ask her to help him make love. . . . She reached up and pulled his head down to rest in the curve of her neck so that he couldn't see her blink the tears from her eyes.

He allowed her to hold him like that, but only for a moment. He could feel how fast her heart beat, how tightly she held him, and he knew that she had not really refused him. She wanted him, too. For some reason that he did not understand—a reason the arrogant man he had once been would have brushed aside—she would not respond. Feeling again that he was in new territory with no map, he pulled back and allowed her to gather her composure. As she sat up, adjusting her wrinkled dress and smoothing her hair, he groped his way into an apology.

"I'm . . . sorry," he said. "Not for telling you that I love you, which is the truth, or that I want you, which is also the truth, but for forgetting that you were ill." He felt the blood leave his pulsing groin and rush to his face. He couldn't even remember the last time in his life he had been embarrassed, but he had the grace to be embarrassed now for his omission. He should have thought to ask her this before. "How do you feel? Physically, I mean."

"I, ah, I think I'm all right now. A little weak and a little sore, that's all."

"Sore? What happened to you, Bruce? Did someone, something at the party . . . ?"

Bruce stretched, carefully. The special silence of the room was gone; the house now seemed alert around them, watchful. "I think I ate or drank something that didn't agree with me. I was suddenly, violently ill. I've never been that sick to my stomach before. Maybe it was food poisoning, I don't know."

Sandor pondered this. "You got sick at the party, didn't you?" Bruce nodded. He went on, "Could it have been something you ate here, before the party?"

"No," said Bruce without hesitation. She had a strong impression, a kind of hunch, that her illness and the party were somehow connected. Yet Sandor's question made sense. Food stays in the stomach for a couple of hours, and very few things are so toxic that they cause an immediate reaction. So she thought about it before adding, "I hadn't had anything to eat since lunch, and then I ate the same thing you did. You seem to be all right."

Sandor nodded gravely. Was it happening? Had the long arm of the curse that Bruce didn't believe in reached them in New Bern, reached her because of her proximity to him? The accidents that had happened on the tour had not included anything like this, nothing physically threatening. Not, that is, until the plane crash.

Bruce could see the wheels of thought turning behind Sandor's eyes. She hastened to say, "If it wasn't food poisoning, then it was probably some particularly virulent strain of G.I. bug. Those things can come on very suddenly, and be just as quickly over. I'm pretty sure that's what it must have been. Once I'd gotten rid of all the contents of my stomach, I was fine. Except I guess I was pretty exhausted!"

"Mmm-hmm." Sandor searched her face, noted her uneasy smile.

"Thank you for staying up with me. For loaning me your afghan."

"You're welcome."

"And now, we should both go to bed." Bruce consulted her watch for the first time, saw that it was 2:30 a.m. She and Sandor couldn't have been talking for more than half an hour, which meant that she'd been in that comalike deep sleep for almost seven hours!

"Not yet," said Sandor.

Concern for him creased her brow. "But, Sandor, you must have been sitting on this couch for a long, long time! You must be very uncomfortable, to say the least."

"Uncomfortable passed into numb a couple of hours ago," acknowledged Sandor, with a wry pull to one side of his mouth. "As I sat here for your sake, perhaps you will humor me by staying here a little longer."

"Well, if you put it that way...."

"I do." He reached across the cushions and took her hand, lacing their fingers firmly together. He looked down at their joined hands, and then up at her face. She had a wary expression in her blue-gray eyes. "I don't know how I'm going to say this," he admitted, "but I'm going to do it somehow if we both have to sit here all night!"

Bruce swallowed hard. She was afraid she knew what was coming, and she dreaded it.

Sandor forged ahead. "I know that you know I'm attracted to you. You've managed to avoid me for weeks, God knows how you can avoid me when not a day goes by that you don't touch me more times than I can count, but you do. You know that you do, you know what I mean."

Bruce nodded. How well she knew! She swallowed hard again. She looked away from his face, unable to bear the intensity she saw there. She looked down at their joined hands, which was a mistake. Her heart lurched in her chest.

"All right," said Sandor. He took a deep breath and plunged on. "I could understand that. I have, I guess...something of a reputation with women. But I seem to have changed. Not just the physical change that you are helping me learn to live with, but here—" he splayed his other hand against his chest "—inside. In my heart." His voice softened. "What I feel for you, what we could have together, is different than anything I have ever known before. I do love you, Bruce. I realized it only a couple of days ago. And I think—look at me, my love—"

Bruce all but dissolved in the tenderness with which he said "my love." She looked at him, though God knew how she would be able to keep her true feelings out of her eyes, as she must.

"I think," said Sandor carefully, "that you are at least attracted to me. I think you might love me, if you allowed yourself to."

Slowly, Bruce shook her head. Achingly, she unlaced their fingers. She did not, could not, speak.

Sandor trapped the hand she had taken from him and crushed it to his breast with all the fierceness of his Hungarian nature. No wild Hussar had ever more passionately refused to be denied. "No! I won't let you go! Why, why must you always pull away from me?"

"B-because," spluttered Bruce, "it isn't real, what you feel. It won't last."

"Not real?" Sandor looked down the beak of his nose, his heavy brows raised in disbelief. "How can you say that what I feel is not real? Are you telling me you know my feelings better than I do myself?"

"Yes," Bruce said miserably. He let go of her hand then. She was not surprised; she only hated herself.

Sandor, wounded, withdrew into the powerful persona of the Maestro that was his most effective mask. "Perhaps you would care, since you know so much, to enlighten me as to the real nature of my own feelings."

"What you feel is gratitude," Bruce said, her voice flat. "I've helped you, we've worked closely together. There's a certain, ah, illusion of intimacy sometimes in physical therapy. Then there's also the fact that you're getting better, much better. You aren't depressed. You've been without sex for a long time, it's only natural that you should be attracted to me."

As she spoke, she grew stronger. She had been taught these things so long and so well that she believed them. Nobody had ever told her there could be exceptions. Her chin came up. "I admit it, I'm attracted to you, too, but that's only because I'm living here, working exclusively one-on-one with you—"

"No more!" commanded Sandor. There was ice in his voice.

Bruce shivered, though the room was not cold. Sandor had made a distance between them somehow, had removed himself as surely as if he had ascended a wintry mountain and left her at its foot, with miles of empty snow between.

"You may leave now," he said.

He needed help in order to get to bed, he knew it and Bruce knew it. He was too proud to admit it; she didn't know how to cross that vast icy distance, which was much, much worse than the withdrawal of his old depressions. So Bruce left Sandor.

She climbed the stairs in the dark slowly, noticing that her legs were weak. She did not notice that Vladimir shrank back, back into the shadows as she came on; nor did she know that he lurked there waiting as she went into the bathroom and turned on the water. She concentrated on taking a shower, a shower to wash away the last taint of her sickness, to warm her again.

Under the warm shower spray, Bruce felt her muscles loosen, the icy tension fade and fall. With the release of tension there came also another kind of release, and with sudden, breathtaking clarity she knew two things: the first, that no matter the source of the poison, whether an innocent virus or something else not so innocent, she had been in mortal danger tonight. If she hadn't been able to rid herself of the poison, she would certainly have been very sick, she might even have died. The second was prompted by the first. She knew that if she had died, she would have gone into whatever lies beyond this life being very sorry that she had not given herself a chance to love, and be loved by, Sandor Szelazeny.

Virginia was right, thought Bruce as she hurried to turn off the taps. Sometimes, if you have a good enough reason, you can break the rules! She toweled her hair fiercely and left it looking like a copper storm, pulled her pink terry robe over a still-damp body, and ran out of the bathroom on bare feet. Ran to Sandor. And ran straight into Vladimir instead.

"God, Vladimir, you frightened me half to death! What are you doing down here in the hall at this time of night?" Bruce stepped back and looked at him. The man was fully dressed. Didn't he ever go to bed? Didn't he ever sleep?

"One might ask you the same question," he replied smoothly. Bruce had a sudden, chilling urge to pull him over to the mirror by the front door and see if he cast a reflection. He looked ghastly pale in the faint light that filtered through the windows from one lone, feeble street lamp outside.

She squared her shoulders. This was ridiculous. She fixed him with the stare that she'd learned early on intimidated him, though she was not at all sure it would have the same effect on this awful night when everything seemed to be going wrong. "I'm going to see Sandor. It's important, obviously, or I wouldn't be doing it at this hour." She moved to pass him, but he stood tall in her path.

"I have just assisted the Maestro to bed," he said.

Bruce stared harder. She suspected Vladimir of eavesdropping earlier, and wondered how much he had heard.

Everything, probably; it made her want to throw up all over again. The man was a fact of life that she found increasingly hard to live with. Nevertheless, hearing her mother's voice in her head saying something about catching more flies with honey than with vinegar, Bruce forced herself to smile at him. "Thank you, Vladimir. I know he needed it. We had a . . . a misunderstanding and he wouldn't let me help. Now I find I can't sleep until I admit that I was wrong. So, if you please. . . ."

With a stooped yet courtly bow, Vladimir stepped aside. Bruce swept past, her head high and her heart beating fast. She wanted to turn around and bark at him to go up the stairs and leave them alone, but she didn't. She simply could not risk alienating the man.

Then she reached Sandor's door and gave Vladimir not another thought. She knocked gently, and without waiting for an answer opened the door and closed it behind her.

The room was not dark. A bedside lamp with a parchment shade spread a golden glow about Sandor's bed. He lay propped in a nest of pillows, his striking profile bent over a book. Bruce paused just inside the door, suddenly shy but expectant, hopeful.

All Sandor heard was the faint click of the door's opening and closing. Bruce's soft robe did not rustle, nor did her bare feet make a sound. But he felt her presence. He knew, without a doubt, that she had entered the room. He closed his eyes and put his head back on the pillows in pretended weariness, though his heart in recognition of Bruce had begun to race. He didn't know what he was going to say until he heard his own voice, in weary affectation saying, "So, aren't you satisfied? Have you come to torment me more?"

"No. I came to ask you to forgive me. I was wrong, Sandor. I made a mistake." Bruce approached the bed. Now that she was here, she was no longer sure of her welcome.

With elaborate nonchalance, Sandor looked down his nose and turned over a page in his book. It might have been covered in hieroglyphics for all he'd read of it. "Did you really?" he drawled.

He glanced over at her, and just as quickly glanced back at the book. He had never seen her looking like that, never! Her hair was in flaming disarray and all the more beautiful for it; the pink color of her robe emphasized the rosiness of her skin; and she was naked, he could swear she was naked under it.

"Yes," she nodded, moving closer. Her heart thundered in her chest, she could barely hear herself think. "I don't want to believe the things I told you, Sandor. About your feelings. I was taught that it can happen like that, that a lot of patients mistake gratitude for love. And I had some experiences that confirmed that what they taught me was true."

"So," he said laying the book aside but still looking down his nose, "do all your patients fall in love with you?"

"A lot of them *think* they do. Yes."

A tiny smile played at the corners of Sandor's lips. "It looks like I'm going to have some competition."

"I don't allow myself to respond to them, of course. That's why... that's what I was trying to do with you. Not respond. I, well, if you can forgive me for telling you that you don't know your own feelings... I'm sorry, Sandor."

"Come here, Bruce." Sandor held out his hand and she took it. He pulled her onto the bed with him. She came without objection. He touched the copper tumble of her hair. Held her chin in his hand. With a finger, he teased the corners of her lips into a smile. Then gently, very gently, he replaced his teasing finger with the tip of his tongue. She tasted clean, and very, very sweet. Her mouth opened, and he kissed her. Kissed her long and deep, their bodies moving together, sliding down, down into the softness of the pillows.

"I suppose that means I'm forgiven," Bruce said when she could speak.

"Absolutely. Completely," said Sandor. He turned onto his back, and couldn't help but let out a grunt of discomfort. It had been a long day for him, full of unusual kinds of exertion—climbing steps, sitting for so long on the couch, even the kiss, though it was more than worth the effort—and now he was paying the price.

"It's been a long day for you," said Bruce, understanding. "Do you want me to go? I just didn't want us to go to sleep with what could have been an awful misunderstanding between us, Sandor. I—I want to give us a chance."

"So I wasn't wrong," he said, feeling perhaps the deepest satisfaction he had ever known, as deep as he had ever felt after his finest performances. "You do have some feelings for me, too."

"Yes," Bruce admitted, "I do." *And you're worth the risk,* she added silently. *Even if you do grow out of me and it turns out that what you felt was gratitude after all, even if my heart gets broken in a thousand pieces as I suspect it will, you are worth the risk.*

"Don't go, then. Stay with me for a while. I can't possibly—"

"I know," nodded Bruce happily, stopping his words with a finger to his lips. "We're both exhausted, but I'll stay. I'll lie here with you for a while."

Sandor smiled. He put his arm around her and she snuggled against him. Within the curve of his arm, Bruce felt instantly, blissfully comfortable, as if she had been traveling for a long, long time and had now come home.

Vladimir found them there in the morning, Sandor beneath the covers and Bruce on top of them, curled against the Maestro with her head upon his chest and his arm about her shoulders, protectively. The corners of Vladimir's mouth turned downward in a sneer. He did not wake the couple. He closed the door on them and went outside to brood over the river.

Chapter Eight

They had been up for less than an hour when they had visitors. Celeste, bearing the gift of a coffee cake so fresh that its fragrance lingered about it, and the Ramsay brothers. Vladimir, on Sandor's direction, brought them all into the kitchen where he and Bruce still lingered at the round oak table.

"Sit," said Sandor expansively. Nothing, not even an unwelcome interruption, could mar his wonderful mood this morning. "We were just finishing breakfast. Join us in a cup of coffee."

All three sat. Ronnie Ramsay knocked his chair into Celeste's and got a severe frown for it, but he managed to get sugar and cream into his coffee without spilling. Bruce watched him with amusement—her mood was as wonderful as Sandor's—until she realized that Celeste was staring at her. Staring, yet trying to cover up the fact that she did so.

"Yes," Celeste was saying to Sandor, while Bruce was the object of her piercing sidewise stare, "the tour turned out to be quite a success. I'm sorry you felt unable to visit the other houses, Maestro."

"A delight, an absolute delight," said Reggie.

"Quite," agreed Ronnie, happily splashing about in his coffee cup with his spoon.

"I'm surprised you enjoyed it so much," Sandor commented, "seeing as how England has houses and gardens far surpassing in beauty anything this country has to offer."

"Oh, not at all!" Reggie said. "Little jewels here in New Bern. Gives one a sense of what the colonies were like in the eighteenth century, don't y' know."

"It has its own particular kind of enchantment," added Ronnie, waving his spoon in the air for emphasis. "And the restorations of these exquisite small homes are so meticulously done. Quite a lesson for us Brits, why—"

He might have gone on in this vein for hours if Celeste had not interrupted him. She turned her thick-lashed violet eyes directly on Bruce and said, "I was so surprised when you didn't come back to my party, dear. And I did think that you were going to go along to the other houses with us, even if the Maestro couldn't come. Whatever happened to you?"

"I was sick," Bruce replied.

Something flickered in the violet eyes. "Really?"

"Yes, really."

While the Ramsay brothers offered a flurry of sympathy, Bruce silently bore Celeste's further scrutiny, and thought about the other woman. Now that Bruce had opened her own heart to Sandor, she recognized that Celeste was awesome competition. She was almost as beautiful as Elizabeth Taylor in one of her thinner periods; Celeste's face didn't quite have the perfect features, but her coloring was the same, and those remarkable eyes were a distinct advantage. Her figure too—small, but with such full breasts. And then there were the clothes. Did she always, always look so feminine? Today she wore a lavender dress with a big lace collar at a neckline that came to a vee, showing an enticing cleavage. Bruce, in jeans and a bright green cotton sweater, felt like a peasant.

In a sudden silence, Bruce realized that everyone was looking at her. They obviously expected her to say something, so she said, "Really, I'm just fine. I think it was one of those quick stomach viruses that seem so much worse at first than they turn out to be."

"You surely don't look like a woman who's been ill," said Celeste with a little sniff and an upward tilt of her chin. Disbelief, disapproval, what? Anyway, Bruce could see that Celeste wasn't pleased about something.

Sandor reached across the table and put his hand over Bruce's. "No, she doesn't," he said, smiling. Bruce had to smile back at him, company or no company. His face was alight, he had never looked more well or happier, and Bruce knew that she probably looked the same.

The Ramsay brothers looked at one another, then nodded as if they had had a telepathic communication. The communication had apparently not told them who was to speak next, because they both said more or less together, "So glad to hear it." Then Reggie's voice dropped out and Ronnie continued, "Shall we share a bit of this coffee cake? It smells so delicious that m' mouth is positively watering."

"Yes, of course," Bruce agreed with alacrity, jumping up from the table to get a knife. Vladimir had gone off elsewhere in the house, and she was not sorry. Returning with the knife and taking her place at the table, Bruce said, "I don't know where my manners are! Celeste, thank you. It really does smell lovely."

"Oh, it's nothing," said Celeste with an airy wave of her hand. "I didn't make this one myself, I just ran over and got it at the bakery. I thought if Bruce hadn't been feeling much like eating, this might tempt her."

Celeste's words sliced through Bruce's consciousness like the knife in her hand cut the cake. Suddenly she remembered the party, the cup of punch, handed to her by the hostess. By Celeste. Punch, the only thing she had had to eat or drink before getting so violently ill. True, everyone had had the same punch, but still. . . .

Bruce fixed the other woman with wide gray eyes. "You mean, you knew before you came over here that I was sick? How could you know?"

"I—" The dark eyelashes swept down like furry curtains, concealing Celeste's expression. "I assumed that you were. You would have come back otherwise." Then she looked up again with the brightest of smiles. "Now, I won't have any coffee cake. I have to go open my shop. Sandor, dear Maestro, do say that you'll come and visit my little old place of business sometime soon."

All graciousness, Sandor inclined his head. "Of course, I will. As soon as I am physically able. Thank you for thinking of us this morning, my dear Celeste."

Ugh! Bruce thought as she addressed herself to the brothers. "You'll stay, won't you?" As both Ronnie and Reggie were practically salivating in anticipation of the coffee cake she had cut but not served, she had no doubt that they would.

Celeste left, escorted to the door by Vladimir, who appeared in the kitchen at just the right moment. As if he had been eavesdropping, Bruce thought as she handed plates around the table. She didn't doubt for a minute that he had. She told herself that he was harmless, that he couldn't help the way he looked. If Sandor's calculations were correct, the man was almost eighty years old, for heaven's sake!

Shaking off an eerie, uncomfortable feeling that she couldn't define, Bruce gave herself a piece of the delicious-smelling cake. She looked at it on the plate. Looked at the three men, chewing contentedly with their conversation.

There is nothing wrong with this coffee cake, she told herself, nothing! Yet she got up from the table and took the plate with her. "You men go on talking," she said, "I think I'll just clean up in here a little." They weren't watching her; she surreptitiously slid the cake into the garbage. It would be a long, long time, if ever, before Bruce would feel comfortable consuming anything that came to her from Celeste Stanhope's hand.

Sandor was disturbed—Bruce could feel it all the way across the room. She stopped in her rinsing of dishes to listen to what was being said.

"Where, exactly, did you hear that?" Sandor was asking. His eaglelike visage was dark, scowling.

Reggie seemed to be handling the questions. Ronnie's eyes were wide, his expression eager in his red-cheeked, mustached face. Reggie tipped his chair back and tucked his thumbs into the pockets of his vest. "Oh, 'round and about."

"We do get about a bit," Ronnie ventured hopefully.

Hear what? Bruce was longing to ask.

"It's true, isn't it?" Reggie persisted. "When we arrived here to visit our Celeste and learned that y' were here in New Bern of all places—"

"Why, we couldn't believe our luck. Could we, Reg?"

Quietly, unobtrusively, Bruce took her place at the table. Sandor's disturbance drew her like a beacon. She must be there to help him, no matter what was wrong.

"You were misinformed," growled Sandor.

The brothers looked at one another, both pairs of eyebrows raised in disbelief. Then, simultaneously, they looked back at Sandor. "Surely not," they said in unison.

"We would pay," said Ronnie eagerly, "pay handsomely. We understand that there are manuscripts—"

"Priceless artifacts—"

"Secrets of, ah, alchemy and such, don't y' know!" concluded Ronnie, his whole face flushed bright red.

Sandor released the brakes from the wheels of his chair with an audible snap. He wheeled rapidly away from the table, across the room where he stopped with his back to them.

The Ramsays appealed to Bruce with their eyes. She shook her head, still not understanding what was going on. "You've upset him," she said quietly. "I don't know what this is about, but I think you'd better go."

Sandor heard her. With a twist so vigorous that a pain, as intense as the old pain, shot along his spine, he spun his chair around. He glared across the room; his golden eyes had never looked more raptorial. "You have made a mistake!" he thundered. "My presence in Europe at the time you heard that this material might become available was only a coincidence. My mother's name was Bator. Do you hear that? *Bator!* And if we are to retain the pleasant relationship we have so far had, you will forget all about the things you have just said to me and never mention them again!"

"Oh, yes, quite so," agreed Ronnie hastily. He got up out of his chair so fast that he upended it onto the floor.

"Do accept our apology, Maestro. We are sorry to have offended y', as we so obviously have," said Reggie. He was the fixer, the picker-upper, the peacemaker. He restored the chair to rights and took his brother firmly by the arm. "Be assured that we shall never mention it again."

"Already forgotten," said Ronnie over his departing shoulder.

Bruce accompanied them to the front door. "I still don't understand, but Sandor said something about Europe. You must not forget that he almost died in a plane crash there. Naturally his feelings are still fragile and anything that recalls that time to him...."

The brothers looked at one another with their wordless communication. They seemed to mutually conclude that Bruce might be a valuable ally. Reggie said in a low, conspiratorial voice, "If, when he does fully recover, y' should learn anything about the artifacts, do give us a call." He produced a business card and slipped it into Bruce's palm. There was something covert and practiced about the way he did it, yet when she looked at the card it was quite ordinary, with a London address and telephone number.

"We'll reimburse any expense, o' course," Ronnie was saying.

"I—" Bruce was only just beginning to frame a reply when she heard the hum of the tires on Sandor's wheelchair coming down the hall, and he called, "Wait!" Bruce slipped the card into the pocket of her jeans and forgot all about it.

The brothers turned, with brightened expressions on their faces. But their obvious expectations were soon dashed.

Coming to a stop, Sandor asked, "Did Celeste Stanhope bring you here? Where does she fit into all this? What does she think she knows?"

"Fit? Celeste?" Ronnie squeaked.

"She, ah, she invited us here quite innocently," said Reggie.

"Innocently. That's the ticket," said Ronnie, bobbing his head. "House and garden tour, don't you know."

Reggie continued smoothly, "She knows almost nothing. She isn't interested in manuscripts and such, as we told y' before."

"We do antiquities, she does antiques," affirmed Ronnie, almost in a singsong.

Bruce began to wonder about their honesty. She gave herself a mental shake. Really, she was getting as paranoid as Sandor used to be.

"Don't worry," Reggie assured Sandor, and with a sweep of his glance included Bruce, "we will tell her that we were mistaken. I know how much she desires and would, ah, treasure your friendship, Maestro. And yours, too, o' course, Miss MacLaren. Now kindly allow us to go our way before we commit any more faux pas."

"Faux pas. Quite. Ta-ta," said Ronnie, and stumbled on the threshold on his way out of the door.

When Bruce turned back from closing the door after the departing Ramsays, she had a smile on her face. It was impossible not to be amused by Ronnie. He had a childlike quality that was endearing. But her smile disappeared when she saw Sandor's gloom.

She went to his chair and turned it about, sighing. "Okay, Maestro. Oops—" she leaned over his shoulder, her hair falling forward to brush his cheek "—forget I said that."

"Hmm," was all Sandor said. He was so distracted that Bruce decided to leave him to his silence.

She pushed him down the hallway, back to the kitchen, over to its seating area, which at this hour of a May morning was bright and sunny.

"My canes!" he barked absently. Bruce noticed, not for the fist time, that Sandor's natural mode of speech was the terse command. A normal conversational tone required conscious thought on his part. Usually this irritated her, but now it did not. She got the canes and handed them to him. A part of her made some purely professional observations: how automatically he now performed motions that had been so laboriously learned, as he moved from the wheelchair to stand, to walk a few steps, to sit on the couch. He was even acquiring a certain grace of movement that she was thrilled to see.

She joined him on the couch. "Sandor...."

"I know," he sighed. "You want to know what that was all about."

"Yes, I'm curious," she admitted. "But mostly I'd like to know because whatever they were talking about was so obviously disturbing to you."

Sandor flashed her an enigmatic look, then took up one cane and pounded it on the floor as he raised his voice, "Vladimir!"

Such projection, he should have been an actor, mused Bruce with a smile.

Some time passed before the man appeared. For once, he had not been listening outside the door.

"Maestro?" he inquired.

"I want you to go out. There must be a decent tobacconist in this town—look until you've found one. Then buy me some tobacco and a decent pipe, you know the kind. And if you can't find my usual in this hopelessly provincial place, make sure whatever you do get is of acceptable quality. Do you understand?"

"Yes, Maestro." Apparently recognizing his master's mood, Vladimir bowed almost obsequiously and backed away.

Bruce said, "I didn't know you smoked."

"They made me quit when I was in the hospital. I've decided to take it up again."

"Oh," said Bruce. "Well, at least it isn't cigarettes."

Sandor raised a thick eyebrow. He was in no mood to be opposed.

Perversely, Bruce couldn't resist adding, "You can get oral cancer from smoking a pipe, you know."

Sandor said, "If I live long enough to get cancer of any kind, I'll consider myself lucky."

Chastened, and a little alarmed, Bruce kept silent. So did Sandor until they heard Vladimir start the car and drive away. Then, with a heavy sigh, Sandor said, "I lied to them."

"I gathered as much," said Bruce.

At this, Sandor raised both eyebrows. "Do you think they knew?"

Bruce wanted to hedge, to smooth things over, but she sensed that this would in the long run not be a good idea. She said honestly, "I'd be surprised if they didn't. You were too angry for what you said, a simple misunderstanding."

Sandor brooded over this.

Bruce cautiously tried to draw him out. "I didn't hear what they said to you that, ah, set you off. I guess I sort of came in the middle, after you were already pretty upset."

Sandor leaned his head back and rubbed his hand over his eyes. He took a deep breath. His chest, which with the re-development of his muscles had grown broad, expanded. Then he expelled the breath in a shout, a protest directed to unseen gods, full of tragic fury. "Will I never be free of this?"

The room rang; the walls reverberated with the timbre of his voice. On the last dying vibrations Bruce asked, in barely more than a whisper, "What, Sandor? What is it that you fear you will never be free of?"

"A legacy. A blasted legacy, from a family I never knew I had until a little over a year ago."

"Your mother's family?" Bruce guessed.

Sandor nodded ponderously, as if his head had grown too heavy to move. He did not want to talk about this, not even to Bruce.

"Is it . . . the curse, Sandor?"

"Not exactly," he said reluctantly. "You've convinced me that I was wrong to blame everything on the supposed curse. But you see, even without it these things continue to haunt me."

"What things?" When he did not reply, Bruce made a calculated guess. "Your mother's name was not really Bator. Was it, Sandor?"

"No." The sigh he uttered was so heavy that it was more of a groan. "All my life I thought my mother was Maria Theresa Bator Szelazeny. Actually, in spite of her coming to this country, in spite of her marrying my father, she was the Countess Bathory." He pronounced it Ba-tor-ee.

The names were so similar, it was a clever switch, Bruce thought. But why? She said nothing, she waited. Sandor looked at her piercingly. "Does the name Bathory mean nothing to you?"

"Not a thing," said Bruce.

Thank God! thought Sandor. He turned his face away from Bruce and felt the heaviness in his chest lessen. Perhaps, with luck, even if she were to stay with him as he still dared to hope, she need never know.

No, he was not quite that lucky. Perhaps she need never know all, but she must know some. If the Ramsays didn't give up, he might have to have Bruce's help one of these days. He certainly wasn't going to involve Vladimir; he had already gone to untold lengths to keep Vladimir in the dark as to much that he himself had done.

Sandor turned again to Bruce. This time he bent toward her from the waist, not realizing that this was a motion he'd been incapable of until recently. Now that the first, and worst, hurdle was past, he felt childishly eager to get this out of the way and have her approval. "We talked once of Transylvania, I'm sure you remember."

Bruce nodded.

"The Bathorys have had a castle there for centuries. My mother apparently grew up in the old castle, and she had the hereditary title. The Bathorys have some, ah, unusual customs about the title and the castle remaining with the ma-

ternal line, and my mother became the countess when she
was very young, before she married my father. But she
didn't want the heritage, and the upheaval in Europe before the Second World War gave her the chance to get away.
She and my father left Hungary in time to take out most of
their wealth, and somewhere in the process of settling here,
she changed her maiden name to Bator."

Sandor stopped, waited, and when Bruce once again
nodded understanding, he went on. "I knew she and my
father had been some kind of aristocracy, but it didn't interest me because it hadn't interested them. Mother loved
America with a passion, and so did Father. They made sure
that I had no romantic ideas about being a titled aristocrat.
They died a few years ago. As far as I knew, I was it, the last
of the line. I never knew of any other Bators and the few
Szelazenys I'd heard of were not blood kin. But I had a
grandfather I didn't know about."

The going became rough for Sandor. He leaned back,
carefully stretching the tension out of his shoulders in a way
Bruce had taught him. He took a couple of deep, calming
breaths, another technique learned from her. She observed
these things without realizing that she observed them, she
was so focused on his story and eager for him to continue.
She guessed, helping him along, "He was your mother's
father."

Sandor completed stretching his neck before he replied.
"Yes. He was there at Castle Bathory. As it were, the keeper
of the flame."

"Guardian of the legacy," contributed Bruce, completely fascinated.

Sandor clenched his hands into fists and a hard light came
into his eyes as he forced himself to go on. He simply trusted
that his love for Bruce would guide him to say what he must
and withhold the rest—the horrible—for her sake. "My

grandfather knew of me, Bruce. Whether my mother knew that he knew, or not, is a question I would like to have answered, but it never can be. I was told only that my grandfather left instructions how to find me after his death. And they found me on that European tour. When I took hiatus, I went to Castle Bathory. I took Vladimir with me, because of his long association with the family. I was, and am, the heir." *God help me!* he added silently. For a moment he could not go on.

"You are the . . . the Count Bathory?" Bruce asked.

"No." Sandor roused himself. "As I said, the title passes only to females. If you and I were to marry and we had a daughter, she would be the countess. That is, if I had stayed there, if I had accepted the burden of this inheritance. And I did not. Now," he went on briskly, before she could ask any more questions, "where the Ramsay brothers come in is that I did take steps to break up the estate. I deeded the castle and its contents over to the town. It seemed only right, considering that for hundreds of years the townspeople paid taxes and tribute to the castle. I wanted to sign legal papers renouncing the title, but in the time I had available I couldn't find anyone willing to draw them up for me. So in the end I wrote my own document and sent it to be put with my papers in the bank back here. Only. . . ."

"Only?"

"Only there were certain things, what the Ramsays call artifacts, and manuscripts, that I didn't want to leave. I took them with me. However, I must caution you that not even Vladimir knows I have them. He suspects, I think, but I have refused to say anything, and Vladimir is much too well-bred to pry. Vladimir, if truth were told, knows much more about how to be an aristocrat than I do." He smiled, relieved, intending that to be an end to it.

But Bruce was not quite satisfied. "The Ramsays must have heard somewhere—maybe there's a sort of grapevine for people who collect things the way they do—that you took these things. Are they valuable?"

Sandor laughed harshly, out of nervousness. "Only to the wrong sort of people!"

Bruce narrowed her eyes. A prickle at the back of her neck told her to beware. "What do you mean, Sandor?"

"I mean, my dear Bruce, that the Bathorys of long ago were not exactly nice people. There are . . . legends. There is the infamous curse that we agreed we are not going to acknowledge, and that is fine with me. You cannot imagine, once your good sense had talked me out of all that silly superstition, how relieved I was. And am. I intend to stay that way."

"Where are they now, these papers and things?"

"In a safe place. Only I know where they are, and I'm not telling anyone. The curious Ramsays will just have to forget all about the Bathorys. As far as I'm concerned, the Bathorys and all their legacy no longer exist. Since I am the last of them, I should be able to accomplish that. Now, if your curiosity is satisfied, I would like to do some exercises, please. After all yesterday's exertions, I feel stiff as a board!"

BRUCE WAS SATISFIED, and more than pleased with Sandor's progress. In every way he was improving by leaps and bounds. Well, maybe not exactly leaps and bounds, but he was making steady progress. The fact that he would not dwell on this legacy thing, that he continued to take her realistic denial of the "curse" so to heart, were all good signs.

So why wasn't she content? Why couldn't she settle into a new, relaxed kind of exploration of the possibilities of their relationship, as Sandor seemed ready to do? But she couldn't. She seemed, mental healthwise, to have traded places with him. Bruce felt watchful, and watched.

Things were happening in the town. In the week following the house and garden tour, Celeste developed an annoying habit of dropping over at any old time, and Sandor didn't discourage her. In fact, he seemed to enjoy her visits. Bruce even began to wonder if Sandor might be the type of man for whom the conquest is all— Now that he more or less had her, at least had her willing attention, had he perhaps lost some of his interest?

At mid-week the Ramsays left to go to an antique show in Charleston and then on to another in Savannah. They would be back, they assured Bruce and Sandor, seemingly anxious to repair whatever damage had been done to the new friendship. And when they returned, they were going to be guests in Celeste's house rather than go back to the bed and breakfast where they had been staying, so they would be just across the street. Bruce did not think this was quite so jolly as she was supposed to; even Sandor was more enthusiastic. He mused on whether or not one of the brothers might play chess.

And in the town at large, within the week following the house and garden tour, every single house on the tour was broken into. Bruce's heart went up into her throat when she heard. The papers had scant information; she went to the drugstore where so many people gathered and she frankly gossiped with them. Rumor had it that, yes, things had been stolen. But they were the most peculiar kind of thefts. Nothing big or important had been taken, only small objects, the kind of thing a person could slip into a pocket undetected.

Other houses, not on the tour, also fell victim. Bruce was grateful that this time they had been passed by. She did not want anything to disturb Sandor's hard-won peace of mind.

She sensed, in spite of the brave face he put on, that Sandor's serenity was fragile.

At the end of the week there was an episode of senseless vandalism right in the middle of town, in the heart of the historic district. Someone, or a group of someones, overturned old grave markers at the Episcopal Church. The newspaper reported that police were baffled; such vandalism just did not happen in New Bern.

Sandor, behind his serene mask, wondered. His palms pricked with memory of the many senseless acts that had plagued people around him before. Over and over again he told himself that Bruce was right, there was no curse....

And Bruce, when she went out for one of her customary early morning runs and slipped on an unaccountable slick spot on the sidewalk, just about at the point where she usually broke into full stride, did not at that moment think it was anything other than a nasty accident. She picked herself up and went on with her run, being grateful that she hadn't sprained or broken anything. If she had been in less than top physical condition, if she hadn't had the kind of physical training that had taught her so well how to fall without injuring herself that it had become instinct, she would have suffered serious harm. There was no doubt of that.

Chapter Nine

"You have to let me call the police," Bruce was saying, but Sandor could feel himself blocking her out. The great gray veil was descending, wrapping him, muffling, insulating. With an effort so huge that he knew it would be his last for some time to come, Sandor raised his head, looked right at Bruce, and said, "I will not allow it. Our would-be thief is very likely the same one we did not report before—"

"You can't know that. There have been all these other incidents all over town, and just when it looked as if we weren't going to be touched—"

"—Kindly do not interrupt me, my dear Bruce," continued Sandor. His jaws had involuntarily clenched; every word was an effort. He knew this kind of tension was bad and brought inevitably with it the pain he had been nearly free of, but he could not help himself. "Since my room and the library were the obvious targets, and since those rooms were less disturbed than the others those previous times, I believe this to have been no more than a continuation of that previous search."

"Search!" Bruce pounced. This was what she herself believed. "There, you see, you believe it, too—"

Sandor cursed himself for his slip of the tongue and doggedly continued on. "A search for anything valuable, no more than that. I repeat, and I do not intend to belabor this matter further, that neither I nor you nor Vladimir will call the police. I do not wish the further disturbance. Above all, I do not wish and will not tolerate the publicity! And that is an end to it!'' The Maestro snapped the brakes off his chair and began, heavily, to wheel himself from the room.

Bruce started to go after him; then, with her bright hair flying, whipped around to Vladimir who stood solemnly by. Her urgent need for action made her put away pride. ''Vladimir, you've known him so much better and so much longer than I have. Can't you do something to make him see reason?'' she pleaded.

The valet's usually impassive face registered surprise. ''No, Miss MacLaren. When the Maestro is so definite, nothing can sway him. Certainly not I.''

''Oh, damn!'' swore Bruce under her breath. She watched Sandor pass through the doorway into the hall, then started after him.

Vladimir stopped her with a light restraining touch on her arm. ''If I may say so, miss, it will only make him oppose you all the more should you continue to plead your case.''

Bruce looked over her shoulder at the man. Her gray eyes were clouded with worry. ''I just thought I'd point out to him that this time is different. Something was taken, even if it was just a letter opener. We really ought to report it.''

A pained expression crossed Vladimir's white, skull-like face. A look of loss, grief so obviously genuine that it put Bruce off-balance. He said mournfully, ''That letter opener was solid silver and very valuable. Very old. It has been in the Maestro's family for a long time. It bore the family's initial. Yes, I would be glad if we could report the letter opener stolen and if the police might recover it. But the Maestro has said otherwise and I will not go against his wishes.''

"Which side of the family? His mother's, or his father's?"

"His father's, of course," said Vladimir, looking very superior. "The letter opener was inscribed with an elaborately scrolled *S.* If it had been his mother's, there would not have been a mere initial, but the family crest!"

Out in the hall, across the way, a door closed with a decisive thunk. Sandor had shut himself into his room.

"Oh, of course," said Bruce; then she regretted her slightly sarcastic tone. She turned back to Vladimir. "I'm surprised that the loss of it would mean so much to you when it came from the father's side of the family."

Vladimir looked down his nose scornfully. "I abhor stealing. I abhor all forms of intrusion. Valuable objects should remain with their owners, no matter their origin!"

Bruce sighed. There, she had done it again. Just when she thought she had detected a streak in Vladimir that she could sympathize with, she'd managed to blow it. Or he had. Or... well, with a toss of her head she decided for the thousandth time that life was too short for the intricacies of dealing with Vladimir. "Whatever!" she said. "I'm going to leave his royal majesty in his room to brood, which is no doubt what he's doing, and I'm going for a walk. I suggest, Vladimir, that you do the same."

"I will stay in the house," said the man stiffly, "I have my work to do."

"Suit yourself," muttered Bruce. Vladimir might not be able to bring himself to go against his Maestro's wishes, but she had no such compunction about opposing Sandor—provided that her opposition had good cause. She intended to think about it as she walked.

SANDOR STAYED in his room for two whole days. On the evening of the first day when Bruce went to get him for supper, he had glared at her with a fierce raptor's glare and said in a grating voice, "I want to be left alone!" So she left him alone. So, for the most part, did Vladimir.

She also decided that she would not go against Sandor and call the police. When she had calmed down she could admit that Sandor's desire to avoid publicity was understandable, and that she would do well to respect it. It was just that she found it so hard to do nothing; doing nothing was all against her nature.

On the afternoon of Sandor's second day in his room, Bruce and Virginia were in the kitchen. Bruce had made bread in the morning, and now the whole house was filled with the wonderful smell of its baking. Virginia was teaching her how to make coulibiac, a dish Virginia said she thought was Hungarian in origin and might tempt Sandor out of his lair. They had disassembled a whole head of cauliflower, prepared a spicy stuffing, and were in an intricate process of assembling the cauliflower head again.

Virginia said, "But aren't you worried about him, in there all by himself for so long?"

"No," said Bruce. Actually, she was absorbed in what she and Virginia were doing, and enjoying herself. She hadn't known that cooking could be such a creative, rewarding, even healing activity—one her strong hands and nimble fingers were good at. If nothing else, she was going to return to New York a gourmet cook.

"But what if he's depressed again?"

Bruce straightened up and brushed the hair back off her forehead with the back of her hand. Her fingers were sticky and smelled wonderfully of herbs. "He isn't," she said. "If I thought he was, then yes, I'd be worried."

"I don't know." Virginia shook her head. She stepped back and walked around to the other side of the counter-divider where she could see their cauliflower in the round.

She said, "This is coming along nicely. But back to Sandor…how can you be so sure if you haven't even seen him?"

"I think what Sandor is doing is having a final battle with himself, and I think he needs to have it. Any long recovery process has at least one major setback, when the person questions whether it's worth all the work to be well again."

"And you think that's what's going on with Sandor."

"Yes. In a way, it's easier to be depressed. Depression makes action impossible, it kind of insulates you from people and the world around you. Sandor no doubt would prefer right now to let the depression claim him, just give himself up to it. But from what I saw last night, I believe that's not going to happen."

"And what," Virginia asked, giving the assembled cauliflower an approving pat, "did you see last night?"

"An angry man," said Bruce with a smile, also admiring their handiwork. "He glared at me. Nobody can be both angry and depressed at the same time! I expect he's in there brooding over things and feeling a bit sad, but as long as the anger is there, too, I'm not particularly worried. If he doesn't come out on his own pretty soon, I'll go in after him. And I'll work on the anger, which is what I did when I first came here."

"You did?" Virginia's eyes were round with wonder. "You actually tried to make him mad? I should think Sandor Szelazenys anger would be something…something truly awesome!"

"I didn't make him *that* angry. I just challenged him a little bit, and it worked." Bruce finished washing her hands and whipped off her apron. "Now, if we're done here, come and tell me who these people are who have sent Sandor all these invitations."

"Invitations?" Virginia was intrigued. She washed her own hands and joined Bruce at the kitchen table.

"Mmm-hmm. Since the Maestro has been refusing to read his mail, I've taken it upon myself to play secretary. It seems everybody at Celeste's party was enthralled by Sandor Szelazeny and now they all want the pleasure of his company for dinner or cocktails, or both. And there's one from a Mrs. Dimes for high tea, if you can imagine!"

"Oh, I could tell you about Mrs. Dimes!" said Virginia with a roll of her eyes.

"Exactly what I was hoping! So let's get to it."

In the midst of Mrs. Dimes, Vladimir came into the kitchen announcing, "Mrs. Celeste Stanhope."

Celeste was right behind him. Her high heels clicked across the floor. "Hello, girls," she said, smiling brilliantly in her progress through the big room.

Bruce winced at the word "girls" but made a little shrug of resignation; no point correcting the very feminine but not feminist Mrs. Stanhope. Virginia didn't notice; she was busily gathering up the little pile of invitations and putting a big, heavy cookbook on top of them just as Celeste reached the table. Virginia looked at Bruce with a wise eyebrow raised; Bruce was sure she would have winked if she'd thought she could get away with it without Celeste seeing her do it. "So what's this about Sandor being indisposed?" asked Celeste.

"Do sit down," said Bruce as Celeste began to do so without being invited.

"We've been cooking," said Virginia, "we're just taking a little break."

"So I can see, and smell," said Celeste, wrinkling her nose in a parody of daintiness. She rearranged the pastel silk scarf at the neck of her periwinkle blue cotton knit dress so that one end fell behind and the other end over her shoulder. Satisfied, she flashed the smile again. It was patently false this time. "Quite the little domestic pair, aren't you?"

A knowing look passed between Bruce and Virginia; they were both suppressing laughter.

Impatient, Celeste prodded, "Well, what about the Maestro? I wanted to see him."

"I'm afraid you can't," said Bruce, trying not to sound too happy about it. "He's keeping to his room. He doesn't want to see anybody right now."

"Why?" Celeste raised her perfectly arched eyebrows. "He isn't ill, I hope?"

"Not really," said Bruce.

"He had a setback," supplied Virginia, "but Bruce said it isn't serious."

"Are you really qualified to judge, Bruce? Perhaps you should call a doctor. I'd be glad to call my own doctor for you, he's the very best in town."

Bruce bristled. Her Scots temper was rising. She tossed her red hair. "If Sandor needs a doctor, I'll send Vladimir. You really need not concern yourself, Celeste."

"We-e-l-l," Celeste drawled, surveying Bruce slyly out of the corners of her eyes. "I think I'd just like to see for myself that he's all right. Yes, I definitely think that would be best. I'm sure Vladimir will agree with me, and will announce me to the Maestro." She turned to the man, who hovered just inside the kitchen door. "Won't you, Vladimir?"

Vladimir cleared his throat and drew himself up to his full spindly height. "I do not think that would be wise, Mrs. Stanhope. As Miss MacLaren said, the Maestro very definitely does not wish to be disturbed."

He sounded very definite, but Bruce saw that the man was nervous. He clinched and unclinched his hands, and darted his eyes from Celeste to her. *How interesting,* Bruce thought, *he seems almost afraid of her and wants my sup-*

*port. Yet I would have bet that the old vulture wasn't afraid
of anyone or anything that walks the earth!*

For spite, either of Celeste or Vladimir, she wasn't sure
which, Bruce gave a shrug that looked much more casual
than she felt. "Of course, he probably would feel different
about you, Celeste. I can't guarantee that he'd really want
to see you, he might bite your head off. Or he might be
coming down with some virus and you'd be exposing yourself to it, but if you really want to try...."

"It's on your head!" inserted Virginia with happy pes-
kiness.

"Really, I just thought I might try to cheer him up," Celeste pouted prettily.

Vladimir had advanced with his phenomenally quiet tread
and now he startled Celeste, just as he had so often startled
Bruce. Right behind her, he said in his sepulchral tone,
"That would, in my opinion, be most unwise."

Celeste jumped, but she held her ground, turning a venomous look on the man. She managed to moderate the
venom before turning back to Bruce and Virginia. "Well, if
you're all going to gang up on me, I guess I'll give up. But
it's against my better judgment, you hear?" She rose carefully, not quite gracefully. "I'll just run along now."

Virginia needled with barely concealed glee. "Are you
sure you don't want to stay and have tea with me and Bruce?
We were just going to make some, weren't we, Bruce?"

"Yes, we were," agreed Bruce, though she would far
rather have seen Celeste leave.

"No, thank you," said Celeste over her shoulder. But she
paused in the door to look at them once more, her gaze
resting longest on the valet. "But if I hear that that poor,
dear, talented man is really sick and you haven't called a
doctor for him, then I'll ... I'll—I'm really going to be upset with all of you!" Not waiting for a response, she

flounced out of the room, and the tall but stooped Vladimir stalked after her.

"You know," whispered Virginia across the table, "Celeste and Vladimir make a good pair. They're vultures, both of them!"

And Bruce nearly collapsed in silent laughter.

THE COULIBIAC did not lure Sandor from his lair. For the second night Bruce ate alone, picking at the elegant dish and drinking two glasses of white wine with it, when one glass of wine was usually more than enough for her. She thought rather wistfully that even Vladimir would have been welcome company... and then wondered how she could have changed so much in such a short few months. She was accustomed to eating alone, she ate alone in her apartment almost every night, and she had almost always enjoyed her solitude. But no more. She missed Sandor dreadfully, and admitted as much to herself.

The next morning she decided she had left him alone for long enough. She had a plan, which she announced to Vladimir, and told him he could take Sandor's car and have a day off. Somewhat to her surprise, Vladimir seemed pleased, and left in the car while she was making her preparations.

It was Saturday and Sandor's building site should be deserted. The men didn't work on Saturday, she knew. She was going to take Sandor on a picnic, whether he wanted to go or not. Since he loved the place where his new house was being built, she would take him there. Sandor wasn't yet flexible enough to sit on the ground, so she would put a card table in the trunk of her car, and there were already folding chairs out there....

Bruce hummed as she worked, gathering all sorts of goodies from the refrigerator. Virginia was always bringing delicious tidbits from the deli where she worked, and soon Bruce had a true movable feast put together. She decided that she would stow everything but the perishables in her car before she approached Sandor the Lion in his den.

As she was hefting the card table into the trunk, Bruce heard an unwelcome sound: the tapping of high heels on pavement.

"Hey," said Celeste. "What are you doing? Need some help?"

"No, thank you," said Bruce, gritting her teeth. The last thing in the world that she wanted right now was for Celeste to invite herself to go with them, which the woman was perfectly capable of doing. So, after slamming the trunk shut, Bruce without a moment's regret did a very uncharacteristic thing: she lied. "I'm going to visit some friends in—" she thought rapidly, frantically; her lack of knowledge of the area was about to do her in when she remembered all the brochures from the Visitor Center "—Beaufort."

"You're taking a card table?" Celeste was frowning, a worried look on her face.

That's the trouble with lying, thought Bruce, *it just gets more and more complicated.* She wondered why Celeste should care so much anyway. With sudden inspiration she said, "My friends have a rented condo and a bunch of people are coming. They needed the extra table."

"Oh. Not that it's any of my business." Celeste's frown cleared a bit, but she still looked worried. "How is Maestro Szelazeny today?"

"He's much better, thank you."

"I'm glad to hear it." But somehow she didn't look glad. "I, ah, I don't suppose he's going along to, ah, to meet your friends?"

"No, of course he isn't." *One more lie,* thought Bruce, *and then please God I'll be out of this!* "He went out with Vladimir, earlier. I do take a day off now and then, Celeste."

Now the frown cleared completely and the brilliant smile appeared like sun coming from behind a cloud. "I'm so glad he's better! And I hope I wasn't too awfully rude yesterday, or if I was you'll forgive me, won't you, sweetie? I just care so much about the Maestro, I certainly want to see him continue to get better and better."

"I know you do, Celeste. Think nothing of it."

Impulsively the older woman leaned over and pecked a kiss on Bruce's cheek. "You just run along and have a wonderful day off. I'm going off in just a minute, to an estate auction in Kinston. So, bye!"

"Goodbye," Bruce acknowledged, trying hard not to wipe her cheek where Celeste's lips had been. She watched her cross the street, then resumed the packing of her car. But slowly. She did not want to take a chance that Celeste might see her bring Sandor out, and know she'd been lied to.

SANDOR COULD NOT understand what had happened to his comfortable gray cloak of depression. No matter how often in the past two days he had tried to draw it round about him, to cover himself in it, the cloak would not keep him covered. He would feel himself enveloped in its comfort, and sink into its nothingness, and then it would be gone. He kept losing it. Losing it in brooding thought, or in a ripping fierce anger, which was worse. He didn't understand.

And he was getting tired of his own company. He missed Bruce. He had begun missing her almost as soon as the door shut behind him. He had missed her terribly that first night when he'd barked at her to go away, and she did. He'd had some moments of near panic when he'd thought she might have gone all the way away, back to New York, but then he'd heard her voice talking to Vladimir and knew she was still in the house.

By the second afternoon he had, without realizing it, given up trying to reclaim his depression. He settled for brooding thought instead. He admitted to a feeling of doom. He could not understand why the thief, whoever it was, had taken his letter opener and nothing else. There were gold cuff links and a gold tie bar, and a ruby ring he seldom wore, and for that matter there was a considerable stash of cash in a drawer that had been rifled. So why take only the letter opener? It made no sense.

He brooded on. No doubt the thief had not been looking for that sort of valuable; no doubt the thief was looking for the things he had hidden far away from here, the evil artifacts of his inheritance. Artifacts...it was the Ramsay brothers who had given him that word for them. Could the Ramsay brothers be the thieves? Not likely, they weren't in New Bern, they'd gone somewhere. But they could have come back. But he didn't believe it had been the Ramsays, and if not them, then who?

In the dark, small hours of night a terrible anger had seized Sandor. With the irrationality those small hours can bring, he had once again decided that the curse was real, and was working on him. He raged against it. Raged against a legacy that could deprive him of happiness, the happiness he wanted to have with Bruce. He had just begun to believe in happiness, begun to believe that a man previously obsessed by music and fame could at a late age really, truly fall in love. But he, Sandor Szelazeny, son of Maria Theresa Bator, who was no Bator after all but an accursed Bathory.... He couldn't fall in love. He couldn't marry like a normal person. The curse had to be real, things were happening again to prove it. The thief was no ordinary thief but some instrument of ancient vengeance who would never, never let him be. And he couldn't involve Bruce. If he really loved her, he must make her go from him, for her own safety.

With this unwelcome thought, the much desired gray cloak had once again claimed him. But only for a little while. Soon he was brooding again, and soon again raging, and so it had gone on for two whole days and nights. Sandor was thoroughly sick of the process, and more than sick of himself.

Nevertheless, when Bruce stuck her head in the door, her hair shining like a new copper penny, he glared and summoned the sourest facial expression he could manage.

"I'm coming in," she warned, "whether you like it or not!"

"Humph!" Sandor was in his wheelchair, and he spun the wheels so that he faced the window. Then he allowed himself a small turning up of the corners of his mouth. She would soon see that he had done a moderately good job of taking care of himself, though his face was disreputably prickly with unshaven black beard.

"Maestro Grumpy," said Bruce, a cheerful note in her voice. She came and leaned against the windowsill, looking at him critically. "Well, Grumpy, I don't think you'll make it as one of the Seven Dwarfs, in spite of your name. With all that growth of beard, you look more like a troll."

"You're not exactly Snow White yourself, you know," Sandor growled.

Bruce laughed. *Yes, yes!* she inwardly exulted. She had been right about what was going on with Sandor. Getting him back into the world again was going to be a piece of cake. On impulse, because she simply could not resist, she reached over and playfully tousled Sandor's unruly hair. As she touched him, a lump formed unexpectedly in her throat.

Just as unexpectedly, she heard herself say in a voice hoarse with emotion, "I've missed you, Sandor."

Her touch went like a bolt of hot, searing lightning from his head down through his entire body. Forcing his shaggy eyebrows together, he jerked his head down and pulled back hard on the wheels of his chair. He shot himself away from her. It was all the rejection he could manage. If he'd tried to say anything, he knew he would have betrayed himself. God, how much he had missed her, too!

Bruce squared her shoulders, thinking that she shouldn't be so disappointed. She had expected more opposition than this. She walked over to his wardrobe and began to assemble a change of clothes, talking in the pleasantly professional manner she used with reluctant patients. "I hope you've enjoyed your time alone in your room these last two days, but it's over. Now get dressed, please." She threw the clothes on the bed.

"I am dressed," said Sandor with a hint of pride. He was indeed dressed...in the same wrinkled clothes he'd worn two days ago. Bruce had no way of knowing how laboriously he'd worked his way out of them at night and back into them each morning, even if he had slept in his undershorts instead of pajamas. He didn't really like pajamas anyway, he'd only started wearing them after his injury because anything was better than those awful hospital gowns.

"So you are," Bruce acknowledged. "But you've obviously slept in those clothes, and they look it. You need to change."

"I did not sleep in these clothes. I took them off at night," said Sandor indignantly. "And put them back on."

Bruce was all professional now. She came to him, knelt in front of him as she used to, and unbuttoned his shirt. The brace was in place; it was even laced properly. "You did it alone? Including the brace?"

The rage, the brooding, thoughts of the horrible legacy and the curse, all fell from Sandor like the tattered wrappings of a shroud. In the shining of Bruce's clear blue-gray eyes he felt himself like Lazarus, called from the grave. Reborn. He said with unusual humility, ''I did.''

''Oh, Sandor!'' She leaned up and hugged him, tears of victory pricking at her eyelids. ''Congratulations!''

Sandor clasped the back of Bruce's head, holding her fast to prolong her embrace. He breathed her clean scent; the silkiness of her hair and the softness of her cheek made him dizzy. ''I missed you, too,'' he murmured. Like a blind man, he moved his face against hers, seeking her mouth. And found it. All the passion he had told himself in the dark nights to deny surged into that kiss. His tongue sought hers, plunging, tasting, twining. The soft cave of her mouth was a place he wanted to lose himself in completely, forever.

He took her off guard. She had not expected this kiss, nor had she ever known another like it. So instantly all-consuming, so deep, so steeped in passionate splendor that she could not get enough of him. His tongue felt huge in her mouth, yet she wanted more; she wanted to make herself deeper, wider, so that she could draw all of him in....

''Ah, no more,'' she heard herself groan at last. She was shaking as she pulled away from him.

''Don't leave me,'' Sandor murmured, ''not yet. Let me hold you, just hold you.''

Bruce understood; she felt the same. They had been so deeply joined in that kiss that the world outside momentarily seemed cold and strange. So she sank down there, where she had bent to his embrace, between his legs and rested her head on his thigh.

Sandor stroked her hair, rhythmically. Finally he found his full voice. And with it, a resolution so fierce it was like the old, strong, powerful man he had been. ''Bruce, I am going to make a promise to you. And to myself. No, don't raise your head, let me keep on stroking you, and just listen.''

Bruce lay still, feeling his rhythmic touch, welcoming the deep conviction of his voice. It was like velvet, but like velvet covering marble.

''I think we may be in some kind of danger. This is real. I don't understand it yet, nor do you. But I feel it. I promise you, whatever it is, I will fight this danger and I will defeat it. Or else I will die fighting with every ounce of strength that remains in my body!''

''Sandor . . .'' Bruce tried to raise her head, but his rhythmically stroking hand did not allow her.

''Ssh, my darling, my love. All I ask is that you not leave me, even if it gets bad, don't leave me. I won't let you be hurt, I swear it!''

''I won't leave you, Sandor. I'll help you. Whatever this danger is, or turns out to be, I'll be with you.'' Bruce wondered what had been going on in Sandor's mind during the two days alone in his room; but she also believed every word she said. From this moment on, wild horses, acts of God, nothing in the universe could drag her from his side.

A moment more she lay with her head on his thigh, and then her practical nature asserted itself. ''Now,'' she said, rising in a graceful unfoldment of long legs, ''since you have become so proficient in dressing yourself, I'd like to see a demonstration. You and I are going on a picnic!''

In a minimum of pain, and with only a little more than the minimum of grumbling—especially when he found that Vladimir was not there to shave him and he had to do it himself—Sandor was ready. Bruce took the perishable food from the refrigerator and stored it with the rest of the movable feast in the back seat of the car. Then she returned for Sandor, and assisted him down the steps. He had his canes in hand. He had opted, for the first time since his accident, to leave the wheelchair entirely behind.

"Okay," said Bruce, beaming at Sandor across the front seat, "away we go!" Sandor beamed back. They both glowed with good health and great love.

The drawbridge was up across the Neuse River, and they had to wait. When Bruce touched her foot to the brake, the pedal went down a little closer to the floor than it should have. But she was so carried away with happiness that she didn't notice.

Chapter Ten

In the turn just on the other side of the bridge, from the main road onto the less traveled state road, Bruce did notice that her brakes felt a little soft. But, being from New York City, she was an inexperienced driver and she only thought, *I'll have to remember to get the brakes checked.* The day was sunny and so were her spirits. There were as few cars as usual on the two-lane road and she thought nothing of it but zipped merrily along, intent on enjoying Sandor's companionship, determined to show him a good time.

She felt it was absolutely necessary to get him involved in a conversation, because the memory of that burning, devouring kiss still lingered in her body; and from the sidelong glances that Sandor sent her way, she guessed he was in the same condition. She was not yet ready to have their relationship take such a blatantly physical turn. After a few false starts at topics Sandor would not pick up on, she cast about in her head for one that he couldn't resist. The state road narrowed, the trees loomed up on both sides, and Bruce paid no heed.

At last she had an inspiration of sorts: she asked him if he liked country music. He said with a perfectly straight face. "There was a time in my life when I thought Johnny Cash was a pay toilet, but I've learned better," and when they'd both finished laughing uproariously, Bruce no longer had to worry about getting Sandor to talk. He did like country music; and as with any kind of music that gained his attention, he'd studied it, with the result that he knew more about it than she did.

The road went on, a straight shot with no obstacles, no stop signs. In what seemed like no time at all, while they debated over whether Kris Kristofferson was better at acting or at singing and song-writing, the turnoff appeared on the right.

Bruce braked. Or thought she did. She pushed at the brakes harder, the pedal went farther down to the floor and slowed the car just when Bruce feared she would overshoot the turnoff. She steered onto the narrow, bumpy gravel track. Sandor continued to make his point; Bruce frowned and hung onto the wheel. She had the Volvo crawling now, and she thought about the other times she'd been out here, when she'd felt that this particular stretch was a trap. Just two rutted tracks the width of one car or truck; scraggly pine trees right up the edge of both sides, and no place to turn around. Gingerly, Bruce pushed at the brake pedal again, and she got no response until her foot was all the way to the floor. The next time, she was afraid she would get no response at all.

What to do? Sandor was silent, she could feel him looking at her. Perhaps he had asked a question, and she had failed to answer. If so, it couldn't be helped. Bruce's entire consciousness was occupied with her dilemma: should she go on to the end of the track, where it widened into the sandy parking area, turn off the ignition key and hope they would coast to a stop before running into anything? Or should she do it here, now, where they were completely hemmed in but at least were a couple of miles closer to a real road, no matter how little traveled? She opted for here, and turned off the motor.

"Uh, Sandor," she said, pushing the now unresponsive brake pedal all the way down, "we have a problem. I've lost the brakes. They're completely gone, no action at all. Zero, zip, zilch, *nada,* nothing!" The eyes she turned on him had gone gray and wide with concern.

All the color slowly drained from Sandor's face. He said, "You're absolutely sure? Of course you are, you must be."

The first wave of near fear left Bruce, and she found that she was angry. She pounded the steering wheel with the heel of her right hand. "Why the *hell* didn't either one of us think about getting a car phone in case of emergencies like this? I am so stupid! Here I've been complaining for weeks and weeks about you building a house so far out of touch, and I should have known better! The very first time I felt apprehensive, which incidentally was the first time I came out here with you—you remember, we were in your car that time and Vladimir was driving—I should have insisted that you get a phone in your car. And even if I couldn't persuade you to do it, I could have gotten one myself. There is no excuse for this, none! And it's all my fault!"

Sandor absently admired her redheaded fury. He felt strangely detached. At one and the same time he knew that Bruce's anger was good for him, that it helped him keep the resolve he had so recently expressed to her; and he also felt fated, doomed, once again tempted to give up. And like a dying man who suddenly sees life with an awful clarity, Sandor understood that the real evil of the curse, of any curse, was the feeling of helplessness that it engenders. Curses are meant to take away free will—and looking at Bruce, who was all fire and energy, Sandor knew that here was one human being who would not give up her free will under any circumstances.

When her fury abated, he said, "You shouldn't blame yourself, you know. This was not an accident. Someone meant this to happen."

"Nonsense, Sandor. I'm no good with cars, I don't drive enough. The brakes must have been getting bad and I just didn't notice. I did have the car checked before I came down here and everything was fine, but even so...."

"I think, as long as we are stuck here, we might use our time, put our heads together as they say, to figure out who would tamper with your car. And why? Why your car and not mine?"

"You think about it." Bruce twisted around and got up on her knees in the front seat. The edge was off her anger but it had not wholly subsided, and that was fine with her. She reached down behind the seat and found the old pair of running shoes she left in the car for bad weather or whatever. "I'm going to do something more profitable."

"What are you doing, my dear Bruce?" Sandor's lips curved; even in this difficult situation, he liked to watch her move, the lithe, loose, unconscious grace with which she twisted and stretched and turned.

"I'm going for help, of course." She looked down at the silky cotton-polyester slacks she had chosen to wear because she had wanted something nicer than her jeans for their outing, and concluded that they would be cooler for a long run. She just hoped their full cut wouldn't trip her up. And she had no socks, she'd probably get blisters but that couldn't be helped. She turned sideways in the seat and stripped off her sandals, and began to put on the old running shoes.

"Bruce, have you any idea how many miles—"

She interrupted, pushing her hair back out of her eyes angrily. "Yes, dammit, that's what I've been telling you! Yes, it's miles and miles, but I'm a runner. I can do five miles easy, and ten or more if I have to. There's bound to be a house back there somewhere, or a car will come along, or... or *something!*''

''And I'm supposed to just sit here and wait for you,'' said Sandor with a hint of bitterness.

Bruce stopped in the final lacing of a shoe and looked at him. His darkling expression cut through her flurry of purposeful activity and brought her actions, and her plans, to a halt. She reached over and touched his cheek, and her insides clenched in a pang of regret. ''You'll be all right, won't you? I know you'll have to be here alone, and it could be hours....''

''We could both stay here,'' said Sandor, taking her hand from his cheek and kissing the inside of her wrist. ''We could have our picnic right here in the car, and talk, and do...other things. It will get dark eventually, and if we aren't back by then, Vladimir will come looking for us.''

He was stroking her wrist, where his lips had been, with his thumb; Bruce felt her pulse beat more rapidly there in time with her heart. She wavered. Oh, how seductive this man could be. How practiced and skilled a lover he must be....

Just as Sandor began to pull her toward him, his dark-lashed, brown-gold eyes fixed on her mouth, Bruce herself pulled away. She shook her head. ''No. He might not come. I don't want to take the risk. It's one thing to run five or ten miles in the daytime, and quite another to try to do it in the dark. Have you ever thought what it must be like out here at night, Sandor? Pitch black, that's what! No more light than the stars and the moon, if there is one. No thanks, I'm going now!'' And with that declaration, she bent to finish lacing her shoe.

"This is ridiculous!" Sandor wanted Bruce with him. While he wasn't exactly afraid, he did not particularly want to be alone, and his old imperiousness came out in his voice.

Bruce just shot him a stern look and reached across him to open the glove compartment and rummage inside.

"You're being completely unreasonable," he all but bellowed. "Why put yourself through all that . . . that grueling exercise when you could simply stay here *with me* and wait for Vladimir?"

"You forget," said Bruce hotly, "that grueling exercise is my stock in trade, *Maestro!* And besides, I don't trust Vladimir! I'm sorry, I know you think I'm wrong, but I don't have time to stay here and argue with you about it." She finished tying the scarf she'd taken from the glove compartment around her head to serve as a sweatband, and concluded, "I know you can take care of yourself for a few hours."

"Oh, sure I can," said Sandor grumpily. He watched as Bruce opened her door, got out, and slammed it behind her.

She did a few bends and stretches, briefly warming up her muscles; then leaned in through the car window. More softly, she said, "Maybe it won't be long, maybe someone will come by on the road and I can get a lift to a gas station. You will stay put, won't you? You won't do anything foolish like decide to see how far you get walking out on your own?"

"I wouldn't dream of it." He raised his hand in a resigned wave. "Go on. Be careful."

"I will." She blew him a kiss and started off at a slow jog. The track was not good footing, and she wanted to be careful not to pull a muscle or turn an ankle.

Sandor had to fight a desire to get out and stand next to the car so that he could watch Bruce until she was out of sight. He didn't, because if she heard him open the door she might turn her head and stumble, or she might come back to see what he was doing. He reached up and angled the rearview mirror so that he could at least watch her through that. And when she was gone from his sight, he closed his eyes and tried to think constructively. Not to brood. Not to feel helpless, a victim of fate.

For the first time he wondered about Vladimir. Could Bruce be right not to trust that faithful family servant?

OUT OVER THE ATLANTIC Ocean, the wind changed. It swirled up over Nova Scotia and came howling down the east coast, bringing with it a load of moisture unusually cold for the month of May. Down, down the coast came the wind, driving dark clouds and crashing waves before it, across the Outer Banks of North Carolina, to surge up the Pamlico Sound. Where the Neuse and the Trent rivers poured into the Sound the waters thrashed, roiling ominously dark like the sky above. A cold deluge fell on New Bern.

Bruce put a match to the wood that had lain untouched in the kitchen fireplace for more than a month. A little sigh of relief escaped her lips as she held out her hands to the leaping new blaze. Then she curled up in front of the fire and began to brush out her just washed hair for the fire to dry it. She felt good, better than she had expected to feel after the longest run she'd done in she couldn't remember how long.

"I wish you could see yourself through my eyes," said Sandor in the doorway. He was in his wheelchair; the long hours of sitting in the car had done his back no good, but he forgot his discomfort in the pleasure of watching Bruce. The firelight on her hair, the long curves of her arms and legs, the arch of her back as she bent her head to the fire's warmth and exposed the tender, white nape of her neck. . . .

She turned her head but did not otherwise alter her position, and she regarded him through the shimmering copper curtain of her hair.

"I didn't hear you come in," she said. Then she looked away and continued to brush her hair with long, languid strokes.

He wheeled himself closer. He just wanted to be near, he didn't want to talk or even to touch, but just to be with her, safe and secure in the warm firelight while the storm blew and poured outside.

Bruce felt Sandor's nearness. She was glad of it. They hadn't talked about their adventure, other than Sandor's one comment that they were fortunate to have been able to get home before the storm broke.

It had come on so suddenly; one minute Bruce had been running down the side of the road in sunshine, and the next the sun was gone and she could feel the temperature plummet. She had run maybe five miles before she'd seen a house back in the trees, and there had been children and an extremely friendly dog in the yard, and a mother inside who had let her use the telephone. Everything had worked out all right, no harm done. Except, maybe, Sandor had been *too* quiet . . . on the return to New Bern, and now.

The really odd thing was that Vladimir wasn't back.

Reluctantly, Bruce paused in her brushing and broke the silence. "I do wonder what has happened to Vladimir."

"Mmm," said Sandor. He had lately, what with the two whole days in his room and then after only a short idyllic break with Bruce, almost three hours alone in the car, done too much thinking. In particular, too much of it had been circular and more frustrating than profitable. Talking meant that he would have to think again, and he didn't want to do it. All he wanted was to be with Bruce.

"I suppose it isn't all that late," she mused, resuming the brushing, "it just seems like it because with the storm coming it got dark earlier than usual. But still...."

She brushed, felt for damp spots, flipped all her hair forward again and let it hang before her face to get the fire's heat. She felt drowsy, her whole body had that wonderful still tingly feel left after a good workout. Her mind felt fuzzy. But through the fuzziness a thought inexorably pushed its way.

Finally the thought emerged, clear and wholly formed, as dangerous as it was unbelievable. She couldn't hold it back. She flipped her hair back and shook her head to get it out of her eyes. "Sandor, you don't think...surely it couldn't be...that someone tampered with *both* our cars?"

Sandor had been thinking that if angels could have nationalities, then at least one of them would have to be Scottish and would look like Bruce. She had a fiery halo around her head. Her words scarcely penetrated this vision. But, slowly, they did.

He raised his chin, a gesture of defiance, and turned his head away exposing his eaglelike profile. "I don't want to discuss it. We will just have to wait and see what happens."

"Oh." Bruce backed away from the fireplace; the fire was becoming too warm on her skin. She sat with her knees up and her arms curled around them, and her chin on her knees.

The fire crackled. Outside the wind made moaning noises against the windows and rattled the shutters. Rain fell in a steady, unrelenting torrent. Sandor looked at Bruce. He ached now with wanting to touch her.

His voice low, from deep in his throat, he said, "You don't know what I would give to be able to sit there with you on the floor in front of the fire." *What I would give for both of us to be naked, with the firelight playing over our bodies while I make love to you,* he thought. And wondered what her reaction would be if he were to say that thought aloud.

"Do you want to try?"

"What?" he blinked. For a moment he thought she was responding to his unvoiced desire.

Bruce smiled and began to unfold herself. "I think you could sit down here for a while. If you want to try it, I'll help you."

Briefly, Sandor scowled. He knew what it was like, Bruce helping him, and it didn't fit the mental picture he'd had of himself in front of the fire with her. On the other hand, the hard part was the getting down and, later, the getting up. And once he was down there he could touch her....

His pride lost; it was no contest, really. The scowl faded. "Yes, I'd like that."

"I think," said Bruce, with her smiling face close to his as she took most of his weight and lowered them both to the floor, "that you and I had best quit running around the countryside and spend more time on your leg exercises. Remember what I told you, it's all in the thighs!"

And Sandor, thinking vividly of thighs, bestowed on her that special slow, very sexy smile.

They sat side by side, not talking, not touching except to hold hands. Eventually Bruce moved behind Sandor so that he could lean against her. She loved the feel of his weight on her body. She let herself dream, dream of a future filled with night after night like this, the two of them together safe and secure and warm while the world outside did whatever damage it might do; but not to the two of them, inside the magic circle of their own fire of love. He leaned upon her upraised knees; she let her drowsy head drop and rest on his shoulder.

Neither of them much cared when Vladimir came home about an hour later, looking like a huge drowned bird. He said he'd gotten lost driving around in the country, and they both nodded and grinned at him. Sandor cut through any further apologies by ordering Vladimir to go upstairs and get dried off.

Then Sandor said into the fire, quietly as if to himself, "When I'm fully recovered we're going to need a separate wing in our house for him—with a lock on the door!"

Bruce giggled softly, and slipped her arm around Sandor's chest, snuggling him to her. Did she dare hope? She did.

Chapter Eleven

When the next day Sandor said, "We have to talk," Bruce was not surprised. Somehow as they had sat by the fire, not talking, barely touching, an invisible bond—an intimacy more than merely sexual, almost telepathic—had woven itself between them. Yes, they had to talk; she knew this as well as he did. Also, she had new information of her own.

"You're right," she said. "I have something to tell you, too. So which of us will go first?"

Sandor looked both healthy and strong as he sat on the couch in a shaft of sunlight that made his yellow sweater glow. Through the windows behind him, the sky, washed clean by all the rain, showed a beautiful blue; the lawn and the bushes near the house were shades of green spangled with diamonds of lingering moisture. He patted the cushion next to him, and Bruce sat there.

He said, "You first, since what I have to say may take a while."

"Okay. But before I get started—" Bruce looked around and then back at Sandor "—where's Vladimir? I'm not too anxious to get into a conversation with him listening in."

"He went off in a huff to do the grocery shopping. I incurred his displeasure by asking him if he had really gotten lost, or if he had had car trouble. He says he did not. I don't know what it was that set him off, a presumed implication that he might not be taking proper care of the car, or just the reminder that he'd gotten lost. Anyway, he's gone.''

Bruce nodded. ''Well, I just got off the phone with the mechanic at the place we had my car towed to. You know, I told you, that I know almost nothing about cars, so this doesn't mean much to me, but the mechanic said I'd lost the brake fluid out of all four wheel cylinders, whatever that means. He didn't exactly say it couldn't be a normal occurrence, but he did say it was pretty unusual for all four to go at once. I didn't ask him if someone had been messing with my car, I just told him to fix it.''

''I think there's very little doubt that indeed someone has, as you put it, been messing with your car. Done something to cause slow leaks. It's not the most original, or the most certain way to cause an accident. But no doubt that was the intent. I surmised as much, which is why we have to talk.''

''But Sandor—not that I don't want to hear whatever you're going to say—this was directed at me, not at you. It was my car, and no one knew you would be with me. No one except Vladimir, and he left himself right after I told him, so I don't see how he could have done it.''

Slowly, gravely, Sandor shook his head. ''From the beginning, as soon as I left the old castle, whatever it is that has plagued me has affected those around me, as well. If I am serious in wanting you to share my life, Bruce, and I am, then I think the time has come when I must tell you *everything*.''

''I couldn't agree more!''

Sandor rubbed his hand across his eyes. He hated doing this, but was determined. He took a deep breath and began. ''This ancestor of mine, the Countess Elizabeth Bathory, was born in 1560 and died in 1614. She died by being walled up, sealed into her part of her castle by local authorities as punishment for crimes so horrible that I hate to tell you. But I must, because the legacy and the curse I have mentioned both come from her.''

He paused. He felt a shuddering deep inside his body, but he conquered it before it could reach the surface, and continued. ''The Countess Elizabeth Bathory was called in her own time both vampire and werewolf.''

''What?'' Bruce was more than shocked, she was incredulous!

''Yes,'' Sandor acknowledged, a sardonic smile twisting his lips, ''no matter that now we tend to think such creatures were the product of overactive imaginations, it is still a shock to think of one's own blood relation described in such a way. Nevertheless, what she did to earn such a reputation is truly horrible.''

''I can't imagine!''

''No, you cannot. Nor could I, even when I read of it in the family record handed down to me after my grandfather's death. Elizabeth Bathory was a monster by whatever name. She tortured and killed at least fifty and perhaps as many as six hundred young women, virgins.''

''Oh, my God.''

''She wanted their blood, that's why she did it. And she probably would have gotten away with it, except that apparently she ran out of virgins in her own village and started in on young noblewomen that she was able to lure to her castle. Their families, when they figured out what was going on, put a stop to her.''

''She must have been insane!''

Sandor shifted uncomfortably on the couch. He stared across the room, at nothing, his face darkening with the darkness of his thoughts. ''Not insane, no. She was probably a very intelligent woman. But horribly twisted. Evil. Elizabeth Bathory studied alchemy, not an easy subject to understand, and a particularly unusual subject for a woman in those times. So there's no doubt that she was brilliant."

"Alchemy," said Bruce. "The Ramsays mentioned that."

"Yes. There is an enormous, and to me undecipherable, alchemical book among the things I brought out of Hungary with me. There is also a kind of diary, begun by the male heir she left behind and maintained by the chosen males since, which is where I got my information."

"I thought alchemy had to do with things like—oh, what do you call it?—looking for the philosopher's stone, turning base metals into gold and all that. So why the... the—"

"The blood? Why the killing? Alchemists also sought something they called the elixir of life, which would bring eternal youth to the one who found it. Elizabeth Bathory believed that she would stay eternally young if she bathed in the blood of virgins. According to the family chronicler, no one knows exactly what methods she used. But the bodies of the young women, when the servants took them away for burial, showed evidence of torture, and sometimes, teeth marks on torn flesh. Hence, the stories that the countess was vampire or werewolf, or both."

Bruce felt the color drain from her face. She said in a hushed voice, "How horrible."

"Yes. I believe, as did my male ancestors before me, that Elizabeth Bathory had taken the alchemical knowledge of the time and transformed it into a kind of black magic, much tainted by the evil of her character. Other alchemists, before and after her time, were more benevolent. At any rate, during the three and a half years after she was walled up until her death, she continued in isolation to practice her black arts, and recorded what she did in another book I brought out with me. She also established, in her will, both the legacy and the curse."

"Ah," said Bruce.

"It was Countess Elizabeth who, before anyone knew how evil she was, had made whatever legal arrangements had to be made in those times so that the inheritance came through the female line. Probably she was able to do this because the king owed her a lot of money. The legacy, therefore, consisted of the Bathory lands and the castle and all its contents. These contents included, of course, the two books—the one on alchemy and Elizabeth's own book— and other objects that she used to practice her black magic. These were placed in a large, metal-banded wooden box. And the curse..."

Once more Sandor shifted. His discomfort was not physical, but still it was almost more than could be borne while sitting in one place. A fine sheen of perspiration broke out on his forehead. Bruce saw, and was concerned. "Are you all right?" she asked anxiously.

Sandor grimaced. "As all right as I can be when thinking about this, much less talking about it!" He tossed the unruly hair back off his forehead and wiped at the perspiration with the back of his hand. "Let me go on. The sooner I get this out, the better I'll feel. Elizabeth Bathory must have had ambivalent feelings about men. She didn't trust them enough to leave her possessions to them, but at the same time she realized that men in general were stronger and regarded as such by others. She wasn't married herself, but she had a consort who was her heir, the one who began the diary. He records the pertinent terms of her will, and the curse. The will requires the inheriting woman either to marry or to have a male consort. The consort or husband is a kind of guardian of the legacy. In the event that there is no female to inherit, then the inheriting male of the Bathory line becomes the guardian. There must, always, be a guardian."

"And you became the guardian," whispered Bruce.

Sandor inclined his head gravely. "So I did. Without my knowledge and against my will, I was chosen. This guardian may never leave the castle, and he must protect the legacy—no doubt Elizabeth meant primarily the castle and her precious box of belongings—with his life. Or the curse will descend upon him—he will be pursued, tormented, and finally killed and carried off by 'hell's minions.' Demons, in other words. I, my dear, Bruce, am the first so-called guardian to break the will and invoke the curse upon himself."

"Oh," said Bruce inadequately. She was for the moment too stunned to think of anything else to say. She got up from the couch and began to pace back and forth. Sandor, at last unburdened of his tale, heaved a great sigh of relief and sank back into the cushions.

"Do you suppose," he asked, watching Bruce eat up the length of the room with her long-legged striding, "that as long as you're up you could get me a glass of water? I need it."

"Of course you do." She complied, and as she handed him the glass, she said, "What about your father? Didn't he break this curse when he left with your mother?"

Sandor drained the water before he replied. "My grandfather wrote in his portion of the diary that he volunteered to stay on and continue as guardian in my father's place. He took some kind of oath to that effect."

Bruce paced some more. Eventually she turned and asked, "Did they believe in it, the curse? I mean your grandfather and your grandmother, and your mother and father?"

Sandor shook his head. "I don't know, Bruce. My mother probably didn't believe, or else I doubt she could have left the castle in the first place, at least, not with my father. I think over the years maintaining the legacy became something the family took for granted. A matter of honor. They did it not because of the curse, but as their kind of sacred duty. I certainly didn't believe in it, nor did I feel bound to live in a crumbling old castle and spend the rest of my life guarding a box of ugly secrets. No matter how much it was expected of me."

"I'm sure you didn't." Bruce stood in front of him, her hands planted on her hips. "This is the twentieth century, almost the twenty-first! Surely no one in their right mind would have been surprised that you didn't stay."

"Ha!" Sandor barked sharply, remembering. "Spoken like a true American, my dear. You have no idea, nor did I until I got there, what one of those little isolated villages is like. They expected me to stay, all right. There was a dark undercurrent of superstition all around. I was bucking hundreds of years of tradition when I announced that I would decline my inheritance. Much talk of gloom and doom, even from educated, seemingly modern men like the mayor and the lawyers. Not to mention the servants! Even Vladimir, who could not have been more faithful to my mother and then to me, wanted me to stay there and assume my inheritance."

"That's so unreasonable!" Bruce began pacing again.

"I thought so, too. But I figured out that the villagers and the servants at some point in time had begun to have their own beliefs about the Bathory legacy. They believed the family curse was their protection, that as long as there was a guardian, none of the old evil could escape the castle to harm them. It's hard to sit here in New Bern on a sunny morning and explain, but..."

Sandor lapsed for a moment into brooding silence, then roused himself to continue. "But it's a whole different world there. They seem for the most part to live in another century entirely. You very seldom see a single car, Bruce. Around the village and the castle it's all farmland, and the people farm as their ancestors did, with rakes and hoes, horses and oxen pulling wooden plows. The women dress in long dresses and tie kerchiefs around their heads. On holidays both men and women wear traditional costumes. The village still has a marketplace and they come to it on foot or in wagons, bringing produce and eggs and live chickens in baskets. I even saw a band of Gypsies in a caravan, looking like something out of a movie.

"After a while, it got to me. I seemed to absorb their superstitions through my very skin. So when it was time for me to leave and I'd done everything I could do to divest myself of the legacy, I told the lawyer that I would take Elizabeth Bathory's metal-bound box, the one with the ugly secrets, away with me. I convinced him, at least I thought I did, that as long as those things didn't remain in the castle everyone would be safe."

Sandor began to laugh harshly, almost hysterically. Bruce whipped around, her hair flying, as he said in the midst of his laughter, "What I didn't realize is that *I* wasn't safe. Not by a hell of a long shot!"

"Stop it," Bruce said, running to him, "just stop it!" She bent and picked up his canes from the floor by his feet and handed them to him. "All this talk of superstition and legacies and Gypsies and curses, not to mention demons, is making us both bananas. We have more talking to do, I know that, but I can't think straight right now and I doubt you can, either. So we're going out. I'll take you for a walk. Maybe the fresh air will clear our heads and we can be more constructive."

Sandor, sobered, accepted her decision. He stood up rather easily and walked to the front door while Bruce retrieved his wheelchair from his room and came after him.

NEW GREEN LEAVES made dappled shade in the little park on its point of land between the two rivers. Sailboats were out, gliding gracefully over the wide water, their spread sails like white wings.

"It's so beautiful," murmured Bruce. "I've missed New York, but I admit I'm beginning to love it here."

"Yes," Sandor agreed. He was idly twirling one of his canes like a baton. "Manhattan seems like another planet. I never thought I could appreciate small town America, but—"

"But New Bern is different, isn't it?" Bruce picked up on his thought. "It's small but somehow it doesn't seem like a small town. It's rather—"

"Cosmopolitan, in its own way," Sandor finished. "The art galleries do help. Some of the works displayed are very fine. I have you to thank for my enjoyment, Bruce." He looked at her. A gentle, steady breeze wafted her hair into her eyes and he reached over to smooth it back behind her ears. "If you had not come, I would have stayed forever behind the closed doors of my rented house and I would not have gotten to know this jewel of a little town. Thank you."

"You're welcome." She raised her eyebrows and cocked her head to one side. "Although, I think you give me too much credit. No doubt if I hadn't come, Celeste would have eventually worn down your resistance, and even Vladimir's, and she would have had you out and about."

"Perhaps." Sandor smiled lazily, and stretched his left arm across the top of the bench behind Bruce. "Celeste is a rather determined sort of woman."

"Yes, she is." Bruce narrowed her eyebrows. "Especially where you're concerned. Which reminds me—"

"We have more talking to do. Yes. The question being, if we both continue to hold to your belief that I have not invoked any curse and therefore am not pursued by the minions of hell, then by whom am I pursued?''

"Exactly. Do you have a likely candidate?''

"No, my dear.'' Sandor gave his cane a last debonair twirl and planted it in the ground between his feet. "I do not. If it were not that your car was so obviously tampered with, I would be inclined—that is, if one must put the curse theory aside—to think that the various occurrences were in fact merely unfortunate coincidences.''

"Mmm-hmm. Well, for sure we have to put the curse theory aside. As dramatic as your story is—and I appreciate how you must have been horrified—I still can't believe in black magic and stuff like that. In fact, I think maybe you, Sandor, have nothing to do with any of the things that have happened here. I think it's Celeste, and she's simply after me. She wants me to leave, because...because...'' Bruce couldn't bring herself to finish the sentence.

Sandor, his eyes twinkling, said, "Because she is interested in me, is that what you're trying to say? And I think you, my Scottish paragon of strength, may just be a tiny bit jealous. Eh?''

"Me? Jealous of that overdressed, too sweet, high-heeled example of exaggerated femininity? Never in your life!''

Sandor chuckled, then said, "Seriously, Bruce, I doubt that Celeste would know enough about cars to be able to sabotage yours.''

"Maybe,'' she admitted grudgingly. "But she certainly could have had something to do with me getting so sick at her party. The only thing I had to eat or drink for hours before was the one cup of punch she gave me herself. And nobody else at the party got sick.''

"I thought you said it was some kind of a virus.''

"That's what I said. It seemed easier at the time. Even now, it does seem bizarre to think that she...well, poisoned me. And she certainly wouldn't want to do anything to hurt *you*...so okay, we forget Celeste. For the moment.''

They were both quiet for a while, watching the boats. It was hard for either of them to concentrate on dark possibilities when surrounded by so much loveliness.

Sandor ventured, "The Ramsay brothers."

"Are you kidding?" Bruce turned to him, surprised. "Those two middle-aged innocents?"

"They knew about the Bathory connection, and they suspect that I have the box of the Countess Elizabeth's things."

"Yes. I admit that. Which reminds me, where is it, Sandor? What did you do with it?"

"I, ah..." Sandor stared down at the tip of his cane and slowly began to twist it more deeply into the rain-softened grass. "I don't believe I should tell you, my darling. Just in case there is anything to this business of the curse, I don't want you touched. I don't want you to know. Like you, I have never believed in black magic, but there is no doubt in my mind that Elizabeth Bathory was evil. I hate the very thought that I am her descendant, that her blood runs in my veins—"

"All right," Bruce interrupted hastily, not wanting Sandor to start to brood, "I don't need to know. Back to the Ramsays—I can't believe either of them would hurt a fly. Can you, really?"

"I think it's possible. Appearances can be deceiving, Bruce. And they are the only suspects to present themselves."

"Not quite," said Bruce, her mouth pressed in a grim line.

Sandor ignored her, still thinking aloud about the Ramsays. "For one thing, it's a bit too much of a coincidence that they should know about my inheritance and turn up here in this charming but out of the way place. It suggests that they may somehow have tracked me down. Which they could hardly have done without help. A private detective, perhaps.... And all these suspicious break-ins—"

"Which began before they arrived on the scene."

"Yes, but how do we know when they actually arrived? We have only Celeste's word for it, and she is their friend. And by far the largest number of these break-ins, and the ones which resulted in some theft, happened after they came. Yes, definitely I think we should suspect the Ramsay brothers."

"I don't know, Sandor, I'm not convinced. Don't forget that the last break-in of ours happened after the Ramsays had left for Savannah. Besides, can you imagine Ronnie Ramsay trying to be a thief? He'd fall all over himself five times trying to get into the house, much less out of it."

"Probably. Again, I must point out that we do not know for certain that they left for Savannah when they said they were going to. And concerning Ronnie's bumbling nature, you may recall a particular phrase the newspaper quoted from the policeman who investigated those incidents after the house tour. 'Clumsy attempts at theft,' it said. Now does that, or does it not, have a sound of Ramsay to you?"

"Maybe," Bruce admitted. "And Reggie is smart enough, and clever enough, to pull off a bit of theft I suppose. Even if Ronnie isn't. But why, Sandor? Why would they do something like that? And how does it have anything to do with the things that have been happening to you? To us?"

"A kind of smokescreen, perhaps. I have been thinking this ever since our last break-in, the one in which my own possessions were the most disturbed. If it was the same person all three times, Bruce, then someone has quite methodically searched my house. I presume he, or they, are looking for clues to the whereabouts of Elizabeth Bathory's box—or for the box itself. And as I said before, the Ramsays are the only suspects to present themselves.''

''And as I said before, not quite.''

Sandor raised both bushy eyebrows. ''Not quite?''

''There's Vladimir.''

''Oh, are we back to that? I thought I told you—''

''Yes, and told me and told me. But I'm not convinced. If you can just take off your blinders for a minute, you might see that Vladimir has been the one constant presence from the time you learned of your inheritance until now. He has been on the scene, Sandor. He could have sabotaged your European tour. He...he—'' Too late, Bruce saw where this train of thought led.

So did Sandor. His face darkened. ''He could have arranged for my plane to crash, is that what you were about to say?''

Bruce didn't reply. She couldn't. As much as she disliked and suspected the valet, even so she could not imagine that he might have done that.

Sandor stood up slowly. ''I cannot possibly entertain such a thought. I honestly believe that Vladimir would give up his own life willingly before he would allow anything to happen to any member of my family...and I am the only one left. My dear Bruce, if we are to go on, you must learn to accept the man. He will never leave me, and I would never ask him to go! Your continuing dislike of my valet must cease, immediately.''

With this, for Bruce, appalling pronouncement, Sandor stalked steadily back to where they had left his wheelchair and sat himself in it. Bruce seethed with thoughts she was no longer allowed to express.

She had pushed Sandor halfway home before she had her temper well enough in hand to speak again. "So," she said as casually as she could, "what do we do now?"

"We cultivate the Ramsay brothers, of course. As I had already intended to do."

"And Celeste, too," said Bruce gloomily, "in case she's part of their little scheme. If they have one."

"Yes. Oh, I don't doubt they have some sort of scheme. We will trip them up, eventually. You know, Bruce, they could have been on my trail all the way back in Europe."

"That's possible, I guess." This was not a happy turn of events. More unpleasant evenings with Tweedledum and Tweedledee and the Pink Fairy Princess loomed in her mind.

She just couldn't stand it. She could see their house and the black Mercedes in the driveway, and she knew Vladimir was at home. She had so many thoughts about Vladimir that Sandor hadn't yet heard, and if he would only allow her to express them, perhaps he would change his mind. She stopped on the sidewalk to give it one last try. "Sandor, please, about Vladimir—"

"I have told you," boomed Sandor in his Maestro voice, pounding his cane on the pavement for emphasis, "you are wrong to suspect him, and you will just have to accept my word, for once in your life, Bruce MacLaren!"

She jumped and bristled, but she held her tongue. Vladimir was the one, perhaps the only, topic on which she was afraid to argue with Sandor. And, she thought as she pushed him to the steps and watched with a degree of pride as he climbed them on his own, in this case Sandor was probably right. She had nothing to go on where Vladimir was concerned but intuition. Both reason and common sense told her that Vladimir must be as faithful as Sandor assumed.

It was not until she was in bed that night, in the dark, with the complete silence of the house and the town surrounding her, that she had a new thought about Vladimir. What if the man were faithful only to the Bathorys? What if Sandor, having divested himself of his inheritance, could no longer be considered a Bathory? How faithful to Sandor Szelazeny would Vladimir be then?

Chapter Twelve

May turned into June in a blast of heat and humidity that made Bruce grateful their rented house had been updated with air-conditioning. Sandor, oblivious to the heat, turned from a lone eagle into some sort of social animal. He accepted invitations selectively, and was much in the company of Celeste and the Ramsays, who had returned from their trip. He encouraged Bruce to be his companion on his outings, but she declined, and he went with Vladimir instead.

"He's neglecting his exercises," Bruce complained to Virginia one afternoon. She had been spending a lot of afternoons alone in Virginia's company these days.

"He seems much better anyway," Virginia said tentatively.

"Oh, his back is better, but his legs aren't anywhere near strong enough yet," Bruce grumbled.

"Bruce, you can't pound biscuit dough like that, you'll ruin it. What's the matter? Are you really worried about Sandor's legs, or is it just that the romance isn't going well?"

"The romance, if you want to call it that, is on the back burner. And if dear Celeste has her way, it will soon be derailed entirely!'' Bruce resisted a further blow to the biscuit dough and reached for the cutter.

''Well, you aren't entirely blameless there. I've heard Sandor with my own ears ask you more than once to go out with him. So why don't you? Why stay here and ruin a lot of perfectly good food with your bad temper when you could be out there defending your interests with the Maestro?''

''Oh, Sandor has his reasons for cultivating Celeste and the Ramsays, I do understand. But there is still this part of me—a rather big part—that can't forget what happens when patients get well. I've seen it too many times, Virginia. Sandor is developing a more normal life-style and I have to let him do it. If, after a while, he still wants me to stay here with him.... Well, we'll see.''

Virginia nodded her understanding. ''I, for one, hope it works out, Bruce. I've been really excited ever since you confided that there was a possibility you might stay on. I meant what I said about wanting you to think about being business partners with me.''

''Thanks, Virginia.'' Bruce smiled at her. She was seriously considering that perhaps the time had come when she should confide even further in Virginia—the suspicions about Vladimir had become almost more than she could bear to keep to herself—when they heard the front door burst open to Sandor's booming voice.

''Get that chair up here, Vladimir! I've been on my feet too much this afternoon.''

Bruce and Virginia looked at each other. ''Leg exercises,'' whispered Virginia, and Bruce nodded her head.

Soon they heard the thrumming sound of the chair's wheels in the hall and Sandor thrust his vigorous presence into the room. To Bruce's surprise, the Maestro's face was positively wreathed in smiles.

"Looks like you had a good time." Bruce smiled, too; when Sandor was this pleased about anything she couldn't help but share his pleasure.

"Yes, yes, I can hardly wait to tell you! Hello, Virginia. I hope you've made a lot of whatever it is you're cooking for tonight, because I'm starving!" Not giving Virginia a chance for response, Sandor wheeled himself right up to Bruce and grabbed her hand. "They've asked me to conduct, Bruce, and I'm going to do it. I said yes!"

"That *is* wonderful news. Congratulations, Sandor. Tell me more." Even as she said the words, her heart—or maybe it was her stomach—did a flip-flop. He was indeed resuming a more normal life, and what was for Sandor normal must be alien territory to Bruce. But this was no time for selfish thoughts. She returned the pressure of Sandor's hand on hers and forced herself to keep smiling.

"I only have a month to get ready, I must work like the devil. And that reminds me—" Sandor spun the wheels and expertly turned his chair to face Vladimir who, as usual, lurked near the door "—Vladimir, call Bernie Gross in New York. Tell him to go to my apartment, he has the key, and have my harpsichord brought down here by air express. I don't care how much it costs! Tell him to get someone from Julliard, or from the symphony, from anywhere, but an expert—to supervise the packing and to come with it to reassemble and tune it for me. Do it right now!"

"Yes, Maestro." Vladimir bowed, but Bruce saw that he shot a black look Sandor's way as he raised his head and turned on his heels.

"Harpsichord?" asked Bruce, bewildered.

"Yes, yes. Come over here and sit down—I'm sure Virginia can spare you—and I'll tell you all about it."

Virginia smiled and waved them on their way.

"Now," said Sandor when they were both seated on the couch, "at this afternoon's gathering I learned that there is to be a Fourth of July celebration at the Tryon Palace. Not your usual hot dogs and all that, but a colonial period kind of thing. And they want to have eighteenth century music on authentic instruments. There is to be a chamber concert in the afternoon inside the palace, and then in the early evening the ensemble will move outside on the lawn for dancing. Period dances, of course, dancers wearing colonial costumes—minuets, et cetera. I will help the committee select the music. They're going to make a dance floor on the lawn in that oval behind the palace, where the grass goes down to the river."

"How exciting," said Virginia. She leaned over the counter listening. "I know about the Fourth of July. It's important, because we've never done anything like it at the palace. But this is the first I've heard of music and dancing."

Sandor beamed. "Naturally! If the rather formidable matron who is in charge can be believed, it was my presence here in the community that gave them the idea. Though I do understand that there are some fine musicians...I suppose it remains to be seen how fine they are." He frowned for a moment, but the frown soon cleared and he looked as enthusiastic as before. "I will conduct, as Mozart often did, from my harpsichord. Mozart, of course, preferred the fortepiano but since I do not have a fortepiano and I do own a harpsichord.... At any rate, there is no doubt—is there Bruce?—that I can both conduct and play from a seated position."

"None whatever," Bruce agreed. She looked away, thinking that even though this was certainly good news, now there would be rehearsals and even less time for Sandor's exercises. Maybe he never would regain the strength of his legs. Maybe he didn't care anymore; and maybe she shouldn't, either. Maybe the time had come for her to give up on all this, her dreams and the unsolved mystery of whether Sandor—and she herself—really was in danger from unseen forces or unknown persons. She looked back at Sandor, and could see behind his eyes the wheels of thought, of plans, turning. She said, "I really am happy for you. It's wonderful that you're returning to your music, Sandor."

Later that evening, with Vladimir nowhere in evidence and for once, no visiting Ramsays or Stanhopes, they were alone in the comfortable seating area of the kitchen. Sandor looked at Bruce's coppery head bent over the book she was reading, and realized that she had been unusually quiet.

"I will give you a penny, to match your hair, if you will share your thoughts with me," he said.

"Hmm? I wasn't thinking, I'm reading."

"But you have been so quiet. There is something on your mind. Come now, Bruce, I know you too well. You must tell me."

There was a hint of sadness in her blue-gray eyes as she regarded him consideringly. "I'm a little concerned, that's all."

"About what?"

"About you. About your progress in recovery, Sandor. You're always putting me off these days, you don't lift your weights, don't work with me on strengthening your legs, you're always going somewhere or doing something else."

"Nonsense!" he declared. Then he realized there was some truth in what she said, and tried to explain himself. "I feel almost entirely well. I have very little pain. I don't feel that I need the exercises anymore, so of course I tend not to do them."

She raised her eyebrows, but made no comment. She had expected that he would say what he did.

"You are concerned that I'm neglecting *you,* not your exercises, isn't that it?" Sandor ignored the thunderous look that was developing on Bruce's face. "That could be easily changed, my dear Bruce. You could come with me, but you always refuse. I begin to think that I'm all alone in my attempts to get the Ramsays to reveal something incriminating about themselves, and to learn who else there might be in this town who is a threat to me, to us. Why else do you think I've been going out so much? Going alone is not my choice. I would much rather have you with me. I've told you that."

Bruce exploded. "I think it's all over, *everything* is all over, that's what I think! It's been two, going on three weeks since the incident with my car, and nothing else has happened. I think we've been making mountains out of mole-hills, except, except—" She bit off "for Vladimir," which was what she wanted to say, and changed her tack. "Except that your recovery is a long way from over. Physical recovery, I mean. The rest of you seems to be doing just fine!" She tossed her head and her chin came up.

"The danger is still there. It is merely quiescent," said Sandor gravely. "I can still feel it sometimes, in the night. You know as well as I do that the focus may have changed to the building suite of my new house. There have been unexplained delays in the construction, materials disappearing, and so on. All this is, as I have told you, much like the persistent little disturbances that occurred when I was on tour."

Bruce knew; she, also, often felt a threat in the night, and did not know whether this was intuition or imagination. But she said, "I'd rather talk about your physical recovery. If I feel that you're neglecting me, it isn't personal so much as it's that I'm still your physical therapist. You seem to keep forgetting that.''

Sandor's most sensuous smile slowly played across his lips. ''If I do forget, it is because you have become so much more than a mere physical therapist to me.''

Bruce steeled herself against his attraction, though that smile did things to her insides. ''Hear this, Sandor Szelazeny. You are capable of complete recovery. You do not need to stay in that wheelchair for the rest of your life. If you'd work a little harder, you could stand for hours and walk for blocks! About six weeks of concentrated leg work, twice a day, that's all it would take. But, oh no, now that pain is no longer a problem you'd rather be off running around town, and now I suppose you'll be rehearsing every day—'' She got up out of her chair in a huff. ''If that's your choice, there isn't much I can do about it. I don't like to leave when I know the job is only two-thirds finished, but perhaps it's time!'' And she strode past him on her way out of the room.

''Wait! Stop!'' Sandor reached for her but she eluded him, and he let her go. She had these little flares of temper, it went with the color of her hair, and soon she would get over it. She wasn't seriously thinking of leaving. In the meantime he had plenty of other things to think about. He began to review musical scores in his mind. His harpsichord would arrive in less than forty-eight hours—he could hardly wait!

''IT'S SO SMALL,'' said Bruce, looking at the harpsichord, which had been set up in the library. ''So few keys. I've never seen one of these things up close before.''

''The ancestor of the piano,'' said Sandor, seating himself and flexing his fingers. ''I will give you my lesson on the evolution of modern musical instruments another time, dear

Bruce. Now, though I must be horribly rusty, I will play. And if you like, you may stay and listen.''

Sandor played. Bruce knew that the instrument, with its slender shape, tapered legs and scrolled gold leaf decoration, was in a way her enemy—it took him away from her, perhaps would take him all the way away. But, she admitted, it was a lovely little thing.

Sandor's fingers caressed the keys of the harpsichord, then flew across them, producing tones like silver bells, cascades of shining, crystalline sound. And his face... Oh, God, his face as he played! Such naked emotion! With eyes closed, his was the face of a lover reunited with his beloved, in ecstasy making love to her after an absence of a long, long time.

A lump formed in Bruce's throat, and her own love for Sandor plunged into a deeper dimension. She could not take her eyes from his face, that incredible, expressive face. She had not known the whole man until now; as powerful and compelling as he had been before, he had been incomplete without his music. The little harpsichord was not her enemy, nor her rival, but in a strange way, it was her teacher. It now showed her the whole of the man she loved as much as she loved herself. Tears came and poured unchecked down Bruce's face.

Sandor finished his piece. In the still ringing silence of the room he opened his eyes. His face was wet with tears. He looked at Bruce and saw that she, too, was crying.

''Oh, Sandor,'' she whispered, ''now I understand. Your legs can wait, will wait. Now I understand...''

He did not smile. His passion ran too deep for smiles. He held out his arms to Bruce and she came to him, into his open arms. He smothered her with kisses, her wet cheeks, her eyelids, her warm, soft mouth; he buried his hands in her glorious hair. She kissed him in return, more deeply and more passionately than she had ever done before.

At last, panting for breath, Sandor said, with his face buried in her hair, "You have given me back my music. You are my life, Bruce!"

"No, no," she protested, but her words were a moan and her heart leapt with joy that he should credit her with this miracle. "This, the music is your life and you gave it to yourself. I . . . I—"

But he stopped her mouth with another fierce kiss. "You are my life," he said again when at last he let her go.

BRUCE WAS ALONE in the house when the call came. Vladimir had driven Sandor to the evening rehearsal and stayed to bring him back.

"I'm not hearing you too well," she said, frowning. "There's some sort of interference on the line."

"It's a mobile phone," said the voice. "I said, this is the foreman. There's trouble out here at the construction site. Somebody better come."

"George, is that you?" It didn't sound like George, who had a deep voice. His voice was high, and rasping.

"George ain't here. This is the other foreman." A brief silence, which crackled with interference. The voice faded in and out. "Pete. Who's this?"

"This is Bruce MacLaren. I'm Maestro Szelazeny's assistant. The Maestro is not at home. What kind of trouble?"

"Somebody done broke in the construction shed. I needs a witness for the insurance company. If'n yore his assistant, you better come on out, right away!"

Bruce sighed. "All right. I'll be there just as soon as I can."

What a bother! She'd just settled down with a new murder mystery, and about the last thing in the world she wanted to do was drive all the way out there. But she supposed she had to. Certainly she didn't want to interrupt Sandor's rehearsal, which was the most important thing in his life right now.

Bruce grabbed her keys and her pocketbook and a sweater. She realized when she got outside that she didn't need the sweater, and she'd forgotten to leave a note for Sandor, but she decided not to go back. The sooner she got out there, the sooner she could get back. It wasn't even dark yet, these days with daylight saving time it didn't get dark here until almost eight o'clock, and it was only 7:45 now. Sandor had said he would be back after nine, so with luck she could take care of this and be back before he got home.

Since their accident with the brakes, Bruce had driven Sandor out to his building site a couple of times. Like learning to ride a bicycle, she'd told herself, if you fall off you have to get right back on or else you'll be afraid to ride the thing.

She wasn't afraid to do this drive alone; nothing would happen, her car had been checked and re-checked. She reached down and touched the new cellular telephone she'd had installed. She had used it a couple of times, just to be sure it worked. Probably she'd never need it now that she had it, but its presence was reassuring. She hummed "Me and Bobby McGee" and sang a few bars as she pushed the car up to sixty, as fast as she dared go on the almost deserted road. Blue shadows turned to purple and finally to black before she turned off onto the dirt track.

It's black as pitch! thought Bruce when she had stopped the Volvo and turned off its lights. She was tempted to turn them back on, but she didn't know how long this would take and she didn't want to run the battery down. From long habit, she locked the car when she got out.

"Hello? Anybody here? Ah—" What had the man said his name was? "Pete?"

No answer, and nobody came to escort her from the car.

"Oh, heck," Bruce grumbled aloud. She had a tiny penlight on her keychain and she switched it on. The little point of light seemed ridiculous in all the darkness, but at least she could shine it on the ground directly in front of her feet.

Bruce hesitated, listening hard. Night sounds. Some cooing kinds of birds called to one another. Small rustles, like little animals in the undergrowth among the trees. A faint lap, lap, lapping of water against the shoreline.

"Pete?" she called again. How could he not hear her? The tiny hairs on the back of her neck stood on end. She was scared, whether there was reason to be or not. She considered turning around, going home and waiting for Sandor.

Bruce looked in the direction of the Pamlico Sound. Her eyes were becoming accustomed to the near total darkness now. There was no moon, but by the faint light of the stars she could just barely discern the water from the land. The water too was dark, but it rippled with a motion she could see. For some reason this gave her courage.

Her common sense told her this could be a trap. The only foreman she knew of was George, not any Pete; and the voice had sounded strange...but that had probably been the distortion of the interference on the line. Bruce was stubborn. She swept the penlight across the ground until she found the path, and took a few steps. Stopped, listening. She had heard a sound, not one of the night sounds.

"Pete, answer me!" she called as loudly as she could.

From ahead there came a muffled, rather high-pitched reply that she interpreted as "Yo!"

Encouraged, Bruce walked carefully on. She rounded a curve in the path and saw the construction shack a few feet away, its door wide open and a faint light within. Immediately she felt relief and let out her breath. She hadn't realized she'd been holding it. She switched off the penlight and went more confidently toward the shack's open door.

"I didn't think there was anyone here," she began as she was in the doorway. But she didn't say any more, because she was suddenly, violently shoved from behind into the shack, and the door slammed shut after her.

Bruce stumbled and fell to her knees. "Hey!" she yelled reflexively, scrambling up. She started pounding against the door, but soon realized that she was only hurting her hands. If someone had gone to all the trouble to lure her out here and shut her in, they surely weren't about to let her out.

So she listened. She strained to hear, even shutting her eyes. Nothing, not a sound.

Bruce uttered a few choice swear words and kicked at the base of the door for good measure. Then she dropped her purse and her keys on the bare earthen floor, gathered her strength, and hurled all of her considerable height and muscle sideways against the door. The door shook, and so did the walls of the shack, making jangling metal sounds from the implements that hung there. But the door held fast.

Bruce stood off and was gathering herself for another assault at the door when she remembered that the door was secured with a padlock. She wasn't likely to be able to break through that. She would have to find another way out.

There didn't seem to be any. And as Bruce was examining the windowless walls for cracks, she heard an unmistakable sound and smelled an unmistakable smell. The sound of pouring liquid, and the smell of gasoline!

Oh, dear God in heaven, she thought. She froze. Now she heard steps, too, someone slowly walking around the shack and pouring gasoline as he walked.

She shoved a knuckle into her mouth and bit down on it to keep from crying out. Whoever was out there intended to burn her alive!

Bruce stayed silent for as long as she could stand. It seemed like a million years that she held her tongue, thinking frantically that there must be something she could bargain with, something she could say...! But there was nothing, nothing, and when she couldn't bear to be silent any longer she yelled, "Don't do this! Whoever you are, please, don't do it!" The only reply she got was the sharp scratch of a striking match, followed almost immediately by a gigantic, ominous, crackling, terrifying whoosh!

Bruce heard the fire ring its way around the shack. Suddenly she was no longer terrified but very, very angry. With fierce, rapid determination she scanned the contents of the little room, looking for anything heavy enough to batter her way out with. An ax! But there was no ax. There was a mallet with a heavy metal head, the kind used to pound stakes. She grabbed it; it would have to do.

Rather than batter at the door with its heavy padlock, she turned. The fire helped her now, it illuminated cracks in the walls. This shack had been hastily thrown together. She chose the largest crack, on the back wall opposite the door, and dropped the mallet to scrabble away at removing ropes and hammers and implements she didn't take the time to identify. Precious, precious time was passing, it was getting hotter.

Bruce hefted the mallet, then almost wrenched her back as she remembered her purse and keys. She couldn't get away without those keys! She lowered the mallet and grabbed for them, shoved them into a pocket of her jeans and slung the strap of her purse over her head, then hefted the mallet again.

She didn't know how long she pounded at the crack in the wall before the boards gave and splintered outward; but the fire was there to leap in at her through the opening. No time to think! Bruce dropped the mallet, backing away, giving herself as much distance as she could to get a running start. She put her arms up in front of her face, bare arms, all she wore was a T-shirt and jeans and canvas shoes. Bruce ran and hurled herself through the flames.

She rolled as soon as she hit the ground. Her arms smarted, she could smell the singe of burning hair. She rolled and rolled, over all kinds of bumps and stones and sharp objects. Finally she stopped and sat up. Gulping and sobbing, she untangled her purse from around her neck and turned to look at the fire. The whole shack was ablaze, it lit up the formerly dark night. Bright orange sparks shot from the roof. By the fire's light she looked at her own arms, her legs; she felt carefully at her hair. She was singed, almost all over, but not really burned. At least as far as she could tell. The skin of her forearms smarted, and the smell of burning was in her hair and in her clothes, but she was okay.

Sore, though, she noted as she got to her feet. She took a few steps. Then she realized that the person who had tried to burn her up might still be around.

Well, let him be here, she thought grimly, starting to jog in a wide curve around the burning cabin toward her car. *I'll beat him up with my bare, burned hands!*

But no one was around. The fire, which crackled spectacularly, had been the only witness to the flash of silver that signaled the departure of the one who had given it birth.

Chapter Thirteen

Bruce had stayed at the building site until the volunteer firemen arrived, after she called the operator on her new car phone and reported the fire.

With the fire engines had come the sheriff and a reporter and photographer. Bruce, by then in mild shock, had told them all the truth. She was sure she had, even if she couldn't remember exactly what she'd said; lying came so hard to her that she had to think to do it and she'd been unable to do much thinking. The only thing she was sure of was that she hadn't said anything about this being only one of several suspicious incidents.

The deputy sheriff had taken her statement and then insisted that he accompany her to the Craven County Hospital in New Bern. Nothing would dissuade him, though he did agree to have his partner drive her car along behind them.

The doctor in the emergency room told her she was a very lucky woman to have escaped with only first-degree burns on her forearms; but still he had slathered her arms in antibiotic ointment and bound them with gauze.

Through all this Bruce had not thought to call Sandor, which may have been just as well. He was so relieved to see her, when she finally was able to drive herself home around eleven o'clock, that it seemed nothing else mattered to him. Relieved, and then angry when she told him the bare bones of what had happened. Ferociously angry.

He appeared to be more upset about the state of her hair than of her burned arms, and this seemed funny to Bruce. Very funny. She started to laugh. And continued to laugh.

"Vladimir," Sandor barked, "get brandy! Right away!"

They were in the living room, since it was nearest the front door. Bruce, gulping for air through great whoops of laughter, noticed that her charred jeans were making black marks on the brocade sofa. That wouldn't do; that wasn't funny at all, so why was she still laughing? She struggled to stand up, but Sandor who was standing on his own two feet, canes forgotten, pushed her gently back and sat down beside her.

"Bruce, my darling, you're a little bit hysterical. You've been through a terrible experience—" he glanced up just as Vladimir came back with a short glass containing a hefty dose of brandy, and took it from the man "—and I want you to drink this."

"I d-don't—ha!—like b-bran—ha!—dy! Ha, ha!"

"Tonight, you do," said Sandor, looking down his nose like an eagle down its beak, wearing his most severe expression for her sake. "And you are going to stop laughing and drink this brandy if I have to pour it down your throat!"

"Yes, Maestro," Bruce managed to say before she went off into another gale of laughter.

Sandor rolled his eyes. "The things we have to go through before you're willing to call me master!"

This remark, which had its funny side, for some reason sobered Bruce. She took the brandy from him and choked on the first sip. "It burns!" she complained, "I'm already burned on the outside, now you want to burn me up on the inside, too!"

"Just drink it!" Sandor commanded, and she did.

And later, she didn't know how much later, she found herself lying in Sandor's bed with him beside her. She was wearing one of her own nightgowns. A single beside lamp bathed the room in a soft glow.

Memory slowly returned. She turned her head on the pillow. He was gazing at her with an astonishing depth of tenderness in his golden eyes. Though her arms stung, she felt wonderful deep down inside. "You bathed me," she said, marveling, "and you cut my T-shirt off, with scissors."

"I didn't want to take it off over those arms, my darling. The back of the shirt was all black anyway, and covered with tiny holes. Do you have any idea how close you came to going up in flames yourself?"

Bruce reached out her hand and traced the outline of Sandor's face, backlit by lamplight. She was remembering something that at the moment seemed much, much more important to her than the fire. "You were so gentle! And Vladimir came with a nightgown, only the one he brought had long sleeves and you made him go back and get another one," she looked down at the gown she wore, which was her best. It was pink and sheer and trimmed with lace and ribbons, so feminine that she hardly ever wore it and had often wondered why she'd bought it—but now it seemed just right. "Now I am the Pink Fairy Princess," she murmured.

"What?"

"Nothing. I was just being silly. I'll never forget how gentle you were. Except when you made Vladimir go away."

Sandor smiled. He caught her hand and brought it to his lips, kissing each of the fingertips. "I didn't think you'd remember. You got very tipsy, my dear, on just one glass of brandy."

"I never could drink that stuff. I think maybe I still am a little tipsy. But it feels good. Thank you for taking such good care of me. However," she added, not believing a word she was about to say, "don't you think I should be in my own room?"

"No." Sandor raised his arm invitingly. "I think you should be a few more inches over this way, lying against me, with my arm around you. Yes, like so. Because tonight I came very close to losing you, and I don't want to let you out of my sight. Or away from my touch."

"Mmm." Bruce stretched her length against Sandor's side. Her bandaged arms bothered her a bit, but she was determined not to notice. These few hours she would savor, and worry about the consequences later.

But there was something, something she had meant to say to him before the brandy.... What was it? She reached for the words that niggled at her until they came to the surface. "Sandor," she said quietly, "I'm sorry. I've blown your cover. I know your house was a secret, I know I should have lied to them and said it was mine, or something, but I just couldn't think fast enough. And there was a reporter there, and a photographer, besides the sheriff. The sheriff will come, I know he will, and ask you questions, and maybe the reporter will come, too. I'm sorry."

"Hush, my darling." Sandor kissed her forehead.

His lips were warm and gentle, as his hands had been earlier. Bruce remembered his gentleness again and a delicious tingle spread all through her.

"That doesn't matter," said Sandor. "None of that matters now, only that you are safe and you are here, with me. Let tomorrow take care of itself."

They were silent. Bruce hovered on the edge of sleep but she did not want to sleep. She wanted to be awake, aware of

how wonderful it was to lie next to Sandor, to be alive, safe
and warm in his arms.

He shifted onto his side while keeping his arm around
Bruce, a movement that caused him some discomfort and he
waited until it subsided. Her eyes were closed, her lashes lay
in crescents of deepest auburn on her cheeks. Her full lips
curved upward at the corners in a tiny smile. He lowered his
head and claimed those lips in a long, gentle, tender yet
thorough exploration.

When he lifted his head he saw that her eyes were still
closed, yet she did not sleep, for she had responded to his
kiss. Sandor had never, ever felt the tremendous yearning
tenderness that heaved and surged within his body. Its
strength astonished him, even frightened him a little. For he
knew that he welcomed this feeling, yet it was so powerful
that he was almost overwhelmed. He yearned toward completion, which he had always before sought to find in his
music, but now, here, was his completion: the woman who
lay smiling in his arms.

"Bruce," he whispered, knowing that he spoke the words
but not quite sure when he had decided to say them. "I want
you to marry me. Now. Tomorrow, as soon as the sun comes
up."

Her eyes opened, clear and gray and honest. "Maestro?" she asked, still smiling. "Have you lost your mind?"

Sandor felt his own smile stretch his lips. "I don't think
so. I must be doing something right, if you've willingly
called me Maestro twice in one night!"

"Not tomorrow," said Bruce seriously. He opened his
mouth to speak, to argue, but she stopped his lips with her
fingers. "Maybe when this is all over, but not tomorrow."
And she burrowed her head into the hollow between his neck
and shoulder.

Carefully Sandor turned onto his back, holding Bruce as if she were the most precious thing in the world. He knew now that she was, to him. All he could think was that he wanted her now, because when this thing was over it might be too late. For both of them.

Chapter Fourteen

Much to Bruce and Sandor's surprise, there was almost no publicity. If a fire had occurred on Sandor's Long Island property or in his Manhattan apartment, it would have made a splash. That the same was not true in New Bern seemed to be largely because, when Sandor was asked his profession by the deputy sheriff the next day, he replied, "Retired." Thus Sandor Szelazeny became, to both the law and the press, just another wealthy northerner who had chosen to come south for his retirement. The fire, which had been contained before spreading to the house under construction, thus eventually rated only a couple of lines in the local paper's daily police blotter.

The deputy had a little more trouble deciding what to do about Bruce. She identified herself as Sandor's personal assistant and said, stretching the truth but not much, that she didn't really know anybody in the area and couldn't suggest anyone who might want to harm her. Sandor shrugged and didn't give a verbal reply when the deputy asked him if anyone had a motive to start a fire on his property.

Finally, looking unhappy with the whole process, the deputy said that he didn't think he would be able to get enough evidence to come up with a charge of attempted murder. His hunch was that Bruce had gotten mixed up in a case of somebody having a grudge against the property owner. He would interview all the workmen and especially this man Pete that Bruce said she'd talked to, and see what he could come up with. He departed with the words, "I'm not too hopeful that we can find out who's behind this, but we'll try."

"Why did we both do that?" Bruce asked Sandor when the door closed behind the deputy.

"Why didn't we tell him more? All our suspicions? I expect your reasons were the same as mine. We simply don't know enough to be able to accuse anyone, and if we tip the law enforcement people off to the ones we have our suspicions about, they're likely to go underground and we'll never catch them. There's work to do, Bruce. And I intend to enlist Vladimir's help."

"Vladimir?" Bruce tried to keep a note of alarm out of her voice.

"Yes. So far in my probing of the Ramsays, the only thing I've come up with is that they were definitely, both of them, in Europe at the time I was there. That's a start, but we're running out of time. I'm not taking any more chances with you, my dear."

"Listen, Sandor, you're forgetting something. This is a lot like the thing with my car. I was the target, not you."

"You seemed to be, yes. But I believe that is only because of your close association with me. You are perhaps an obstacle that must be removed. At any rate I'm still not taking any more chances. We have to do something, fast, and I came up with a plan while you were sleeping so peacefully last night." Sandor lovingly caressed Bruce's hair for a moment.

"All right," she said, smiling at his touch, "let's hear your plan."

"I will ask the Ramsay brothers to accompany me some-where, and perhaps Celeste, as well, and while we are gone I'll send Vladimir to search their rooms in Celeste's house. He may be able to find some evidence we can use against them. If he does, I will report it to the New Bern police. I want to keep you out of this, my dear."

Bruce fixed Sandor with her clear gray gaze. Her chin was set at a stubborn angle. "You and I are supposed to be partners, if you recall. Vladimir is too old, he'd be no good." As hard as it was, she refrained from saying that she didn't trust him.

"Physically he's on the frail side, I admit, but the man still has all his mental faculties. And there is the fact that he will do exactly what I tell him to do. I don't think we have time to hire a private detective, nor do I have any confi-dence that I could find one down here. Vladimir can follow my instructions. It's a beginning, Bruce, and would be bet-ter than nothing."

Bruce held up her hand, palm out, like a warning. "Now don't get all upset with me. Hear me out. I agree with most of your plan. I think it's a good one. But if I conduct this search, not Vladimir, we might have more than just a be-ginning. I'd know what to look for, and I'm quick, and physically able. These burns on my arms are nothing, they'll be healing in a couple of days and already they don't hurt."

"I don't want you involved. I don't want you hurt any more than you already have been!"

"You know we're talking about breaking the law, San-dor. Breaking and entering, or whatever they call it. I'm not likely to get caught. If I had to I could even do something like jump out of a second story window and not injure my-self." Bruce hadn't thought any of this through, she was saying whatever came off the top of her head to deflect

Sandor from using Vladimir. She was intuitively sure that would be a terrible mistake.

"If necessary," said Sandor grimly, "Vladimir is expendable. You are not. Not to me."

"I wish you could hear yourself," said Bruce, jumping up from the living room couch where they had both sat for their interview with the deputy. "You sound just like what you gave up the chance to be—the lord in his castle. So the vassals or the servants are expendable, are they? Honestly! Well, I say no. I say I'm your partner and I'm the best one to go and I'm going!"

"Why did I ever fall in love with a redheaded woman?" Sandor complained under his breath.

Bruce pretended not to hear. She paced back and forth, casting about in her mind for more ways to convince him. Maybe she didn't need any more ways. She turned and asked, "Are we agreed, then? I will go, not Vladimir."

"We are not agreed. I'm trying to think of something else."

"There isn't anything else. Not if we're going to act quickly, and I think we must."

Sandor still made no reply.

Bruce threw caution to the winds. She played her one and only card: she voiced the doubt that had been torturing her all morning. She stood before Sandor, looking down at him, and asked softly but intently, "Sandor, when Vladimir takes you to rehearsal, does he stay in the room where you rehearse all the time? Or does he wait outside with the car?"

Sandor blinked at her in surprise. The question had caught him totally off guard. "I've never thought about it. We've only had a couple of rehearsals, but.... He doesn't stay. He brings the wheelchair in, in case I need it, and he's there when we finish, generally in about two hours, but no...he doesn't stay."

"All right. So you don't really know where Vladimir was last night, at the time I was attacked. Do you?"

"N-no-o..."

Bruce bent and took Sandor's hands in her own, bringing her face close to his. "If you care for me, Sandor, don't, please don't tell me again how faithful Vladimir is. Let it be enough for you that I still don't trust him, and you don't know where he was last night around eight o'clock."

"I see your point," said Sandor reluctantly.

Bruce pressed her advantage. "You and I can trust each other, Sandor. We're all we've got!"

Sandor searched Bruce's face, deeply, seriously. Finally he said, "Because I do care for you—more than care, I love you—I accept your concerns about Vladimir. All right. You will go to Celeste's house and search the rooms of Reginald and Ronald Ramsay. And I will worry about you and pray for you every minute that you are gone."

He pulled her into his arms and kissed her with a kiss that lasted until they heard the front door open, announcing Vladimir's return.

SANDOR MADE an arrangement to take the Ramsays on a visit to his under-construction house in the afternoon two days in the future. They had never seen the house, and he could both show it off and watch their reactions—if any— to the evidence of the recent fire. Following the visit to the site, the Ramsays would be his guests for drinks at a tacky-chic little bar in the sailing town of Oriental just a few miles away. Vladimir would drive them. In the afternoon Celeste was bound to be occupied in her antique shop, because, as they had learned from Virginia, she was notoriously difficult to work for and currently had no part-time help.

In the meantime, there had been only the one small mention of the fire in the local paper, which Bruce and Sandor hoped would escape the notice of most people; and they deliberately would not mention it themselves. If the Ramsays seemed genuinely surprised by the evidence of burning on the site, that could tell Sandor a lot.

Two days wasn't long to wait, but Bruce chafed under the restrictions she had imposed upon herself. She didn't want to go out and run into people and answer questions, but it was hard for a naturally active person to stay in the house. Sandor had his music. She became accustomed to doing everything—reading, writing letters, even cooking with Virginia—to the crisp, pure background accompaniment of Sandor's harpsichord.

Bruce trailed idly down the stairs on the second day of her self-imposed confinement. Halfway down the stairs she stopped, enchanted by the melody that Sandor played. She listened, and felt the music reach into her body and pluck a responsive chord deep, deep inside. The rhythm, it was that insistent rhythm in the lower notes that made her throb with desire, while the melody above was all pure beauty. She stood on the stairs still as a stone, breathless with pleasure.

When silence fell, Bruce rushed down the remaining stairs and into the library, eager to interrupt Sandor before he began to play again.

"What was that," she asked, with her face aglow, "that you were playing just now?"

"It was the opening dance for the celebration at the Tryon Palace." Sandor looked up from arranging the musical score of his next piece and saw Bruce's glowing face. "It's a sarabande. You liked it, I see."

"Yes! It was . . . It . . . got to me."

"Got to you, did it?" Sandor raised a bushy eyebrow, amused.

"Sarabande! What an interesting word. I don't think I've ever heard it before, but it fits, doesn't it? I mean, it sounds like the music sounds, sort of—oh, God, Sandor, I'm way out of my depth, I don't know what I'm talking about—"

"Go on, please. You're certainly on the right track, and I find this fascinating."

"Okay." Bruce paused, and felt once again that throbbing deep inside her. "I mean the name, sarabande, it sounds Spanish and exotic, but courtly, too. Like the music, all sexy underneath and yet stately, dignified at the same time. I loved it. Play it again, for me, please!"

"With pleasure, my darling." Sandor played and Bruce listened with closed eyes to the throbbing, measured rhythm.

"Oh," she breathed when he had finished, "that was wonderful. So...moving."

Sandor beamed. His greatest pleasure in music was to invoke an emotional response in others. To be able to do this for his Bruce filled him with a curious, passionate gratitude. He said, "Now I will tell you the history of the sarabande, and you will see how amazingly correct your intuition is about this music. The sarabande I just played is part of a dance suite composed for the French Court in the early eighteenth century. It is a stately court dance, with slow, measured rhythms. But underneath, woven into the music and the history of this particular dance, the sarabande is something else. Something more. It was originally a medieval Spanish dance of Arabic or Moorish origin—a bawdy, primitive, sexual kind of dance. During the late Renaissance in France and England the sarabande acquired its present form, and became a court, rather than a peasant dance."

"But they didn't quite all the way clean it up, did they?" asked Bruce.

Sandor laughed heartily. "Oh, Bruce, your choice of words is priceless! No, they didn't completely 'clean it up.' They overlaid the sarabande's frank sexual message with a veneer of civilization. They slowed down the steps and ritualized the touching of the dance, but the basic, primitive sexuality of it is still there.''

He looked at Bruce, and saw in the widening pupils of her eyes that the music had stirred her just as she now stirred him. He throbbed with wanting her, throbbed like the bass rhythm of the music he had played.

''The sarabande is like life,'' Sandor said, his voice low and deep in his throat. ''On the surface we are civilized, but beneath the surface in each of us there burns this primitive urge, this longing—''

''To be filled!''

For a long, long moment they gazed at one another. Not touching; they both knew that the slightest touch would be like a shattering bolt of electricity.

Finally Sandor broke the eye contact. He said with a shrug and a deprecating grin, ''I think I have had enough of practicing my music for today. Come, my dear Bruce. You have been telling me for weeks that I must strengthen the muscles of my thighs and buttocks. I believe I've just acquired what was missing before—a major motivation. Shall we begin?''

BRUCE WAS NERVOUS. Sandor and Vladimir had left with Reggie and Ronnie Ramsay about fifteen minutes earlier, Celeste had long since gone to her antique shop, and Bruce was now ready to go across the street. Though she knew her cause was just, she felt like a criminal. She was wearing old, weathered jeans and an equally old denim jacket over a sleeveless V-neck undershirt. She had re-bandaged her arms to protect the tender skin from bumps, and she had taped her ankles in case she really did have to jump down to the ground from the second floor, where she presumed the Ramsays had their rooms. She had twisted her telltale bright hair into a knot on top of her head, and covered it with a dark blue scarf tied pirate-style at the back of her head. Any more of a disguise seemed pointless in the daytime; she didn't want to look suspicious.

She set out walking. The day was gloomy and overcast, and so humid that she was soon sweating beneath all the heavy denim. She had mapped out her route in her mind—she wanted to approach Celeste's house from the rear. To simply walk across the street and up onto that broad porch seemed far too obvious.

Bruce turned the corner onto Johnson Street. No one was around, though there was no way to tell who might be looking out of a window. With her heart in her throat, she started to jog, and in a quick, planned motion she cut into the driveway of a house she knew was unoccupied. The backyard of this house was adjacent to Celeste's.

She had come equipped in the inside pockets of her jacket with a small screwdriver, a hammer and wire clippers. Not that she was sure how much use any of them would be for breaking and entering. She just hoped Celeste didn't have a burglar alarm.

Bruce dashed across the yard and up the back steps. She tried the obvious first, and to her amazement the back door opened when she turned the knob. Not locked! She couldn't believe her luck!

In the next breath, Bruce wondered whether this was really good luck, or bad. What if Celeste had a cleaning woman who was here, and that was why the door had been unlocked? Well, if so, then she would just have to brazen it out. She'd think of something.

She stepped into the kitchen and waited, closing the door carefully behind her. No one came. She listened. She heard only the steady, slightly resonant tick-tock of the tall-case clock she remembered seeing in the hall. Otherwise there was nothing—only the hushed, watchful silence peculiar to old houses, as if their many former occupants hovered, expectant and invisible, in the air.

Bruce *felt* there was someone in the house. She advanced slowly into the hall, keeping to the side where the old boards were less likely to creak. Next to the tall clock she flattened herself against the wall, suddenly afraid to go on.

Nonsense! she told herself. *I should keep moving and get this over with. Zip in, zip out, that's the ticket!* and she winced as she realized she was thinking in Ronnie Ramsay's language.

Her thoughts were running wild: what if Celeste wasn't in the shop? What if she'd suddenly come home? Why hadn't she thought to check if Celeste's car was outside?

Wow, thought Bruce, rubbing perspiration from her forehead with the heel of one hand. *I really am letting my mind run out of control here. For one thing, Celeste walks to work, and for another she has a garage, she doesn't leave her car outside. Come to think of it,* Bruce added to herself, *I've never even seen Celeste's car, I wouldn't have the slightest idea what to look for! I'm just procrastinating, that's all.*

Determined to move on, Bruce kept edging her way along the wall to the foot of the stairs. The only thing she was sure of about Celeste's house—aside from the fact that the rooms were large and wonderfully proportioned, but for an antique dealer, sparsely furnished—was that all the bedrooms had to be upstairs.

A stair creaked underfoot, and Bruce froze. She held her breath, once again irrationally convinced that she was not alone in the house. Yet she heard nothing, not the slightest rustle of movement. She went on.

At the top of the stairs she scanned the hall. Even in her tension she could not help but notice its perfect proportions. There were six doors, three on either side. To her left, two doors were closed; all the rest stood open. Bruce headed for the first of the two closed doors. Very cautiously, she opened it. And let out a startled squeak that had almost become a shriek before she contained it.

Celeste, violet eyes wide, face white as a sheet, whipped around to face Bruce. At the same moment she thrust one hand, in which she concealed an object, behind her back. "B-bruce! It is you, isn't it? You look so, so... well, rather peculiar." With each word she regained more of her composure.

Bruce was completely at a loss. "I—" She gulped. "I guess I owe you a tremendous apology. The back door was unlocked, but I—I would have come in anyway."

Celeste narrowed her eyes and tapped her high-heeled foot. "This is Reggie's room," she said.

"And Ronnie's is next door," Bruce guessed.

"That's right. They, ah, they keep them locked, which I don't particularly like. After all, it is my house. But of course I have the master key." Celeste reached into the pocket of her full skirt with her unoccupied hand, and pulled out a long, old-fashioned key.

Bruce felt greatly hampered by her instinct to tell the truth. She was desperately sure that she would never be able to lie her way out of this. "I, ah, Celeste, I don't suppose you would just accept my apology and forget I was here this afternoon?"

Celeste appeared to be thinking hard. Her little foot tapped and her red rosebud mouth pursed. Suddenly, all in a rush, she apparently made up her mind. "No, no," she crossed to Bruce, petticoats flashing under the full skirt, "I think I'm glad you're here, Bruce! You're going to be the most marvelous help, because I can just tell you're here for the same exact reason that I am!"

"Wh-what . . . ?"

"Look at this!" Celeste whipped out the hand she'd held behind her back.

Bruce looked. The object in Celeste's palm was a fancy glass paperweight.

"It's one of the things that was stolen after the house tour," said Celeste in a conspiratorial tone, "I'm just sure of it because I've seen it myself in the Palmer's living room. This is a Victorian paperweight, not hugely valuable but valuable enough. Don't you see, Bruce? I started to suspect, and you did, too, didn't you? That's why you're here, isn't it, to search Reggie and Ronnie's rooms?"

"Yes," Bruce nodded. Celeste took her by the arm and Bruce let herself be led to a chest of drawers beneath a window.

"Well, you know I'd heard rumors that Reggie was a plain kleptomaniac, but I just never believed it until recently. Just look at all this stuff!"

Bruce looked. Among socks and shirts and the usual things men keep in drawers were tucked objects of the sort the newspapers had described missing: enameled ashtrays, bud vases, figurines, a mother-of-pearl comb and brush set, more paperweights . . .

Celeste pounced on a small porcelain vase in the shape of a swan. "Why, would you believe it? And after all I've done for those two! Well, I never!!! Bruce, this is mine. Those bloody Englishmen even stole from me, their dear friend and hostess. Such a disappointment!"

"Yes. I'm sure it is." Bruce opened all the drawers once more in turn. She was looking for Sandor's silver letter opener, but something, she wasn't sure what, cautioned her not to tell Celeste. She closed the bottom drawer and straightened, asking, "Is there more of the same in Ronnie's room?"

"I don't know, dear. I started looking in here. Let's go together and see, shall we?"

Ronnie's room looked altogether different. On almost every flat surface there were piles of books. Some of them looked very old. Moldy, even. "You look in the drawers," Bruce said to Celeste. "I really wouldn't have felt right doing it even if I'd had to, if you hadn't been here."

"Well, of course you wouldn't," said Celeste sweetly, "you just had your suspicions the same as I did." The chest in this room was a highboy, next to the bed, and she began to open and close drawers one by one.

A long, thin, portfolio-sized book lay on the floor in front of the fireplace's summer brass fan. Bruce crouched down to examine it. The covering was leather; the maps were old, and fascinating. "This must be priceless!" she exclaimed. "Do you know anything about maps, Celeste?"

"No," said the other, rifling through drawers, "that was more in their line. The Ramsays, I mean. They're the ones who know about tatty old books and maps. Speaking of maps, Bruce, if I were you I'd take a look at the one on the bed."

While Bruce went to the bed and looked down at the map unfolded on the pristine white surface of a candlewick spread, Celeste closed the bottom drawer of the highboy with a swift kick of her stylishly shod foot. "Reggie's the kleptomaniac, all right!" she declared. "There's nothing like all those little things that were taken after the tour in here. Of course, there's no way to tell whether they actually bought and paid for all these books and things . . . What do you make of that, Bruce?"

The map was a recent one, the kind you get in gas stations, of the coastal counties of North Carolina. The route to Sandor's house site, and the site itself, was marked in red. "Not much," said Bruce. "What about you?"

Celeste squinted down at the map as if she were trying very hard to remember something, or to figure it out. Then she shook her head, saying, "Well, they were either planning to go somewhere or they've already been. But there's just nothing over there! Nothing beyond Oriental worth seeing at all!"

As hard as Bruce might stare into the violet eyes, they remained wide and innocent. And Bruce decided that Celeste was on the level. She didn't know where Sandor's house was, she hadn't had anything to do with these thefts or any of the break-ins, she was truly upset that her houseguests had stolen things and hidden them in rooms of her own house.

"Well," said Celeste, never blinking once, "we discovered all this together. My dear friends the Ramsays are nothing but common thieves! So are you going to call the police, or will I?"

"You, I think," said Bruce in a rush of relief. "After all, it is your house and it's really your find, even if I did have the same idea. You call them. You know where Ronnie and Reggie are right now, don't you?"

Celeste nodded. "Out somewhere with Sandor."

"That's right."

"Any idea what time they'll be back?"

"Between four and five, I should think."

"That should be close enough for our little old police department. They can send an officer to arrest them the minute they get back," said Celeste. She sounded satisfied enough to purr as she laced her arm through Bruce's and led her to the stairs. "Why don't you stand right next to me while I telephone them?"

Chapter Fifteen

"That's an interesting-looking outfit you have on, Bruce,"
said Virginia. She had been sitting on the steps of Sandor's
house. Far more interesting than the outfit was the fact that
Bruce had walked away from Celeste's house and across the
street with, apparently, so much on her mind that she didn't
even notice her friend's presence.

"Oh!" Bruce started, saw Virginia, and forced what felt
like a foolish grin onto her face. "Yeah. Much too hot
though. Let's go inside."

Once inside the coolness of the house, Bruce pulled the
scarf off her head and shook out her hair. Gathering her
wits, she asked, "What are you doing back here? I thought
you'd gone for the day. Not that I'm not glad to see you,
I'm just surprised."

"I have a good reason. We'll get to it in a minute. I have
a feeling I'm missing something. What's up, Bruce?"

Bruce hesitated. She couldn't think of a reason in the
world why she shouldn't tell Virginia, yet she was cautious.
"I . . . well, you'll find out soon enough anyway. Come on
up to my room while I change into something cooler, and I'll
tell you."

As she peeled out of all the heavy denim and put on a
khaki cotton skirt and a pale blue cotton-knit shirt, Bruce

told Virginia as much as she could without revealing Sandor's side of the story. Virginia heard it all quietly and interrupted only to insist on seeing for herself, when Bruce removed the protective bandages, that the tender too-pink skin of her friend's arms was really not badly burned.

Stepping into sandals, Bruce concluded, "If you want to stick around, there will be some action across the street pretty soon. Celeste has already called the police. They'll be waiting in her house when Sandor gets back with Ronnie and Reggie Ramsay. I expect they'll arrest both of them, though it looks like Reggie is the thief. At least, all the stolen things were in Reggie's room."

"Hmm," said Virginia. She was frowning. Then she muttered, barely loudly enough for Bruce to hear. "It takes one to know one."

"What?"

"I said, it takes one to know one!"

"One what?"

"One thief, or two or three, small difference."

"Meaning what? Be more specific, please, Virginia."

Virginia got up off Bruce's bed where she had been sitting. She looked troubled. "I shouldn't, I really shouldn't. I don't have a shred of proof and I'm not really a gossipy sort of person. Oh, I talk, but I hope I never say things that could cause another person harm—and this could."

"All right, just between us, then. I'm sworn to secrecy," promised Bruce, "cross my heart and hope to die."

Virginia shuddered. "Don't say that, Bruce! You came entirely too close the other night and you didn't even tell me about it. How could you not tell me?"

"Never mind, I just used what I thought was my best judgment. And you know, cross my heart's just an expression. You're procrastinating, Virginia. Come on, give!"

"It's just something I remember from when we were kids. You remember I told you what Celeste was like when she was in school. Well, she had a reputation for taking things. She'd see something she liked and she'd take it, just like that."

"You mean, like a kleptomaniac?"

"No, I don't think so. At least I never heard that. I'm not being fair, Bruce, I'm really not. I was so much younger than Celeste and it's all just hearsay. I probably don't know what I'm talking about. She certainly never got arrested for shoplifting or anything. Just forget I said it, okay? The trouble is that I don't like Celeste, I've tried to and I can't. And unfortunately for her, I'm not the only one. The poor woman is doing her darnedest to break into the social structure of this town and people only tolerate her. As hard as she's worked to overcome her past, it wouldn't make any sense for her to have had a part in stealing those things."

Bruce mused, searching Virginia's gentle features. At last she said, "I don't like her any better than you do, but I think we have to give credit where credit is due. She really did seem sincere, Virginia. And she did call the police herself, though she offered to let me do it. And don't forget, I did break into her house, legally speaking, even though the back door was open. She could have gotten me into a lot of trouble over that, but she actually seemed glad to see me instead."

Virginia sighed, as if she were putting aside a great burden, then brightened. "On to happier things! I have the greatest surprise for you. How would you like to be one of the dancers at the Fourth celebration at the Tryon Palace?"

"Me? Dance? I don't exactly have two left feet, but I don't know any of those old dances and I hardly look the part. I'm too tall, for one thing—"

Virginia hastened to interrupt. "That's just it, you are tall! And none of us are professional dancers, you know I'm doing it so you can, too. One of the women has had to drop out at the last minute and she's tall, Bruce, she's just about your size and I think the costume would fit you, so I said I knew someone who could take her place. Oh, say that you'll do it! I'll teach you the dances, you can catch up to the rest of us in no time."

"Well, maybe." Bruce smiled. The idea was appealing. Sandor would be playing and conducting, and this would give her a part, too. "I could learn the sarabande," she said.

"Yes! Not to mention the minuet and the gavotte and Lord Henry's reel! And the costumes are great. Wait till you see!"

"All right," Bruce said with a laugh. It was no surprise that Virginia, whose clothes often looked like costumes to begin with, should take such pleasure in the prospect of wearing period clothes. "I'll do it, but I'm holding you to your promise about teaching me. I don't want to look, or feel, like an idiot!"

"You won't, you'll be great. Trust me!"

"I do," Bruce affirmed, taking her friend by the arm. "In fact, you're just about the only person around here that I really do trust. Except Sandor. And now, let's go back downstairs and wait for him. He and the others should be home any minute now, and they're all in for a big surprise!"

THE RAMSAY BROTHERS were arrested and remained in jail pending further investigations. They protested their innocence, but nevertheless were being investigated for thefts of antique objects up and down the east coast, and as far south and inland as Atlanta. The things they had taken in New Bern had been returned to their rightful owners, and Celeste's part in the affair had given her a sudden celebrity status that made Virginia's small suspicions seem ridiculous.

Sandor's silver letter opener, however, had not surfaced. Since he hadn't reported its loss, there was not much to be done. He declared it unimportant, and Bruce knew she should be satisfied.

But she wasn't. She carried with her through the days and nights a suppressed, eerie feeling, like waiting for the other shoe to drop. She was continually wary, often felt that she was being watched. Her peripheral vision began to bother her—she kept seeing bright flashes out of the corners of her eyes. These she tried to dismiss as aftereffects of her recent traumatic experience. The residue of an undiagnosed concussion, maybe, or simply some sort of emotional fallout. Whatever; for Sandor's sake, Bruce said nothing.

Sandor was working incredibly hard, both at his physical condition and his music. And Bruce herself worked at learning the dances. Now they both had rehearsals to attend. The month of June was drawing to a close, the celebration at the palace was only a week away. If Celeste had not been such a perpetual thorn in the side, Bruce could have been happy—for a little while, at least.

She had been in her room, sewing lace ruffles on the bottom of the skirt and edges of the sleeves of her colonial dance costume. The woman she'd replaced had, in spite of Virginia's assurances, been somewhat shorter. But the costume was beautiful and otherwise a good fit. Bruce hadn't let Sandor see, nor in fact had she seen his costume. Perhaps he wanted to surprise her, as she wanted to surprise him. She was thinking about this, a small smile on her face, as she descended the stairs to spend some time with him before retiring for the night.

She heard voices in the living room. Sandor and Celeste. Without the Ramsays to entertain her, Celeste had been spending a good deal of time at Sandor's house. Bruce pretended that this didn't bother her, but it did. She was continually faced with a choice: whether to join Celeste and Sandor and have to watch the woman work her wiles—in which case she always wondered if Sandor were either as indifferent or as amused as he seemed to be—or to leave the two of them alone together, that having its own set of dangers. Tonight she opted to leave them alone.

But the tone of Sandor's voice drew Bruce, against her better judgment, near the open door.

Amused and indignant, Sandor sounded, "Your powers of observation are excellent, Celeste. I am indeed almost fully recovered and ready, as you said, to get on with my life."

Celeste said something in a voice so soft that Bruce couldn't make out the words. She must be sitting very close to him, Bruce thought. Her gray eyes clouded. She was a little jealous, she admitted it, and resolutely took a step away from the door.

Sandor's sexy chuckle—she knew that sound—made it hard for her to keep going. Bruce had a vision of him removing Celeste's arms from about his neck as he said, still indulgent, "Never underestimate your powers of temptation!"

Another enticing murmur from Celeste. Bruce took another step away; then Sandor's next words stopped her cold.

"You put me in an awkward position." He no longer chuckled. His voice was grave, deep and smooth as velvet. "I feel I must, for your own sake, Celeste, tell you something in confidence. I have asked Bruce to be my wife." A little pause after which Sandor said again, with emphasis, "I intend to marry Bruce MacLaren."

"What!" Celeste's shriek could have been heard blocks away. It brought Vladimir running up the hall, to shoulder past Bruce into the living room.

Bruce ignored the shriek's ringing in her ears; she heard only the warmth, the definiteness of Sandor's declaration. She felt her cheeks go crimson with pleasure as a delicious thrill trembled up her spine. She decided this scene was too good to miss, and entered the room after Vladimir.

"Is there some problem?" Vladimir was asking in his obsequious tones.

Celeste, for once, was speechless. Her mouth hung open as she sat in a pastel puddle of skirts on the couch.

Sandor started to reply to the valet, then checked himself as he saw Bruce. Immediately he smiled, stood, and held out his arm to Bruce. "My dear," he said, "I'm glad you're here. Vladimir, too."

Bruce walked up to Sandor, into the circle of his outstretched arm. She knew her color was still high as she asked him, "What's going on, Sandor?"

He turned his face to hers, away from Celeste, and gave her a brief, private, intense look. His grip on her shoulder was so tight that it almost hurt. He said, "I made a unilateral decision. I hope you won't mind. It seemed the proper time. I've told Celeste, and now am telling Vladimir, as well, that you and I are to be married."

"I—" said Bruce, thinking that she hadn't quite agreed to marry him, but absurdly happy nonetheless. "I thought we weren't going to tell anybody yet."

Sandor, still beaming, looked down his eagle's nose at the still astonished dark-haired woman on the couch. "Celeste is such a good friend. I'm sure she will keep our secret until we make a formal announcement. Won't you, Celeste?"

Celeste came to life. The air around her fairly crackled with an angry energy. Her tone of voice could only be described as bitchy. "Oh sure, I'll keep your secret, Maestro." Her bowed lips thinned into a sneer. "Although you might want to go ahead and announce it, the sooner the better. People have been talking, you know, about a female assistant living alone in a house with two men. Isn't that so, Vladimir?"

Vladimir was having his own problem with Sandor's declaration. He frowned, he bowed and then seemed to think the better of it, his hands twitched. The look he cast at Celeste when she addressed him was one of sheer desperation. "I'm sure I don't know, madam," he croaked. Finally his training took over and he turned to Sandor and Bruce, put his heels together and with a jerk of his head said, "Congratulations, Maestro. Miss MacLaren."

"Thank you, Vladimir," said Bruce automatically. How odd, she thought, that Celeste should look to Vladimir for an ally. Of course, he was the only other person in the room....

Celeste meanwhile could no longer contain her anger. Her violet eyes glared and the ugly contortion of her features made her look every year of her age. Skirts swishing, she rose from the couch in a huff. "Yes, congratulations, Bruce. Though in this case you can't expect me to say and certainly not to think that the best woman won!" She flounced to the door.

Sandor gave Bruce's shoulder a squeeze and rolled his eyes, as if to say "Thank God that's over!"

Vladimir recovered himself with a start and rushed to open the front door for Celeste. But she flounced back for a final word. "Just when," she asked, "do you intend to make this engagement public?"

"After the Tryon Palace celebration," replied Sandor smoothly, "when I have had time to select a ring and make arrangements properly."

"I see."

Bruce felt the angry force of Celeste's gaze, and met her eyes. For a moment she felt from the other woman a push of pure, bitter hatred. It was so quickly gone that later Bruce wondered if she had imagined it.

Somehow Celeste managed to smile...at Sandor, true, but the smile looked genuine. She said, "Forgive my bad manners. Your news was just such a surprise, and I—I suppose I've made a fool of myself. Do forgive me. I'll say good night now."

BRUCE AND SANDOR were enjoying the unusual luxury of a nightcap—brandy for him and white wine for her—in the big kitchen. They sat, as they did so often, side by side on the comfortable sofa. Vladimir had gone for a walk after seeing Celeste out.

"Do you think that was wise?" asked Bruce, studying Sandor over the rim of her glass.

"Telling Celeste that you and I are to be married, you mean?"

"Celeste and Vladimir, yes."

Sandor chuckled. This time, the sexy sound was all for Bruce. He stroked her hair. "Yes, I think it was wise. Provided of course that you don't make a liar out of me."

"She was very angry," said Bruce.

"She would have been even angrier, and perhaps with better reason, if I had failed to stop her, and that was the best way I could think of doing it. The woman was quite determined to seduce me, Bruce, and she's good at it. I'm only human. She was damn near succeeding tonight, and not for the first time."

"I can believe that!"

"Bruce, my love, look at me. Not long ago I would have been flattered by the attentions of a woman like Celeste

Stanhope. But no more. I want only you. I'm well aware that you've never actually said the words that you love me, that you will marry me. Don't make a liar of me, my darling. Tell me now.''

Bruce bent her head so that her hair swung forward and obscured her face. She held her glass very tight in her hands. She had that feeling, that horrible eerie feeling. It seemed the wrong time to make such a commitment though she had never wanted anything more in her life.

"I'm not doing this right," grumbled Sandor. "You want a proper proposal, is that it? I should get down on my knees and all that?"

Sideways, through a curve of copper hair, Bruce looked at him and saw the earnestly puzzled look on his face. She doubted that women ever said no to this compelling man. She smiled. "Don't worry, that's not it. Besides, I don't think you'd better try that. You might not be able to get back up again."

"Oh, no?" Sandor had grown increasingly confident of the new strength of his body. He had, in particular, worked hard on the use of his legs, and this was a challenge he couldn't resist. Besides, to have Bruce's affirmation he would do anything.

He was slow, careful, but certain in his movements. With the assistance of one cane, he stood to his full height in front of Bruce. Then feeling the pull in his thigh muscles, knowing by the absence of weakness that they would support him, he sank to one knee in the classic pose. He placed his right hand solemnly over his heart. This physical position, which intellectually he thought ridiculous, he found actually deeply moving. His words, which might have been tongue-in-cheek, were not.

Sandor said, "I burn with love for you, Bruce Mac-Laren, and if you will be my wife I will cherish you all our days. Will you marry me?"

She saw that he was serious. Tears pricked in her eyes. She heard her voice say words she had not intended to say, and knew that she meant them. "Yes, Sandor Szelazeny. I will marry you." She leaned forward and kissed him, only their lips touching in a long, tender kiss.

By mutual accord, their lips parted. "You said yes," Sandor said, "say it again. I want to be sure."

"Yes, I will marry you," said Bruce again. "How could I refuse when you asked me so beautifully?" She grinned. "Now, I'd like to see if you really can get up from there by yourself."

He was so happy, he felt that he could fly if he wanted to. Sandor rose, his legs took the strain, and if his hand was heavy on the cane it did not matter. Perhaps, he thought, he should not wait. Perhaps tonight should be the night!

But no. He had made plans. He had sent for his mother's jewels. He would wait.

"Oh, Sandor!" exclaimed Bruce, "well done!"

"Thank you, my love. However, I will now rest on the couch while you refill our glasses. I think a toast is in order. It's a pity we don't have any cold champagne!"

THE SUN WAS BLAZING hot in a mercilessly clear blue sky. Bruce strode along Pollock Street with the dress bag that contained her costume like a heavy blanket over her arm. She was returning from a dress rehearsal at the Tryon Palace. Sandor was still there, rehearsing with the chamber group. His own harpsichord had been moved there earlier in the week, so that he was often at the palace practicing, rather than at home. Bruce was so used to having him around all the time that she missed him.

She waved at Virginia through the windows as she passed the deli, and continued on to the corner to turn on East Front Street. Only a couple of blocks now and she would be home in the blessed air-conditioning. Perhaps Vladimir, too, would be out. He was gone a lot lately, which was fine with her. She did, though, wonder where he went. Sandor often caught rides home with another of the musicians, so that he didn't rely on his valet for everything. Perhaps Vladimir resented that; perhaps he went off sulking.

Bruce shook her head at herself. She couldn't ever let go of her suspicions of the man, and she was going to have to...if she was going to be Mrs. Sandor Szelazeny. And she was! It seemed like a dream, but it was a dream that was coming true.

The Mercedes and her Volvo were both in the drive at the side of the house. That did not necessarily mean Vladimir was there, but just in case, Bruce called out "I'm home!" as she unlocked the front door and closed it behind her. There was no response; but then, Vladimir often ignored her.

I don't like to be alone with him, that's the trouble, thought Bruce. The eerie feeling was with her again. She shook it off and went upstairs. What she wanted more than anything in the world was a cool shower—even if showering in the house alone with Vladimir made her think of the shower scene from the movie *Psycho.* She hung up her costume, shed her clothes, pulled on her terry robe and locked herself in the bathroom.

As she turned off the taps, Bruce thought she heard the front door open. Dripping wet from head to foot, obeying an urgency she didn't understand, she threw on her robe as she ran to the head of the stairs. She heard Vladimir's voice, but not his words, and a male voice that she didn't recognize. She thought he said, "I promised I'd give it to her in person."

Vladimir mumbled again, in his obsequious cadence, and the door closed. Bruce ran down the stairs, oblivious to the fact that she left a trail of water behind her. She called out "Wait!" as she reached the landing and took the turn so fast that her bare, wet feet nearly skidded out from under her.

"Yes, miss?" Vladimir raised his eyebrows, then composed his cadaverous face and made no mention of her dripping appearance.

"Was that someone to see me?"

Vladimir's eyes flickered. "Ah, yes. I told him you were indisposed."

"You could have had him wait. Who was it, Vladimir?"

"A most improperly dressed person. A stranger," sniffed Vladimir.

"Oh." *How odd,* Bruce thought. She gathered the neck of her robe in one hand, suddenly uncomfortable and aware of the sight she must present. "Did he leave a message?"

"No, miss."

Bruce turned to go back upstairs, and as she did, realized that throughout this entire exchange Vladimir had kept one hand behind his back. She turned back to the man. "You're lying to me, Vladimir. That man gave you something for me. I'll have it, please." She held out her hand and stared at him in the way she had perfected on first coming to this house.

"He was not our sort of person, Miss MacLaren," said Vladimir. He pulled himself up as erect as possible and looked down his nose at her.

"Nevertheless, if he had something for me, then you certainly have no right to it. Let me have whatever is behind your back, Vladimir. Right now!"

The man bowed his head, defeated, and gave her a long white envelope somewhat marred by dirty fingerprints. In the center of the envelope her name was written; in the lower right-hand corner the words "by hand."

"Thank you," said Bruce, "and don't let anything like this ever happen again. Don't attempt to screen my mail, or my visitors. If you do in the future, I shall tell Maestro Szelazeny. Is that clear?" She hated to talk to anyone that way, but apparently Vladimir understood no other language.

"It is clear," he echoed. The tone of his voice gave Bruce the creeps as she turned her back on him and walked up the stairs with her letter in her hand.

She didn't open it until she was dry and dressed. She had an idea who had written it; the quaint "by hand" was almost a dead giveaway. A glance at the signature before she read the text proved her hunch was right. This was a letter written in a jail cell; it was from Ronnie Ramsay.

Chapter Sixteen

Dear Bruce,

I've tried to call you whenever they'd let me, but that man Vladimir isn't giving you the message, I'm sure of it. He and Celeste are very thick, did you know? So I'm giving this to a man who was only in overnight. Drunk and disorderly, he was, and they put him in with me because the jail's full up. You must come and see me, really you must! I wanted to talk it over with Reggie, but they've separated us. They never let me see him, and, Oh my dear, it's such a bother! I hardly know what to do without Reg. But I've thought and thought and there is something I must tell you. I'm sure it's the right thing. You will come, won't you?

Yours most sincerely,
Ronald Ramsay

Bruce didn't hesitate a moment. She brushed her hair and went out with it still wet.

The Craven County Jail was not far, but Bruce drove. She arrived outside of normal visiting hours and had to get special permission to see Ronnie. This took time, but at last a uniformed guard escorted her to a small room with nothing in it but a table and two chairs. All the waiting had her

nerves on edge, but even so it was better than the vague ee-
riness that she had for so long suppressed. Something was
happening, something would come of this interview, she was
sure of it.

When Ronnie was ushered into the room, he didn't
stumble. He shuffled to a seat at the table. He sat without
mishap. His shoulders were hunched as if the clumsiness
had, along with his will to live, been drained out of him.
Bruce's heart went out and she reached her hand across the
table.

"I came as soon as I got your note, Ronnie," she said.

His blue eyes lit up, and tiny spots of pink appeared on his
jail-pale face. "Knew you would. Good of you," he bobbed
his head and looked a bit like his old self.

"You're all right, I hope? You have everything you
need?"

"I suppose. Except I do miss dear old Reggie most awfully. Twins, y' know. Awful for twins to be parted. Not
identical, but we've always been together. I say, Bruce, they
won't let me talk to you for very long so I'd best get on with
it."

Bruce nodded. "I'm listening."

"I didn't steal that stuff, y' know."

"I know you didn't, Ronnie, your brother did. The things
were in your brother's room."

Ronnie looked surprised. "What makes you think that?"

"I was there with Celeste at the house when she found
them. She said it was your brother's room."

"No, no," Ronnie shook his head, "that was my room,
all right. Celeste had it backward. Reggie's room was the
one with all the books and maps and things. Can't resist
'em, he can't. I told him those old maps would be missed,
we'd be in a passle of trouble over that, but he wouldn't listen. Always an eye for the fine old stuff, has Reg. But me, I

don't take things. I'm not clever enough. I'd make mistakes, botch it up. Reg can pull it off, even if it is wrong, but he's very careful, very selective, doesn't do it often. All that stuff in my room, little silly things...why, I never took it!"

The spots of color on Ronnie's cheeks burned brighter with his indignation. Bruce asked, somehow not the least surprised, "You think someone set you up, then?"

Ronnie nodded vigorously. "Quite!"

"You want me to help you prove it, is that it?"

To Bruce's surprise he shook his head no. "Not the point. Got to stay here as long as my brother's here, anyway. I wanted to tell y'... to tell y'—" He broke off, wiped at his forehead with the back of his sleeve. "Sorry. This is damned hard. Wanted to tell y' to be careful. Sandor's papers and things, the ones we came here for, the ones he says he doesn't have...y' know?"

"I know." Bruce's heart was beating fast.

"We were willing to give up on them, Reg and I. Going home, we said. Soon. And then this happens, we get arrested. I'm not too bright. Reggie could figure this out, I can't. All I know is Celeste got interested in the Bathory stuff, didn't want us to give up. Got herself in tight with old Vladimir. He's a strange egg, don't y' know?"

"I do know. Go on."

"Celeste isn't usually interested in stuff like that. Can't figure it out. But she doesn't like you, Bruce. Wants Sandor for herself. Wants his stuff, too. Just felt I had to warn you to watch out for her, that's all. Maybe it's nothing, maybe I made a mistake." Ronnie hung his head and then buried his face in his hands.

Bruce reached across the table and patted his arm. "Thank you for telling me. I had no idea that Vladimir was close to anyone except Sandor, let alone Celeste. Ronnie, do

you think Celeste framed you? And why would she put the
things in your room and tell me it was Reggie's?"

"Don't know," said Ronnie miserably, looking up again
at Bruce. "Thought Celeste was our friend. Best of friends.
Maybe she didn't do it. Oh, I do wish I could talk to Reggie! He will have figured all of this out, he'd know what to
do. But I did think I had to tell you to watch out. Kept
bothering me, it did." His head bobbed up and down.

Having discharged that burden, Ronnie brightened considerably. "Now, until the old guard comes, how about a bit
of a gossip, what say? Tell old Ronnie what's happening
about town?"

Putting her own thoughts and questions aside for the
moment, Bruce complied.

IT WAS LATE, almost the dinner hour, when Bruce left from
her visit with Ronnie Ramsay. Driving home she admitted
to herself that it was something of a relief to be able to suspect Celeste Stanhope again. But perhaps she, as Virginia
had said of herself, was being unfair simply because she
didn't like Celeste. Could Ronnie be believed? Why would
he lie about which room was his? He certainly had nothing
to gain by it, since the objects stolen in New Bern were all in
that room. And why or how could there possibly be any relationship between that vulture, Vladimir, and Celeste?

Of course Celeste didn't like her, Bruce had known that
almost from day one. Maybe she thought if she cultivated
Vladimir, she could get closer to Sandor. From that point of
view the man did make a valuable ally....

Bruce got no further in the short time it took to drive
from the jail to Sandor's house on East Front Street. One
thing she knew for sure, it required no thought whatever:
she would say nothing of any of this to Sandor until after
tomorrow's concert and dance at the Tryon Palace. Sandor

had said at breakfast that he was as nervous about this performance as if it were Carnegie Hall.

So she pasted a smile on her face and went lightly up the steps, as if she hadn't a care in the world. Her smile, when the door was opened for her by Sandor himself, was no longer pretended.

"At last!" he said, taking her in his arms. He nuzzled her cheek, lightly kissed her lips. He did not ask where she had been. Instead, leaning on one cane and his other arm around her, he escorted her down the hall, saying, "I have a very special evening planned for us, my dear Bruce. I was like a horse champing at the bit waiting for you."

"I'd think you would be exhausted. You were at the palace almost all day. Did the afternoon's rehearsal go well?"

"Better than I would have thought possible. Our little group of musicians is quite good. The chamber concert inside the palace will be excellent, I think. I am not so sure about our playing outside for the dancing. That harpsichord is somewhat inferior, but since I do not want to risk my own instrument outside, there is little choice. Our ensemble is not large enough for playing on the lawns, I fear. The sound is swallowed up by the great outdoors."

Bruce smiled over at him. She loved Sandor's absorption in his music. "I thought you sounded wonderful at the dance rehearsal."

"Not as wonderful as you looked, my dear. I was more than a little envious of your partner."

"And I wished I were dancing with you," said Bruce seriously, looking into Sandor's eyes. "Especially for the sarabande."

"I will dance the sarabande with you at our wedding. For tonight, I have arranged something, ah, similar perhaps. A surprise. Close your eyes, Bruce, and let me lead you."

They had walked up the hall to the kitchen as they talked. Now with her eyes obediently closed, Bruce felt Sandor lead her back the way they'd come.

"You may open your eyes now," he said.

He had brought her to the library. Now vacant of its harpsichord, the room was ablaze with candlelight. In the center was a table set for two, gleaming with silver and crystal, centered with a bowl of roses. Soft classical music played from an unseen source.

"Oh, it's beautiful!" sighed Bruce.

"I planned it, but we may thank our friend Virginia for the manner of execution. And for the food, as well." Sandor gestured to a side table, where dishes waited mysteriously under silver covers. "We are alone," Sandor whispered into her ear, "I have sent Vladimir away and told him not to return before midnight."

"Ah," Bruce sighed again. She looked at the loveliness of the room, at Sandor, who wore a cravat and a silk dressing gown over his trousers, and down at her own slacks and shirt. "But you must wait until I've changed my clothes. I can't sit in a room like this dressed the way I am."

"You always are beautiful to me, but if you must change, then hurry."

Bruce did hurry. She thanked her lucky stars for the instinct that had made her recently buy a long caftan that she had not yet had occasion to wear. The material was cotton, not silk, but the fabric was richly patterned in shades of yellow and gold that brought out all the highlights of her hair. She slipped it over her head, and on her feet put the simple gold thongs she'd bought to wear with it.

She was rewarded by the look on Sandor's face when she returned to the library. "You make the candles pale by comparison," he said.

Their meal was a sensual blur of tastes, smells, smiles, tiny touches. The evening was, as Sandor had intended it to be, like a moment out of time.

"And now for dessert," Sandor announced.

"I couldn't possibly," protested Bruce.

"This dessert," he said solemnly, "is different." He reached into his pocket, extracted a small black velvet box, and leaned across the table to place it in front of Bruce.

Bruce looked at him. Looked down at the velvet box. Her heart pounded, her cheeks flushed.

"Open it, my love."

She did. Inside the box was a ring, an oval diamond so large that at first she didn't think it could possibly be real. It was cleverly set in gold, as if the precious gem had been caught and held in a tangle of gold vines. Unconsciously she gasped as the diamond winked and glowed, reflecting the candlelight. "Sandor, it's the most beautiful, most original ring I've ever seen!"

"It's your engagement ring," he said. "I had it made for you and sent here. I hope I got the size right. Put it on."

"I—I've never worn anything like this before! I'd be afraid—"

"Don't be silly!" Sandor leaned across the table and slipped the ring on Bruce's finger. Her reticence touched him. "When you are my wife I'll shower you with much, much more than this. But this ring, I thought it would be right for you. I sent for the family jewels and they arrived—they're in a box at the bank—but when I looked at them I knew that for our engagement I had to have something different. Because you are so different, and so precious to me, my Bruce."

Bruce smiled at him, looked at her ring, and thought once more that this night was like a dream. Her voice was very soft. "If anyone is different, it's you, Sandor. I've never known anyone like you. I can't believe this is happening."

"It is," he said, his face and his voice heavy with emotion, "and there is more to come."

Sandor rose and held out his hand. "Come with me."

Bruce gave him her hand. She was almost, but not quite, mesmerized. "The candles," she said.

Sandor rolled his eyes. "It is hard to make a romantic of you, Bruce MacLaren, but I will succeed yet! All right, blow out the candles if you must, and *then* come with me."

Bruce blew out the candles and then once more gave Sandor her hand. In the almost dark hallway, his eyes twinkled. He stopped, his head to one side. "Listen," he said.

She listened. From down the hall, faint but distinct, she heard throbbing, sensual yet stately music. She recognized the sound of Sandor's playing, the tone of his harpsichord. "The sarabande!" she exclaimed. "But how . . . ?"

"The miracle of modern technology—a tape," he whispered, his lips at her ear. Then his tongue delicately traced the orifice where before he had made soft puffs of sound. Lightly he nipped the lobe, then led her forward again. He brought her to his bedroom and slowly pushed open the door. The bedroom, too, was lighted only by candles. There were candles everywhere.

Bruce gasped; the room was transformed into a bower of golden light. Sandor said, "I am going to make love to you for the first time, my dear Bruce, to the music of the sarabande. Our sarabande."

Slowly, sensually, they moved together. Eyes closed, lips met, tongues caressed, hands explored. The sarabande played on. Clothes fell away; skin met skin. Slowly, Sandor told himself, slowly. He led Bruce to the bed, touched her golden body, her fiery hair. Her hands played over him, and he groaned.

"I'm not going to be able to wait," he said deep in his throat, "it's been too long."

She looked at him, her gray eyes almost blue, wide and very, very deep. "I think we have both waited a very long time already," she said. She opened her legs and guided him into her.

He filled her as completely as she had always known he would. To the cadence of the music, Sandor thrust, and with every thrust Bruce spiraled farther and farther, deeper and deeper into an ecstatic land where she had never been before. Soon she no longer heard the music, she was lost in a kind of madness that was all Sandor. Sandor within her, in her depths, all thrusting power, mounting pleasure; she could not open wide enough, draw him deep enough, ride him high enough.

Sandor forgot himself. He forgot that he had ever been injured, ever felt pain, ever been weak. He knew only the softness, the incredible yielding of this woman. His woman. He yearned, he burned to lose himself in her, to merge with her and be one flesh. And he did: they moved as one, over hills and valleys of most exquisite, ecstatic harmony. And finally, they left the hills and valleys, riding together, and mounted the skies where they exploded among the stars. Together. A new star, a double star, was born.

Chapter Seventeen

They had let themselves be lulled, of course, by the spell of their own falling in love. Bruce realized this, but not in time.

So, on the day of the Fourth of July celebration at the Tryon Palace, Bruce was rosy with the glow of a woman who has been well-loved, fresh in spite of a near sleepless night, and so much in love that she could hardly see straight.

Sandor looked marvelous in his eighteenth century music master clothes. They suited him so well that he did not look as if he had donned a costume. He had let his hair grow in the months since he'd agreed to play and conduct, and since he habitually wore it rather long anyway, he was able to pull it back and tie it with a black ribbon. The silver streaks shone at his temples; the severe style, rather than his usual shaggy look, accentuated the Slavic planes of his face. His long-skirted jacket and tight-fitting, knee-length pants were black; his waistcoat was brocaded silver, his stockings gray; his high-necked white shirt had a stock discreetly trimmed in narrow lace. He walked with one cane only, limping not at all—the only sign of his recent injury was that he moved slowly, but he had developed a certain grace to go with the slowness of his movements.

When Bruce watched Sandor cross the council chamber, the palace's largest room, to take his place for the chamber concert, she was so impressed by his appearance that she got tears in her eyes. In general that day her eyes were not working too well—she was, quite literally, almost blinded by love.

She took care with her own appearance, because she wanted Sandor to approve. Her costume had a tight bodice of pale blue silk, trimmed with narrow cream ribbons patterned by tiny rosebuds. Its neckline was low and square and showed the tops of her breasts. Panniers of the same blue silk fell to the sides of a full underskirt of cream, which she had trimmed, as she had the sleeves, with lace ruffles. She pinned her heavy hair back and up, and tried not to mind the wisps that escaped along the edges. She wore her engagement ring, and from time to time throughout the afternoon looked down at it—the diamond's brilliance further blinded her.

Of others Bruce took almost no notice. She vaguely registered Celeste's presence as a hostess at the door, wearing something frothy and pink that looked like a cross between Marie Antoinette and a birthday cake. Virginia among the dancers flashed in green and white striped silk; but her own handsome young dancing partner Bruce noticed not at all.

She never even saw Vladimir; had no idea that he was present at the celebration until much, much too late. Then, with the brilliant clarity that is a by-product of sudden shock, she saw him all too well. Like Sandor, he looked as if he belonged in the period clothes he wore; all black except for a touch of white at the neck, and white wig with a black-tied pigtail. He came up to her just as the dancing ended, came on his silent tread so that she did not know he was behind her until he spoke.

"You will come with me, Miss MacLaren," he said, bending over her. As she turned her head in surprise, Vladimir grasped her shoulder in a hard, bony grip. At the same moment she distinctly felt the prick of something sharp...in a very vulnerable area of her spine. The sudden shock set in, and everything became too, too clear. Colors were brighter, sounds so loud they hurt her ears, and Sandor, surrounded by a group of admirers, seemed very, very far away.

Still, Bruce moistened her lips, and her chin went up. "I think not," she said.

The sharp pressure at her spine increased. "I have a knife—a stiletto—at your back," Vladimir hissed, "and I know how to use it. One thrust would be sufficient. You *will* come with me!"

She went with him, more to give herself time to think than because she was afraid of him. He was an old man, his reflexes had to be slow, his bones to be brittle...yet the bony hand on her shoulder was latched to her like a claw. Like a death grip.

And with a sickening lurch to her stomach, Bruce realized that Vladimir was a fanatic. Whatever his mission was with her, he would not hesitate to die himself, if need be, in the accomplishment of it. The few self-defense moves she knew immediately paled in her mind by comparison to such crazed determination.

"Where are we going?" Bruce asked as they left the main palace building and Vladimir urged her with his knife point up the cobbled drive.

"You are now a hostage. Although, if necessary, I would not hesitate to kill you. The Maestro will come for you either way...but he is more likely to reveal what must be revealed if you are alive when he comes."

You old vulture! Bruce thought, *I was right to suspect you all along.* The remaining question was, was he in this alone, or was Celeste somehow a part of it, as Ronnie Ramsay had suggested? And why, why had she and Sandor let themselves get so caught up in simply living that they hadn't pushed harder at solving the mysteries? Sandor had a better excuse than she did; she'd had her suspicions and she hadn't done anything much about them, and now it was too late!

Bruce's mind worked hard and fast as Vladimir prodded her along the drive, out on the sidewalk, and to a car he had parked on the far side of the palace parking area. If he really did have a stiletto, then there was no doubt that the blade was long enough and sharp enough to penetrate where it would do the most damage. He *could* kill her with the thing; or, what might be even worse, he could damage the spinal cord and leave her paralyzed for life. Therefore struggling did not seem such a good idea. Better to wait and try to escape later. Perhaps once they were in the car....

But all hope of that was dashed when they reached a car Bruce did not recognize. Rented, she guessed. She was still seeing things with that awful clarity when Vladimir whipped a pair of handcuffs out of an inner pocket in his eighteenth century frock coat—it was such an anachronism that she almost laughed. The sun glinted off the silvery color of the cuffs as Vladimir, one-handed, slipped a cuff over her wrist and clicked it shut without ever having removed the knife from her back.

Bruce frowned and squinted at the flash of silver; it reminded her that she had been seeing such flashes out of the corners of her eyes for weeks now.

Because that made her feel as if she might be losing her mind, Bruce countered her apprehension with a wisecrack. "You must have practiced with the handcuffs. It's hardly a skill one expects of a gentleman's gentleman, Vladimir."

"Yes, miss, I did practice." With those exceedingly polite words, he wrenched Bruce's arms behind her back and cuffed her wrists together. Only then did he remove the knife. It was as wicked and deadly as Bruce had imagined it to be, and so was the glint in Vladimir's beady black eyes when he put it on the front seat between them.

"Are you going to tell me where we're going?" she asked.

"We will not be pursued. This time was chosen because everyone in town is occupied at the palace celebration and will be there until the fireworks display is over after dark. There is no longer a need for secrecy. I will take you to a deserted house some miles away, on the road to a place called Edenton."

"Uh-huh," Bruce observed shrewdly, "no doubt that was where you went the night of the storm, when you got lost and came home looking like a drowned bird."

"As you say, miss."

She didn't seem to be able to shake the man's icy composure, so she gave up trying. She thought instead, trying to find a comfortable way to sit with her hands behind her, of how in the world she could help herself and Sandor out of this mess. But she couldn't think of anything. She concluded she would have to play it by ear, do whatever occurred to her when the time came.

The silence in the car got on her increasingly tight nerves. Bruce decided to try to draw Vladimir out. At least she might get some of the answers that so far had eluded both her and Sandor. "Vladimir," she began, giving voice at last to one of the many suspicions Sandor had refused to hear, "what you want Sandor to reveal—it's the whereabouts of the box of the Countess Elizabeth Bathory's things, isn't it?"

"Yes." The bony white fingers tightened on the steering wheel. "I have searched and searched, and been unable to find what he has done with them."

"Why? What do you want with those things? You know that Sandor will not go back to Hungary, and so it's all over. I thought you truly cared about Sandor—" well, that was a lie, Bruce had never believed it but Sandor had almost convinced her "—and you know what you are doing will hurt him."

"I serve the Bathorys, as my father and my father's father and so on for many generations have served the Bathorys." Vladimir's thin lips curved down in a sneer. "But the Bathory blood has thinned, alas. It is no longer noble. Sandor, the Maestro, is the last of the line. I was to keep watch, to be the guardian of the next guardian. There was hope that even though his mother was so weak that she changed her name, her son would restore the ancient pattern, take his rightful place."

He glanced at Bruce, the malice in his eyes now unveiled. "I did everything within my power to convince the Maestro that he should return to Hungary. I had not given up hope, especially after he was injured. He almost believed, then. But *you* came, and you have ruined everything!"

"You made Sandor believe in the curse, didn't you?"

"I tried to, yes, and if it were not for you I would have succeeded. Eventually."

Bruce shivered. Vladimir was probably right about that. "So you were the one who arranged all those nasty little accidents that plagued Sandor's concert tour."

"I arranged some, yes. Other things that were called accidents occurred in the process of my looking for the great countess's secrets. Even then, so early, I could not find them."

Vladimir was talking almost to himself now, caught in the grip of memory. "When the Maestro disappeared from our midst and then there was the plane crash, that was the worst time. I feared that he had taken the secrets with him, that they had been destroyed in the crash. For all the months he was in the hospital I searched . . . I got permission, finally, to go through the debris recovered from the crash and I searched the site. But I found nothing. I knew then that the box was elsewhere. I have never been able to find out where."

Listening carefully, Bruce gleaned an important fact. "So you didn't make the plane crash happen, Vladimir? That was not part of your attempt to make Sandor believe he was cursed?"

"No, I did not. It was most appalling. I did not, and do not, want the Maestro to die. I want him to live and to return to the Castle Bathory. The plane crash was either caused by the true curse, or it was merely an accident."

"Ah." In spite of her uncomfortable circumstances, Bruce sighed with relief. She enjoyed for a few minutes the simple pleasure of having found out that she was right.

Then she asked, "If Sandor won't ever go back, why do you want the Countess Bathory's secrets? What will you do with them?"

"I will take them back to the castle, where they belong. And then we will meet, the old servants and others who believe. We will see what shall be done." He shot Bruce a venomous look. "Of course, it is still not certain that the Maestro will not go back. You are still standing in the way, Bruce MacLaren."

He did not have to say more; nor did he, for he turned off onto a side road and drove more slowly. Bruce saw they were apparently near their destination. And she knew without asking, that her life was in danger. When her usefulness as a hostage was past, Vladimir would not hesitate to kill her.

The car approached a house that sat all by itself in the middle of flat, unplanted fields. It had been a grand house once, an antebellum mansion, no doubt the center of one of the large plantations of the Carolina coastal plain. It was perhaps not as gloomily atmospheric as one of the hulking rock pile Transylvanian castles in which Vladimir the Vulture would feel right at home, but it would do. All traces of paint had long since vanished from weather-beaten gray walls, porch columns were cracked from top to bottom, lintels sagged, long windows gaped in the facade like empty eye sockets. This vision wavered in a miasma of evening heat; the sky above, darkening to purple with approaching night, roiled with massing clouds.

Vladimir stopped the car, took up his stiletto, and prodded Bruce inside.

The place was nearly airless, dank and dark. A ruined stair rose up and up from a wide center hall. "Whose house is this?" Bruce asked, more from wanting to hear the sound of her own voice than from desiring an answer.

"It is the property of Celeste Stanhope," said Vladimir.

"Oh," she said. So Ronnie Ramsay had been right after all. Vladimir, no matter how much she'd thought him capable of, was not in this alone.

Thunder boomed in the distance. Bruce hated this house, hated the way it smelled, hated the way it summoned up old childhood fears of ghosts, hated how helpless she felt. Her shoulders hurt, her arms were getting numb, and she had shooting pains in her wrists from time to time.

Vladimir left and went into a room on the left. "We will wait here," he announced in his old stiff way.

She followed him. She felt no need to ask for whom or what they waited. Through the gloom Bruce made out a few pieces of furniture in the large, square room, and a fireplace whose Greek Revival-type surround had retained some of its paint and stood out against the darkness like a startling white, open mouth.

"You may sit," said her captor, indicating a moldy old settee.

"No thanks. I sat enough in the car. I'll stand, if you don't mind."

He bowed stiffly, which Bruce found odd. Habit, she supposed. She didn't care. She knew she was near to losing heart. She couldn't for the life of her see how she was going to get out of this, and she did not want Sandor to come. He'd be no good in a physical fight, and if there were any chance of escape at all, it was bound to come to that. She didn't think there was a chance, not for herself; they—Celeste and Vladimir—would use her to get what they wanted from Sandor and then they would kill her. Right before his eyes. Vladimir would step up then, and whisper like a snake into Sandor's ear, "It is the curse!" And Sandor, half crazed with grief, would believe him.

Bruce shook her head so hard that half her hair lost its pins and came tumbling down. *I must not think that way,* she said to herself, *I'll make myself crazy.* She walked over to one of the long glassless windows and looked out. She would watch the road.

The car that came had not been far behind. She watched its approach from far off, before it turned onto the road through the empty fields. Thunder boomed, and afterward a flash of light glanced off the car in a beam of dazzling silver. Silver!

Of course, Bruce thought, excited by the discovery. That was Celeste's car, Celeste with her fondness for silver! Suddenly it all came together, all the times she'd seen silver flashes and not known where they were coming from, what they meant! Celeste had a silver car that Bruce had never seen before in spite of having lived for months directly across the street from her. Never seen head-on, that is, but oh so often from the corner of an eye. Celeste had followed Bruce, watched her, plotted against her, unseen but like a silver shadow—how many times? More than Bruce could count.

The car pulled up, stopped. Another boom of thunder followed by another flash of light revealed that the car was a Jaguar sedan, very handsome, more silver than gray. Celeste popped out. She was no longer dressed like Marie Antoinette; she had changed into a sleek black outfit of trousers and top. She looked like a black cat of ill omen. Bruce reflected ludicrously that this was the first time she'd ever seen her wear anything other than a dress.

Sandor got out from the passenger side. Bruce didn't like the way he moved. He was tired, she could tell. He leaned too heavily on his cane and his movements were stiff. He might even be in pain again; the past two days had been days of unusual exertion for him. With a pang she remembered their night of love and for a moment felt bitter irony—that she and Sandor should have discovered a wealth of happiness and a land of promise in one another, only to have it now snatched away.

As she watched Sandor, slow-moving, still elegant in his eighteenth century dress, Bruce felt tears well in her eyes and one spilled over, down her cheek to her lips. She touched it with the tip of her tongue and tasted salt. The thunder continued, and sheet lightning, more frequent now and yet there was no wind. The coming storm not yet close.

Slowly Sandor mounted the steps and passed from Bruce's line of vision. So did Celeste, behind him…but not before she'd seen that Celeste had a gun in her hand.

Still at the window, Bruce turned. Waited. The room was almost entirely dark; now lit by a single too-white flash of lightning that blinded the eyes. When she could see again she saw Sandor, and he saw her.

"Bruce!" His voice was hoarse with agony. She started toward him, and he toward her. He stumbled, his cane scrabbled, he almost fell.

"Back! Get back!" Celeste commanded, waving her gun at Bruce. "I'll not have you too near each other, you hear? Vladimir, for heaven's sake, light the lamp. You know where it is."

"Yes, madam," said Vladimir. Ever the faithful servant.

Now outside Bruce heard the wind rise. It moaned like a living creature in the boards of the old house.

"Are you all right?" Sandor asked.

"Yeah." Bruce tried to grin. "So far, so good."

Sandor turned his head. Behind him, on the other side of the room, orange light flared from a kerosene lamp and outlined his profile. Like a hawk, Bruce had thought at first; and then later, when she'd known him better, she'd chosen instead a more noble bird, the eagle. Every line of that face was dear to Bruce. Tears welled again. She blinked them back. Told herself that she had to shake the despair that threatened; told herself somehow still there might be hope.

Sandor was speaking to Vladimir and as he spoke his voice gained more and more of his customary authority. "Vladimir! Celeste told me you had brought Bruce to this place. I would not have believed you capable of such treachery! What have you to say for yourself?"

Vladimir bowed. Bruce could sense Celeste's impatience but the woman did not interrupt. Vladimir said, "What I have done, Maestro, I did for the honor of the Bathorys. And will continue to do."

"Yes, yes," snapped Celeste, "but now let's get on with it! Sandor, you sit down before you fall down. On that chair over there." She gestured with the gun. "Bruce, get over here, in front of the fireplace where I can see you better. Vladimir, stay where you are—for the moment."

Bruce did as Celeste directed. This put her within three feet of Sandor. Achingly close. He spoke to her with his eyes; she longed to touch him. As she watched, amazed,

Sandor gathered his strength. She could see the power well-
ing up within him though outwardly he did not move. His
sensual mouth curved, and in that curve Bruce took hope.

"All right, Maestro," said Celeste, "this is real, real simple. Your man Vladimir has been helping me because we had
something in common—we both wanted Miz MacLaren out
of the way. Unfortunately, this ungainly witch—" she
looked Bruce up and down "—has more lives than a cat!"

"*You...*" Bruce whispered, but she said no more because Celeste had only confirmed what she had already figured out from her intuition about the silver flashes.

"Yes, me. Vlad fed me information but I did everything
myself. Except for the brakes on your car—I had to pay a
junkie mechanic I know to do that—"

"Maestro," Vladimir interrupted, coming from the
shadows, and wringing his hands. "I did not know, when I
left the house that morning, that Mrs. Stanhope had already had the damage done to the Volvo's brakes. I did not
wish *you* harm."

"That in no way excuses you," said Sandor severely, and
Vladimir recoiled.

"The fire... the voice on the phone?" Bruce asked.

And Celeste confirmed. "Yes, that was me. I'll never
understand how you got out of that. But no matter. As it has
turned out, it's just as well you're still alive. Since the
Ramsay brothers and Vlad here have all three let me down!"

"I don't understand," Bruce said. She was playing for
time. She'd seen, in the wavering orange lamplight, Vladimir's mouth drop open. He looked like a ghoul with a gap-
ing O for a mouth.

"You will!" declared Celeste. She came closer, past Sandor, her gun trained on him all the time. Then she reached
for Bruce, grabbed her by the arm, and dragged her back so
that they both stood perhaps four feet from the Maestro.

Celeste was small, Bruce registered; in spite of her anger, her grip on Bruce's arm seemed insecure. If it had not been for the gun, Bruce would have tried, despite her hands locked behind her back, to trip and flip the woman. All she needed was leverage, and beneath the long skirts Bruce wore, no one could see how she maneuvered her feet. . . .

Celeste continued, taunting Sandor. "You lo-o-ve Bruce, don't you, Sandor?"

"I do," he said firmly. His hand rested on the top of his cane. A potential weapon, Bruce thought.

Vladimir once more came forward. "You have promised me!" he said to Celeste, a note of warning in his voice.

She laughed, a mocking laugh. "Don't worry, Vlad. I haven't forgotten. My goals have changed, but you'll still get the precious information you wanted."

Bruce worked her feet back until she sensed her heels were within inches of Celeste's legs.

"I don't want you anymore, Maestro Sandor Szelazeny," Celeste was saying, "now that you've displayed such poor taste in women. I want what you have, those secrets of your female ancestor that the Ramsays told me about. I had already decided I'd let Reggie and Ronnie get the secrets from you and then take them for myself. But they chickened out, they made me mad, so I framed them. Then I told Vladimir to look harder, but he didn't accomplish a thing. I only kept the poor decrepit old boy on the string in case he might help me get rid of Bruce."

A long, loud rumble of thunder signaled the storm's imminence. Lightning flared its ghastly glare through the room. Into this, Vladimir's ancient voice cracked, "You can't do that! The secrets are for the Bathorys! We had a bargain. I would help you be rid of Miss MacLaren, and you would help me to find out where the Maestro had hidden the box of books and sacred objects!"

"Oh, hush up, Vladimir!" Celeste glanced over her shoulder at the man, but she kept her gun trained on Sandor. "Things change, and from what Reginald Ramsay told me about that countess, I'd be just the one to take hold of her knowledge."

"And which piece of my ancestress's knowledge is it that you so covet, my dear Celeste?" asked Sandor smoothly.

"All of it!" Her greed was in her voice. She let go of Bruce's arm and worked her fingers. "Secrets of eternal youth, alchemy! I could learn to make silver, couldn't I? I read some old books about it, silver comes before gold!"

Bruce wanted to further distract her, though she hadn't quite figured out when or how to make a move. "You have Sandor's silver letter opener, don't you? You couldn't bear to leave it there, and you couldn't put it out with the other things when you were setting up your friends, either. Isn't that so, Celeste?"

"Yes. I searched one last time myself, for clues in your rooms, Sandor. Now enough of all this talk. I don't like being stuck here in the middle of a storm, I want to get this over with. Here's the deal. You tell me, right now, where this box of Elizabeth Bathory's things is. Or else I will kill your beloved Bruce!"

"I—" said Sandor, but his words were drowned out by a tremendous crack of thunder and a simultaneous flash of lightning, so great that the old house shook.

And into the reverberating air came a hideous, heavy groan, followed by a creaking wheeze, and the sound of a body falling.

Bruce knew it had to be Vladimir but there was no time to think what, how, or why. Now, while Celeste was distracted by the unexpected, was the time to act.

She slammed her right heel into Celeste's leg, hard, knocking her off balance. Then Bruce threw all her weight sideways, against the smaller woman's body. At the same time Sandor stood and lashed out with his cane and knocked the gun from Celeste's hand. The gun hit the floor with a clatter and Sandor, who could not easily bend down to get it, was quick-thinking enough to whack the weapon with his cane to the dark far reaches of the room.

Meanwhile, Bruce body-slammed Celeste again and sent her to the floor. Bruce pinned her down with a foot in the middle of her back. She felt an exultant, primitive surge of victory.

"Can you keep her there?" asked Sandor. "I think I should see to Vladimir."

Celeste, who was not so brave without a gun in her hand, didn't move or make a peep. "You bet I can," said Bruce.

"Your hands..." said Sandor, hesitating.

"Handcuffed. The key's in Vladimir's pocket."

Vladimir was dying. He had stabbed himself with neat accuracy, through the heart, with the stiletto. Bruce heard him croak, "Forgive me, Maestro. I wanted...to restore the guardian...the honor of Bathory...."

Vladimir died. The storm unleashed its full fury.

"WHAT IN THE WORLD is that?" asked Bruce. Celeste now wore the handcuffs. Sandor had tucked the gun into his waistband. The three of them were waiting out the worst of the storm. Now above its crashes and booms and lashing rain, they heard a high, thin, nerve-racking wail.

"Sirens, I think," said Sandor.

"They're getting closer," remarked Bruce. Curious, she risked getting a little wet to look out of the window. "I can't see much except revolving blue lights, but I think they're coming here."

Celeste squeaked, "That's not possible! There's no telephone, no one to see way out here!"

"Nevertheless," said Bruce, "they're coming. Getting closer every minute."

Celeste pouted. She turned her innocent-looking wide violet eyes on Sandor. "Don't turn me over to the police, Maestro! We can work something out."

The look he gave her would have frozen fire. "You can't possibly be serious. There is nothing you could say, nothing you could do, that would make up for the crimes you have committed. And just in case a judge is so foolish as to let you out on bail before you come to trial, let me assure you of one thing. Those evil treasures you, and others, have sought will no longer be in existence by this time tomorrow."

"No!" Celeste screamed.

"Oh, yes. Bruce and I, together, will destroy the last vestiges of the evil heritage of Countess Elizabeth Bathory!"

"Amen to that," said Bruce, and went to meet the police at the door.

A very wet, green-and-white striped Virginia was first across the threshold. She threw herself at Bruce, hugging her friend. "Oh, thank goodness you're all right. I saw you leave with Vladimir, and pretty soon after that I saw Celeste come for Sandor, and I don't know, I just thought something was wrong somewhere so I followed Celeste's car. And then when I saw how deserted it was out here...well, I just didn't like it. I drove on as fast as I could to Edenton and got the police."

Two state policemen, dripping rain from oily black ponchos, stood in the hall while their eyes adjusted to the change in light level. "Ma'am," one of them said to Bruce, eyebrows lifting at the sight of her costume.

"In here, gentlemen," called out Sandor. "We have quite a story to tell."

Author's Note

The Countess Elizabeth Bathory was a real person whose life and death were, according to fact and/or legend, much the same as I have told in this story. Her castle was in Austria-Hungary, but its present day ruins are in Czechoslovakia, rather than in Hungary, near the Transylvanian border, where I have placed it. She did have links with Transylvania, and inspired the gothic imaginations of such nineteenth century writers as Mary Shelley (*Frankenstein*) and Bram Stoker (*Dracula*). However, the Countess Elizabeth, as far as I know, left neither a curse nor a legacy of any kind behind her. That part, and the names Szelazeny and Bator, are all out of my imagination. M.S.

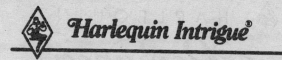

COMING NEXT MONTH

#189 ILLUSIONS by Jenna Ryan
Summoned to the castle of magician Cesare LaFortune
to witness his greatest illusion, Karoline O'Connor
entered a realm of evil that changed her life forever.
Her only hope of survival in Sainte Marie des
Monts, France, a land where madness reigned, was
Nicolas Demos, Cesare's nephew. Did she dare trust
a man whose power to look deep into her soul was
both exciting and frightening?

#190 DOUBLE VISION by Sheryl Lynn
Tarkington Smith felt that Kerry Byfield's testimony
had convicted an innocent man, not to mention his
best buddy. After a grueling trial, the cowboy
Casanova flirted shamelessly with Kerry—all to
convince her there was more to murder than met the
eye. But was there more to Tarkington Smith?

OVER THE YEARS, TELEVISION HAS BROUGHT
THE LIVES AND LOVES OF MANY CHARACTERS INTO
YOUR HOMES. NOW HARLEQUIN INTRODUCES YOU
TO THE TOWN AND PEOPLE OF

One small-town—twelve terrific love stories.

GREAT READING... GREAT SAVINGS...
AND A FABULOUS FREE GIFT!

Each book set in Tyler is a self-contained love story; together, the
twelve novels stitch the fabric of the community.

By collecting proofs-of-purchase found in each Tyler book, you can
receive a fabulous gift, ABSOLUTELY FREE! And use our special
Tyler coupons to save on your next TYLER book purchase.

Join us for the fifth TYLER book,
BLAZING STAR by Suzanne Ellison, available in July.

Is there really a murder cover-up?
Will Brick and Karen overcome differences and find true love?

H A R L E Q U I N
American Romance®

American Romance's yearlong celebration continues. Join your favorite authors as they celebrate love set against the special times each month throughout 1992.

Next month, fireworks light up the sky when Anne Haynes and John Westfield meet in a special Fourth of July romance:

JULY

S	M	T	W	T	F	S
			2	3	4	
5					11	
				7	18	
19	20			23	24	25
26	27	28	29	30	31	

**#445
HOME FREE
by Cathy Gillen Thacker**

Read all the books in *A Calendar of Romance*, coming to you one per month all year, only in American Romance.